IRON
ORCHID

Books by Stuart Woods

FICTION

Two-Dollar Bill[†]
The Prince of Beverly Hills
Reckless Abandon[†]
Capital Crimes[‡]
Dirty Work[†]
Blood Orchid[*]
The Short Forever[†]
Orchid Blues[*]
Cold Paradise[†]
L.A. Dead[†]
The Run[‡]
Worst Fears Realized[†]
Orchid Beach[*]
Swimming to Catalina[†]
Dead in the Water[†]

Dirt[†]
Choke
Imperfect Strangers
Heat
Dead Eyes
L.A. Times
Santa Fe Rules
New York Dead[†]
Palindrome
Grass Roots[‡]
White Cargo
Deep Lie[‡]
Under the Lake
Run Before the Wind[‡]
Chiefs[‡]

TRAVEL

A Romantic's Guide to the Country Inns
of Britain and Ireland (1979)

MEMOIR

Blue Water, Green Skipper

[*]A Holly Barker Book
[†]A Stone Barrington Book
[‡]A Will Lee Book

Iron
Orchid

of

STUART WOODS

**Doubleday Large Print
Home Library Edition**

G. P. PUTNAM'S SONS · NEW YORK

G. P. PUTNAM'S SONS
Publishers Since 1838
Published by the Penguin Group
Penguin Group (USA) Inc., 375 Hudson Street,
New York, New York 10014, USA • Penguin Group
(Canada), 90 Eglinton Avenue East, Suite 700,
Toronto, Ontario M4P 2Y3, Canada (a division of
Pearson Penguin Canada Inc.) • Penguin Books Ltd,
80 Strand, London WC2R 0RL, England •
Penguin Ireland, 25 St Stephen's Green, Dublin 2,
Ireland (a division of Penguin Books Ltd) •
Penguin Group (Australia), 250 Camberwell Road,
Camberwell, Victoria 3124, Australia (a division
of Pearson Australia Group Pty Ltd) •
Penguin Books India Pvt Ltd, 11 Community Centre,
Panchsheel Park, New Delhi–110 017, India •
Penguin Group (NZ), Cnr Airborne and Rosedale
Roads, Albany, Auckland 1310, New Zealand
(a division of Pearson New Zealand Ltd) •
Penguin Books (South Africa) (Pty) Ltd,
24 Sturdee Avenue, Rosebank, Johannesburg 2196,
South Africa

Penguin Books Ltd, Registered Offices:
80 Strand, London WC2R 0RL, England

ISBN 0-7394-5894-9

Printed in the United States of America

This is a work of fiction. Names, characters, places,
and incidents either are the product of the author's
imagination or are used fictitiously, and any
resemblance to actual persons, living or dead,
businesses, companies, events, or locales
is entirely coincidental.

While the author has made every effort to provide
accurate telephone numbers and Internet addresses
at the time of publication, neither the publisher nor the
author assumes any responsibility for errors, or for
changes that occur after publication. Further, the
publisher does not have any control over and does
not assume any responsibility for author or
third-party websites or their content.

**This Large Print Book carries the
Seal of Approval of N.A.V.H.**

DEDICATED TO BROOKE SWENSON

IRON
ORCHID

PROLOGUE

TEDDY FAY HAD ALWAYS BEEN a planner, and he had a plan now. He hadn't expected to be rousted from his cottage in Islesboro, Maine, by the FBI, but when it happened, he had his escape route already prepared. The tunnel had taken him out of the house, and while they were searching the coast, he had headed for the little island airstrip.

For the past few weeks, Teddy had been methodically killing people with whom he disagreed politically, and, as he had expected, the nation's law enforcement agencies had not taken it kindly. But he had been a step or two ahead of them all the way, and he was a step ahead of them now.

He had been in the air for an hour, now, and he was approaching the Kennebunk VOR at six thousand feet. He had been flying the day before at low altitudes, full rich, and he had burned a lot of fuel. He was down to nineteen gallons, now and burning thirteen an hour. He couldn't land at an airport, because the airplane would be discovered when the sun came up, and the FBI would know where to stop looking. He needed to ditch and Cessna where it wouldn't be found. Where would that be? He looked down the Maine coast. There were a few lights on, except in Kennebunkport, a short distance ahead.

Then something roared past him on either side, shaking the Cessna 182 RG and frightening him badly. What the hell was that? When he had calmed himself, it occurred to him that, maybe, he wasn't as far ahead of them as he thought. He switched his radio to the emergency frequency.

"Cessna 182 retractable, do you read me?" a young man's voice asked.

The two jet fighters would have already started their turn back to him. Teddy pressed the talk button. "I read you loud and clear," he said.

"This is the United States Navy," the young man said. "You are instructed to turn on your transponder, your navigation lights and your strobes, then to make a one-hundred-and-eighty–degree turn and fly a heading of zero six zero until you have the beacon of the Brunswick Naval Air Station in sight, then to land there on runway two. Do you read?"

"Negative, can't do it. I don't have the fuel." That was no lie. He was down to almost eighteen gallons. It would take a little time for them to locate him again. Without the transponder on, he was only a primary target on radar, and a small one, at that. The moon was in and out in the partly cloudy sky, and they would have trouble getting a visual on him, too.

"Then you can land at Portland International on the same heading. You'll be met there."

"Negative, Navy. Can't do it." Teddy was a couple of miles from the beach, and he turned toward it, flipping on every light on the airplane. He wanted to be seen now. The two jets roared past him a second time.

"Listen, pal," the young voice said. "I don't

give a fuck if you dump that thing in the Atlantic. My instructions are to force you to land or shoot you out of the sky, and those are my intentions. What's it going to be?"

An excellent question, Ted thought. He was no longer a step ahead of them, and he had no doubt that the young pilot meant what he said. He began tightening straps and unbuckled his seat belt. "Navy, do you read me?"

"I read you," the pilot said, "and I have a visual."

"I'm afraid I can't fly back with you, and it would be best if you stay well clear of me."

"Don't worry, little guy; I'm not going to bump into you."

They would be setting up their shot from landward, so that any rounds that missed would end up in the sea. "That's not what I mean," Teddy said. "Just stay well clear." He was coming up on the coastline, now, and he dropped the landing gear to slow him down quickly. The two jets blew past him again, causing him to laugh. "Sorry about that, fellas," he said into the mike.

Half a mile to the beach. Teddy reached into the duffel next to him and took out a package the size of a thick, hardcover book. He unlatched his door and stood by, watching the beach. The moment he crossed it, he lifted the door off its hinges and let it fall from the airplane. He moved the gear lever to the retracted setting, and while it came up he hung the duffel around his neck and set the timer on the package to thirty seconds.

He didn't waste another moment. Clutching the duffel to his chest, he rolled sideways and out of the airplane, counting. "Thousand one, thousand two, thousand three, . . ." He wanted to be as far below the airplane as possible before it blew. On ten he tucked the duffel under his arm, grabbed the rip cord handle and pulled.

The chute opened with a jerk, and a moment later the sky lit up and the shock wave hit him. Two pounds of plastic explosive made quite a bang. A split second later he heard the noise, but he was too busy trying to control his wild swinging to pay attention.

He finally stabilized as the two jets roared over him, creating more turbulence, but it was manageable. As the water came up toward him he pulled two cords and stalled the chute, nearly stopping his descent. He stepped into the Atlantic Ocean as if into a swimming pool.

His feet touched bottom almost immediately. The water came not quite to his waist. He was already wading in when the chute collapsed into the water behind him. He struggled on toward the beach, maybe fifty yards away, trying to keep the chute from filling with water, while holding the duffel high and dry.

When the water was ankle deep he hung the duffel around his neck again and used both hands to gather up and wring out the chute. He shrugged off the pack and stuffed the chute into it, then put the pack on again and started wading down the beach. He wanted no footprints left in the sand.

A few yards ahead he saw a rocky outcropping running down to the sea and headed for that. When he reached the rocks he stepped out of the water and onto them, then began picking his way toward dry land, careful not to turn an ankle. He needed both ankles now.

He walked through some long grass and came to a road. He looked both ways and saw a darkened cottage a couple of hundred yards away. It was very unlikely that anyone was living on the beach at the beginning of winter, but he had to be careful. He was cold, though, and he needed to get dry and change clothes, so he headed toward the cottage.

He walked up to it slowly and noiselessly; he didn't want to set off some barking dog. People would remember that. He reached the house, put down the chute and the duffel and leaned against the building, catching his breath. He was in excellent condition, but still, at his age . . .

When he had rested, he began circum-navigating the house, looking into windows, some of which had blinds drawn. When he reached the back door, he found it pad-locked from the outside. Nobody home; gone for the winter. He picked the lock in seconds, and he was inside. He retrieved the pack and his duffel and, still treading lightly, he walked through the house and found it deserted.

He found a linen closet and removed a couple of towels and a thick blanket, then he stripped off his wet clothes in the kitchen and rubbed himself down with a towel. He wrapped himself in the blanket, found a flash-light and began exploring. He found a utility closet housing an electric hot water heater and turned it on, then he ran in place for a couple of minutes to get his circulation going.

After fifteen minutes, when the water from the tap was tepid, he turned off the hot water heater, so that it wouldn't be found to be warm when the house was searched, found a shower and got clean. He dressed in the change of clothes from his duffel, then he went through the house to see what he could find.

He came back to the kitchen with a suit that was only a little too big for him, a couple of shirts, some underwear and a presentable felt hat from the master bedroom and a man's Burberry raincoat from the front hall closet. He packed them in the duffel, put his wet clothes and the towels into the washing machine, then he went into the attached garage. There was a ten-year-old Ford station wagon parked there, along with a pair of bicycles. He found a shovel, then he went out behind the house to what, in the summer, would be a very nice garden, and dug a hole four feet deep. He buried the chute, filled the hole, and arranged the soil to match the furrows of the garden, then he went back inside and put the washed things in the dryer.

An hour later, Teddy left the house exactly as he found it, absent the clothes and a bicycle. He strapped his duffel to the rear of the bike and began pedaling toward the lights of Kennebunkport. It was nearly six A.M., and the sun wouldn't be up until eight.

On the outskirts of Kennebunkport he came to a diner, glowing brightly in the predawn, and out front was a sign proclaiming the place to be a Greyhound Bus stop. He checked the posted schedule: a bus to Boston in forty minutes. He went around to the side of the building, found a Dumpster and deposited the bicycle there. Then he went into the diner, consumed a large breakfast and was outside when the bus arrived.

He paid the driver for a ticket to Boston, then put his duffel in the overhead rack, slipped into a seat, tipped his hat over his eyes and fell soundly asleep. The bus made it to the Boston Greyhound terminal at midmorning, and Teddy bought another ticket for Atlantic City, New Jersey, departing immediately.

Late in the afternoon, Teddy left the bus in Atlantic City, went into the men's room, locked himself in a stall and, fishing them from his duffel, donned a wig and a mustache. He found a wireless phone store, bought a throwaway cell phone, then phoned the Algonquin Hotel in New York and booked a room. He then took a cab to one of the casino hotels, went to the concierge's desk and booked a car and driver.

Late in the afternoon, the car dropped him

at the corner of 44th Street and Madison Avenue. He went into Brooks Brothers and, telling a salesman that the airlines had lost his luggage, bought two suits, a blue blazer, gray trousers, some shirts, ties, socks and underwear, a topcoat, a new hat and a suitcase. Teddy was a perfect size forty regular, so the only alterations necessary were hemming the trousers. He paid for everything with a credit card that drew on a large sum in a Cayman Islands bank. That done, he changed into a new suit, tossed his old clothes into a wastebasket and left the store carrying his new suitcase and the duffel. He walked the two blocks to the Algonquin, checked in and was escorted to his room.

He unpacked his new clothes, then opened a secret place in the lining of the duffel and dumped everything onto the bed. He inventoried the contents: a second wig and other makeup, four complete sets of identification and credit cards, plus the ones in his pockets, the pieces of a nonmetallic .380 pistol with a silencer that he had built himself, and ninety thousand dollars in used hundreds, fifties and twenties. He locked them in the safe in the closet, had dinner from room service and went to bed.

ONE

HOLLY BARKER TOOK AIM and squeezed off a round. Her father, Senior Master Sergeant, U.S. Army (ret.) Hamilton Barker, looked through his hand scope.

"High and to the right," he said.

"How high and how far to the right of what?" Holly asked in disbelief.

"An inch high and to the right of dead center," Ham replied. "That's not good enough. Push with your right hand, pull with your left."

"That's what I've been doing since I was eight, when you first taught it to me," Holly said. She took aim and, this time, made a point of pushing and pulling.

"That's better," Ham said.

"How much better?"

"A quarter of an inch off dead center," he said.

"Oh, please," Holly said, laughing.

"How did the Orchid Beach town council take your resignation as chief of police?" Ham asked.

"They were appropriately sad, except for a couple who looked relieved. At least they accepted my recommendation of Hurd Wallace to replace me. They're getting a good man."

"They're losing a better woman. What are you going to do with your house?"

"One of my young policewomen is going to move into the guest house and be my caretaker. I'll need the house to decompress once in a while. Also to remind me of Jackson." Jackson Oxenhandler, Holly's fiancé, had been killed in a bank robbery two years before, an innocent bystander.

Ham went to his range bag and came back with a mahogany box.

"What's that?"

"Something for you to take with you on the new job." He handed her the box and a small key.

Holly set down the box, inserted the key and unlocked it. "Oooh," she said, gazing at the shiny stainless slide with her name engraved on it. "Nice Colt .45."

"It's not a Colt, and it's not a .45," Ham said. "It's a nine-millimeter made of Caspian parts. The lightweight frame was designed by Terry Tussey, and the grip holds a round shorter than standard, but it will conceal nicely. Only weighs twenty-one ounces. I thought it might come in handy."

Holly picked up the small gun and hefted it. "Nice," she said.

Ham handed her a loaded magazine. "See if you can hit anything with it."

The target was still set at twenty-five feet. Holly set herself, pushed and pulled and squeezed off the round.

"Half an inch off dead center," Ham said. "Not bad, considering it's a three-inch barrel, instead of four."

"Sweet trigger," Holly said. "Four, four and a half pounds?"

"Four, exactly. Try it with both eyes open, and use up the magazine, rapid fire."

Holly obliged.

"That target no longer has a center," Ham said, a touch of pride in his voice. He went back to his range bag and came back with some gun leather. "Mitch Rosen made you a shoulder rig, a belt and a holster for it," he said.

"It's beautiful work," she said, caressing the mahogany leather. "Thank you, Ham." She put her arms around him and hugged.

Ham, uncharacteristically, hugged her back, but then he looked a little embarrassed. "What time did you file for?"

"Ten," Holly said. "My stuff's in the car."

"You'll have to clear out at Fort Pierce for the Bahamas," Ham said.

"I know, Ham."

"I don't know why you want to go to the Bahamas alone for a weekend," he said.

"I just want to take Daisy and spend the weekend alone; I have a lot to think about."

"Whatever you say."

"I'll be back on Monday, maybe Sunday night, depending on the weather."

"Okay."

She packed up her things, put her new gun into her range bag and went to the car. She gave Ham a wave and drove off.

AT FOUR O'CLOCK that afternoon, Holly landed the rented Cessna at Roberts International

Airport in Grand Cayman, having flown first to the Bahamas, checked into a hotel, filed a new flight plan and left Daisy in a pre-arranged kennel. She dropped off her bag with the doorman at her Georgetown hotel, then kept the cab for the trip to the bank. Refusing the driver's help, she hefted the two nylon duffels from the trunk of the cab and carried them inside.

A Mr. Dellinger—English, well-tailored and very discreet looking—was waiting for her. He nodded for a guard to take the bags, and the man went into a side room while Dellinger showed her into his office.

"How do you do?" Dellinger said, offering his hand.

"I'm very pleased to meet you," Holly replied.

"The money will be machine counted in there," Dellinger said. "It will take a little while; why don't we get the paperwork done?"

"All right." She sat down at his desk.

He handed her a sheet of paper. "It's a very simple form," he said. "You may use any name you like, and you needn't put down an address, since we will not be mailing you account statements."

Holly put down "H. Barker" for a name. "I'd like two credit cards in the same name," she said. "They may be used by two different people, and I brought a sample signature of the other person." She gave him a photo-copy of Ham's signature. It was illegible to anyone but her. She signed "H. Barker" for her own card.

The guard came back and handed Dellinger a slip of paper.

"Five million, seven hundred and sixty thousand dollars," Dellinger said. "Does that sound right?"

"It sounds exactly right."

"Let me tell you a few things about our service," Dellinger said, "and I hope you won't take offense at what may seem to be our assumptions. We give all our clients this information without regard to the amount de-posited or the source of the funds."

"I won't be offended," Holly said.

"First of all, because of the way we dis-perse cash around the world, these funds will immediately become untraceable. In the unlikely event that the United States or any other country should invade our island and take over our bank, they will not find a name on your account, only a number, which will not be in any way traceable to you. The number will not be coded in any way that would reveal even the nationality of the customer.

"The only thing traceable to you would be the credit card charges. When you view your credit card statement, you'll be given the option of erasing the names of the payees—hotels, restaurants or shops, for instance. Only the amounts and dates of the charges would then appear on your statement, which you may access by entering your account number and a password, which you will designate. You may use as many as three passwords, each from four to twelve letters or digits or a combination of both."

"That sounds good."

"It is very important that you never forget the passwords, because if you do, you will not be able to access your account statements. In order to change the passwords, you would have to come personally here, to the bank."

Holly signed one card and put them both into her pocket.

"The paper I gave you also has instructions for going to your account online," Dellinger said. "Will there be anything else?"

"No, I think that does it," Holly said. She

shook his hand and left the bank. Now the drug money she had stolen from the hundreds of millions confiscated in a huge raid was safe from anyone but her, and no one would ever be able to prove that she had it. At least, she hoped not.

She spent the night in Georgetown, then, the following morning, flew back to the Bahamas. She spent two days there, shopping, eating and walking on the beach with Daisy, and on Monday morning she flew home to Orchid Beach.

She, Ham and Ginny, Ham's girlfriend, had dinner that night at the Ocean Grill in Vero Beach, then the following morning, she gave her house keys to the young policewoman who would be her caretaker, loaded her Jeep Grand Cherokee and drove with Daisy ninety miles to Palm Beach. There, at the Porsche dealer, she traded in the Jeep for a Porsche Cayenne Turbo, and paid for it, not with her new credit card, but with a check on her own bank account. Holly had been a woman of some substance since Jackson's will had made it so.

By noon, she was headed north to Virginia.

Two days later, at the appointed hour, she

turned into an unmarked gate on a country road, went around a bend and saw a road-block ahead. A man in civilian clothes, carrying an assault rifle, stopped her.

"You seem to have taken a wrong turn," he said. "Please turn around and go back to the highway."

Holly, as she had been instructed to do, handed him her U.S. passport. "My name is Barker," she said. "I'm expected."

The man consulted a clipboard, very thoroughly compared her passport photograph to her face, then returned it to her. "And who might *that* be?" he asked, pointing to Daisy, who sat in the front passenger seat.

"That is Daisy," Holly replied. "She doesn't have a passport."

The man checked his clipboard. "Her name is on the list," he said. "Go all the way to the end of the drive, park your car and go into the white house, which is the administration building. You'll be met." He walked to the side of the road, tapped a code into a keypad, and the concrete roadblock swung slowly out of the way.

Holly gave him a wave and drove past the barricade. After five minutes of winding through woods, she emerged at what appeared to be a large farmhouse.

She had arrived at Camp Peary, which members of the Central Intelligence Agency referred to as "the Farm."

TWO

HOLLY ALLOWED DAISY a moment in the bushes, then entered the old farmhouse. Immediately, a trim, middle-aged woman emerged from a side room.

"Ms. Barker?"

"Yes."

"I am Mrs. Colville, the chief administrative officer at this installation. If you'll come with me, we'll get you processed, and then you can have dinner. First, may I have your car keys? What a nice dog." She gave Daisy a pat.

Holly handed the keys over, and Mrs. Colville walked outside for a moment, then returned. Holly followed the woman through a living room furnished with eighteenth-century American furniture, down a hallway and into an elevator, which took them down. They emerged into a perfectly ordinary open office floor divided into cubicles, with a row of private offices along one wall. Mrs. Colville showed her to a seat at a table, upon which rested a fairly thick file.

"The file contains the rather extensive application and personal history that you filled out many weeks ago. You may review it, if you wish, and make any changes you feel are necessary for accuracy. Once you sign the sworn statement, at the end, the Agency will accept what you have entered, and you will be henceforth held responsible for its accuracy, in every respect, on penalty of perjury. Is that perfectly clear?"

"Yes," Holly replied. "I don't feel the need to make any changes." It was as accurate as she knew how to make it, except for the new bank acount in Grand Cayman. She countersigned the document and handed it over.

"Very well." Mrs. Colville put what appeared to be a large identification card in front of her. "Please sign this, and we'll get you photographed."

Holly signed it and was taken down a hallway to a bare-bones photo studio and photographed. Colville left the paperwork with the photographer and returned to her office with Holly, where she handed her a thick envelope. "This is a document explaining all of your obligations and rights as an employee, everything from the health plan to the pension plan to your legal rights. Please read the entire document carefully, then return it to this office, since you are not allowed to have in your possession, after leaving here, any document belonging to the Agency, except your identification card."

The photographer came in and handed Colville a leather wallet. She inspected the contents and handed it to Holly. "This is your identification," she said. "From this moment, you are a probationary employee of the Central Intelligence Agency. When you have completed your course of training here, you will surrender this card and, if you have been successful, given new identification." Colville took a sheaf of typed papers from her desk drawer and handed it to Holly. "This is your schedule for tomorrow; you will be given a new schedule each morning, so that training may be adapted to whatever your special needs may be."

"Thank you," Holly said.

Colville walked her to the elevator. "While we have been speaking, your car and and everything in it is being searched. Your car will be garaged until you have finished your training. You won't need it, since you are not allowed to leave the Farm during training. Your luggage will be delivered to your room presently, and in the meantime, I suggest you walk over to the dining hall, there," she pointed out a barn, "and have dinner. Some-one will escort you to your room after you've eaten. While you are here your code name will be Harry One," she spelled it, "and you are not to tell anyone, neither your fellow trainees nor even an instructor, your real name. Is that clear?"

"Yes," Holly said.

Colville leaned over and patted Daisy. "You will remain Daisy," she said. "Good dog." Daisy received this attention with gratitude.

"Thank you."

"You may take her to the dining hall with

you. When your luggage is returned, so will be her dog food, and you may feed her then."

"Thank you, Mrs. Colville," Holly said. She shook the woman's hand and departed for the barn. During her short walk, she could not see anything that would reveal that the Farm was anything other than a farm. Even the parking lot didn't look like a parking lot.

She walked to a door in a corner of the barn and went inside. She was in a large dining hall with a cafeteria line down one wall. She served herself and took a table alone. The food was good, and no one joined her. When she had finished dessert, a young man approached, as if on cue. "Harry One?"

"Yes."

"Please follow me." He led her to another long, low farm building, which turned out to be a dormitory. She was shown to a decent-sized room containing a queen-sized bed and a comfortable chair. A wall was fitted with built-in furniture: a desk, bookcase and television set. Her luggage was stacked, empty, in a corner, and when she looked she found that everything had been hung up or tucked into a drawer, except her gun, the gift from Ham. She didn't ask about it.

"I hope you'll be comfortable here," the young man said. "Attached to your schedule is a map showing the places you'll need to go tomorrow."

"May I take my dog for a walk after she eats?" Holly asked.

"Yes, but stay on the map. If you wander beyond that, you'll be challenged, and the trespass will go in your record. Good night."

The young man left. Holly fed Daisy, took the map and went outside. There wasn't much daylight left, so she exercised Daisy by throwing her ball, which got the job done in a hurry. When Daisy was finally tired, she returned to her room and began reading the document she had been given, then her schedule for the following day. That took much of the evening, and when she had finished, she watched the eleven o'clock news on TV, then went to bed.

HER PHONE RANG at six A.M. "Yes?"

The young man. "Breakfast now, your first class at seven. This is the last wakeup call you'll get; from now on, you're on your own as to schedule. Don't be late for anything." He hung up.

Holly showered and changed into sweat

clothes, as her schedule had dictated. She would miss her morning run today, and she'd have to ask about that. She fed Daisy, had breakfast in the dining hall, threw the ball for Daisy for a few minutes, then followed the map to her first class, which was in an auditorium below the dining hall. Daisy remained at her side.

She took one of about two hundred seats, near the front. The room was less than a third full. At the stroke of seven o'clock, a lean, military-looking man of about sixty strode onto the stage and switched on a microphone at the podium.

"My name, for the purposes of your visit here, is Hanks," he said. "During the coming weeks or months, depending on the course of your training, you will come to hate me."

Somehow, Holly didn't doubt him.

"Most of you have been here for less than twenty-four hours," Hanks said, "and it may have occurred to you that this installation has been designed to look like a farm, which it has been for a couple of hundred years. Particularly, it has been arranged to reveal none of its secrets in satellite photographs. Most of your classes will therefore be conducted underground.

"For those who, after our physical training, still desire more exercise, there is a running path through the woods. You may not run in the company of more than one other person. There are also two tennis courts, one of them above ground. There is also an underground pool, which will be the site of special training for some of you as well as a recreational facility.

"We discourage your getting to know other trainees; that is why you have each been assigned a code name. You are not to tell any other trainee anything about your personal or professional or educational background, or anything about how you were recruited. If you confine your conversations to the weather and other such innocuous subjects, you'll be fine. If you are questioned by someone not on the staff seeking personal information, then lie.

"In each of your rooms there are books and a television set with satellite service. You may entertain yourself, alone, in your room between dinner and bedtime. If you complete your training successfully, your assignments thereafter may involve long periods alone or with hostile companions. Learn to enjoy solitude.

"There will be no question-and-answer period. Good luck." Hanks stalked off the stage.

Everyone sat still for a moment, waiting for further instructions. None came. Holly got up and started off for the first class on her schedule.

THREE

ROBERT KINNEY ARRIVED at his office at the Federal Bureau of Investigation promptly at nine A.M., still warm from the praise of the president at the news conference of the day before, announcing the resolution of the Theodore Fay affair, and from the extended sexual activity with his paramour, Nancy Kimble, following his proposal of marriage, which had been accepted.

His secretary, Helen Frankel, was just hanging up the phone as he walked past her desk. "Stop where you are," she ordered.

Kinney stopped. "What?"

"That was the White House on the phone. The president wishes to see you immediately."

"Right now?"

"Mr. Kinney," Helen said, sighing.

"Okay, immediately is right now."

"There'll be a White House car waiting for you by the time you get to the garage."

Kinney turned on his heel and headed for the garage. As he was entering the elevator, someone shouted his name. He turned to see one of his agents, Kerry Smith, walking rapidly toward him. "Later, Kerry," he said, and the elevator door closed before Smith could reply.

There was, indeed, a White House car waiting for him in the garage. He folded his six-foot-five-inch frame into the rear seat, and twenty minutes later he was sitting in the office of Cora Parker, the president's secretary.

"It won't be long, Mr. Kinney," Parker said. "Would you like some coffee?"

"Yes, thank you," Kinney replied.

"As I recall, you take it black with a carcinogenic," she said, walking to a coffee pot nearby.

"I wouldn't put it quite that way, but yes," he replied.

"That stuff will eat your insides out," she said.

"If that were true, Ms. Parker, I would have no insides."

She handed him the cup. "If you don't have time to finish it here, just take it in with you," she said.

Kinney took a sip of the coffee, then looked up as the door to the oval office opened. His boss, the director of the Federal Bureau of Investigation, stalked out of the office, red-faced and blinking rapidly. He glanced at Kinney, and his expression changed to one of hatred, then he was gone.

"You may go in now, Mr. Kinney," Parker said.

Kinney stood up and tried to figure out what to do with his briefcase and the coffee in his hand. He set the coffee on her desk and walked into the Oval Office.

William Henry Lee IV, president of the United States, stood up to greet him. "Good morning, Bob," he said, extending a hand.

Kinney shook it. "Good morning, Mr. President. I didn't expect to see you again so soon."

Lee waved him to a sofa and took a chair

opposite him, while Cora Parker set down Kinney's coffee on a table next to him.

"Well, events move quickly sometimes," the president said. "Once again, my congratulations on wrapping up the Fay affair so well."

"Thank you, sir." Kinney didn't bother with any self-deprecating talk about the teamwork involved, since he considered himself principally responsible for the outcome.

"Anything new on the search for wreckage and a body?"

So this was why he had been called over here, Kinney thought. "The Coast Guard has found numerous pieces of the wreckage, none bigger than the size of your hand. It was, apparently, a very powerful bomb. Chances are, the body is in pieces just as small and is fish food by now, so there's not likely to be an autopsy."

"Bob, I'd like you to be the new director of the FBI," Lee said, "effective immediately."

Kinney tried not to choke on his coffee. "Sir? Is James Heller ill?"

"If he says he is. Figuratively speaking, he's dead," Lee replied. "I accepted his resignation five minutes ago for personal or health reasons. Whatever he decides. He'll be out of the Hoover Building inside of an hour."

"I see," Kinney said.

"Do you accept?"

"Mr. President, I'd like to know what my brief as director would be."

Lee gazed at him. "To shake the organization to its roots; to improve every facet of its operations, particularly criminal and terrorist investigations; to build bridges to the CIA and other intelligence organizations; to change its self-serving and standoffish culture with regard to those organizations and law enforcement agencies all over the country; to weed out the deadwood and promote the able. I think that about does it. Sound familiar?"

Indeed it did, Kinney thought. It was virtually a quote from a memo the president had recently asked him to write to him. "It sounds very good, Mr. President. I'd be honored and very pleased to accept."

"I'm delighted to hear it," Lee said. "I'll be issuing a formal appointment today, and someone will be in touch to iron out the details. One other thing: in view of the constant threat of terrorist attack, I want your first order of business to be a thorough review of the Bureau's own security, both in Washington and at every field office. I want it strengthened, where necessary. And I've decided that the director should live in secure government housing, so someone will be discussing a few choices with you. I hear you live in some awful bachelor digs, anyway, so I'm sure you'll enjoy the change."

"Thank you, sir, I'm sure I will, especially since I'm planning to be married very soon."

"Who's the lucky lady?"

"Her name is Nancy Kimble. She lives in Chester, South Carolina, and I met her when I went down there to investigate Fay's murder of Senator Wallace."

"Oh, the innkeeper you were bunking with?"

Kinney blushed. "Sir?"

"Relax, it was in your file. I think Heller took some pleasure in noting it."

Kinney gulped. "I see."

Lee shrugged. "Everybody's entitled to a sex life, but don't quote me as having said that; I'd be explaining for weeks."

"Of course not, sir."

Lee slapped his hands on the arms of his chair and stood up. "Well, why don't you and I take a stroll down to the White House Press

Room and surprise the boys and girls with an announcement, then you can get back to the Bureau and move into your new office."

Kinney stood up and grabbed his briefcase. "Yes, sir."

They walked out of the Oval Office, and Cora Parker snatched Kinney's coffee cup as he passed.

"By the way," the president said as they walked down the hallway, trailed by Secret Service agents, "I hope you'll make a special effort to get along with my wife." Katharine Rule Lee was the director of Central Intelligence. "Because if you don't, there'll be hell to pay at home."

"I'll do my very best, sir."

"See that you do."

The president's press secretary fell into step with them, and they continued on toward the press room.

Kinney couldn't wait to call Nancy.

FOUR

TEDDY FAY WALKED OUT of the Algonquin Hotel and greeted the brisk new day. He hailed a cab. "Take me uptown on Madison," he said to the driver. When they had reached 63rd Street, he told the driver to stop, and he walked across the street to a branch of the Bank of New York. A guard directed him to a desk at the rear, and the young woman behind it stood up to greet him, introducing herself.

"I'm Albert Foreman," Teddy said, seating himself beside the address. "I'd like to open an account."

"Certainly, Mr. Foreman," the woman said,

then began producing an application and signature cards. "Are you new in town?"

"Yes, I just arrived last night, from Chicago. I've sold my business and retired, and I thought I might live in New York for a while. I've always loved the city."

"Welcome to town," she said. "How much would you like to deposit?"

Teddy handed her an envelope. "Five thousand dollars," he said. "I'll be wire-transferring a larger sum as soon as I have an account number."

"Here are some counter checks with your account number," she said, handing him a packet. "Where are you living?"

"At the moment, I'm at the Algonquin, but I'm on my way to do some apartment hunting right now. I'll call you with the address when I've found something."

"Fine. Everything is in order. You may begin using your account immediately."

Teddy thanked her and left the bank. Outside, he used his cell phone to call a number he had memorized.

"This is Mr. Allen," a voice said.

Teddy gave him his account number.

"Password?"

"Cayuse." He spelled it.

"Yes, sir, how may I help you?"

"I'd like to wire two hundred thousand dollars to the following account number at the Bank of New York." He read the number and the routing number, and Allen repeated it.

"And your transfer password?"

"Old Paint."

"Thank you, sir. I'll wire the funds immediately; they'll be in New York within the hour."

Teddy thanked him and hung up. He walked along Madison for a few blocks and went into a real estate office where he had made an appointment earlier, by phone.

"Good morning, Mr. Foreman," the agent said. "I've arranged viewings of three apartments that would seem to meet your requirements. The first is just around the corner."

He followed her to 610 Park Avenue. "This was formerly the Mayfair Hotel," the agent said, "and it was converted to condos a few years ago."

Teddy had requested a condominium building, since he did not want to wait weeks for the board of a co-op building to investigate him. A condo board would only want a credit report.

"It's a full-service building; the restaurant,

Daniel, is on the ground floor and provides room service." They got onto an elevator and emerged on a high floor. "I sold this apartment three years ago, and my clients have gone on a round-the-world tour for a year, so the apartment is available for that time." She unlocked a door.

Teddy walked quickly through the place. It was really a two-bedroom hotel suite, beautifully furnished. "How much?"

"Six thousand a month."

"I'll take it," he said.

"You don't want to see the other two?"

"No, this is fine."

"They'll want a credit check, of course."

"Of course, but I'll pay the year's rent in advance." He took a check from the bank packet and wrote it out.

"If you'd like to take a seat, I'll see how quickly we can get this done," she said.

Teddy took a book of Winston Churchill's speeches from a bookcase, sat down and began reading.

Ten minutes later the woman returned. "Your credit report is fine, and the building manager has approved you," she said. "And in view of your advance payment, I've gotten him to waive the security deposit."

"Then I'm home," Teddy said.

"Yes, you are." She handed him the keys. "Is there anything else I can do for you?"

"Not a thing," Teddy said.

They rode down to the street together, and Teddy took a cab back to the Algonquin. He cleaned out the safe, packed his bags and checked out. Fifteen minutes later, he was a resident of New York City. He called the bank and gave them his new address, then he began looking in the classified section of the newspaper for suitable work space.

AN HOUR LATER, Teddy was looking at a three-room furnished space over a dry-cleaner's shop on Lexington Avenue. "Does anyone live in the building?" he asked the super.

"No, sir. The place is empty by six."

"What's immediately below?"

"A storeroom for furs. The cleaners store them there for clients."

"And above?"

"The roof."

"I'll take it." He wrote the man a check for a year's rent and was given the keys.

Now all Teddy had to do was to begin shopping for tools. He already had a detailed list of what he would need, and he knew where to find them. He walked downstairs and out onto Lexington Avenue and hailed a cab.

FIVE

HOLLY FOLLOWED THE MAP to the room number on her map, which turned out to be an underground firing range. She was issued an electronic noise-canceling headset and shown to an equipment room where she could leave Daisy. Someone had thoughtfully left a bowl of water and a blanket for her.

A dozen trainees had assembled in the range, and shortly, a short, thickly built man in what Holly assumed to be his late fifties, wearing an olive-drab T-shirt, army-issue fatigue trousers, black tennis shoes and a white-sidewall haircut, addressed them.

"You may call me Sarge," he said in a

clipped voice. "I will teach you how to shoot, if you do not already know how. Your employer does not issue a standard weapon, so you will fire many weapons—handguns, assault rifles and machine guns. You will learn how they work and to disassemble and reassemble them in light and dark. You will learn about silencers and flash suppressors. Someone else will teach you how to eviscerate others with knives and kill them with your hands. That is out of my line."

He looked at a clipboard. "Harry One?"

Holly raised a hand. "Here, Sarge."

"Have you ever fired a handgun?"

"Yes, Sarge."

"Come over here and show me how you do it. Ears on, everyone. We didn't bring you here to send you out into the world deaf."

Everyone put on their headsets.

Sarge indicated half a dozen handguns lined up on a bench. "Take your pick, Harry One."

Holly chose a standard Model 1911 Colt semiautomatic pistol. While pointing it downrange she removed the magazine and found it full and the chamber empty. She shoved the magazine back into the weapon, racked the slide, took up a combat position and emptied the weapon into the target, fifty feet away, at the rate of a round per second. She removed the magazine from the gun and returned it to the bench.

Sarge pressed a button, and the target traveled toward the group. He examined the tight group, all eight shots in the bull's-eye, then turned back to his class. "I have been at this installation for an extended period of time, and that is the first time I have ever seen a trainee do that on the first day," he said. "When I am done with you, you will all be able to do it." He turned to Holly. "Harry One, you are my assistant instructor."

Holly spent the next two hours teaching other trainees what Ham had taught her since she was a little girl.

When the class ended, Sarge pulled her aside. "Do you own a little nine-millimeter custom-made with Caspian parts?"

"Yes," she replied.

"I know who made that weapon," he said. "Not because I'm psychic but because he put his initials on the frame. That sonofabitch cost me the national shooting championship twice, and I can see he taught you what he knows. Before we're done, you may learn some things he didn't teach you. Now get out of here."

Holly got out of there. She collected Daisy and made her way to the next room number on her schedule in another underground building. She entered the room and found three other trainees there, waiting. On a low platform at the end of the room was an array of safes and locks and prop doors.

"Come in and sit down, please," an elderly man said. He had a thick German accent and was wearing a seedy cardigan sweater over a bright orange polo shirt, which Holly thought he had probably not chosen for himself. "You may call me Dietz.

"You are in this class to learn how to be a criminal," Dietz said. "You will learn how to pick locks and jimmy windows and crack safes. I say, 'crack,' because you will not be here long enough for me to teach you to open any safe in the world by learning the combination. With some, you will have to employ explosives, and I will teach you that, too. You may comfort yourself with the knowledge that if, by the end of your training, you have not measured up in some way and are dismissed, you will at least be able to earn a good living as a burglar."

Everybody laughed.

Dietz picked up a remote control, pressed a button and a screen came down from the ceiling. He pressed another button and a slide of a cutaway view of a lock flashed onto the screen. "Now, we have here a common, domestic, double-bolt lock, in this case, a Yale." And he proceeded to explain how it worked.

By the end of the class, two hours later, each of the students knew how to pick the lock, open it with a credit card or remove the lock from the door with tools. Holly thought she was going to enjoy this class.

HOLLY EMPTIED DAISY and went to lunch in the cafeteria. She chose her food, sat down and was immediately joined by a young Asian woman of around thirty. She was petite and very pretty.

"Mind if I sit down?" she asked. Her accent was completely American.

"Please do. This is Daisy."

The woman scratched Daisy behind the ears and made baby talk, then she turned to

Holly. "You're Harry One, right? I'm Harry Three. There are five Harrys, and I've already met the others. I have a feeling we're going to be working together when we get out of this joint."

"Well, you're way ahead of me," Holly said.

"You were recruited by Lance Cabot, right?"

"I don't think I should confirm or deny that," Holly said. "How do I know you're not a spy who's just trying to get me to talk."

"Yeah, well you're right. Not that I'm a spy, but they told us not to say anything, right?"

"Right."

"I was really impressed with your shooting," Harry Three said.

"Thank you."

"Where did you learn?"

Holly smiled and shook her head. "I'm not biting, Three."

"Oh, shit!" Three replied, looking disgusted. "This goes against every natural instinct I have. I always want to know everything about everybody, and in this place I can't find out nothing about nobody."

"I believe I can deduce that you were not an English teacher in your past life."

"Ha, ha, ha," Three said, glumly. "You

sound just like my mother, except you don't have a Chinese accent."

"And that you are a first-generation American," Holly said.

"Yeah, sure; big deal, Sherlock. Well, look, it's my guess that all five of the Harrys were recruited by Lance and that we're all going to be working together when we finally bust out of here. Any idea how long it's going to be?"

"All I've been told is that we'll be here until we're ready," Holly said. "I don't think I'm giving away any secrets by saying that."

"I think Lance is hot, don't you?"

"You don't really expect me to answer that, do you? You're probably wired, for God's sake."

"You want me to strip down right here in this weird dining room? You know, they don't even have any noodles here? How can a nice Chinese girl get along without noodles? My mother would really be pissed, if she knew."

"Maybe if you put in a request, they would serve some noodles."

"A request to who? That guy Hanks already said they weren't going to answer any questions."

"It wouldn't be a question; it would be a request. Why don't you write it down and hand it to one of the restaurant workers?"

"Well, all right, but I don't think it's going to work."

Holly finished her lunch with Harry Three without divulging any information about herself, but it wasn't easy. Three would make a great interrogator, she thought.

AFTER LUNCH and a short walk with Daisy, Holly found her way to her next class. Only it wasn't a class. She walked into an office, and a woman at a desk said, "Harry One? Sit down. You are scheduled for a polygraph at this time."

Oh, shit, Holly thought.

SIX

WILL LEE STEPPED TO THE PODIUM in the White House press room. "Good morning, ladies and gentlemen. I would like to announce that I have accepted the resignation of James Heller, director of the Federal Bureau of Investigation, effective immediately. I have no further comment on his resignation. Mr. Heller will be making his own announcement later today.

"I am pleased to announce that I have appointed Robert Kinney as the new director of the FBI. Mr. Kinney began his law enforcement career with the New York City Police Department, where he established an outstanding investigative record and rose to the rank of detective lieutenant, before being recruited to the FBI fifteen years ago. There, he blazed a trail of successful investigations and held increasingly important administrative positions, most recently, that of deputy director for investigations. I have every confidence that Director Kinney will make great strides in preparing the Bureau for a bright new future as our nation's premier law enforcement agency.

"I have one other announcement of importance. In furtherance of the rebuilding of our country's national security, I will today send legislation to the Congress to remove the FBI from the Department of Justice and make it a freestanding agency, with the director reporting directly to the president. Mr. Kinney has time to take a few questions."

Lee stepped aside, and Kinney approached the podium. He had been surprised and delighted by the president's announcement. He wondered why the attorney general had not attended the meeting where he was appointed. He pointed at a woman reporter in the front row who looked vaguely familiar from television.

"Mr. Kinney, what progress has been made in the Theodore Fay case?"

"The search for wreckage of Mr. Fay's airplane is just about over, and the Coast Guard has found, as we expected, only small pieces of the airplane."

"Have you found Mr. Fay's body?"

"We believe that it no longer exists as such," Kinney replied. "The very powerful explosion would have had the same effect on Mr. Fay's body as on the airplane itself."

"Is there any chance that Mr. Fay got out of the airplane before the explosion?"

"Conversations with the two pilots pursuing Mr. Fay's airplane have convinced us that he had no opportunity to escape the airplane before the explosion."

"So the Fay case is now closed?"

"Except for follow-up and adminstrative details, yes."

The questions continued for another five minutes before the president's press secretary called a halt. The president walked Kinney to the White House portico and his car.

"Your announcement came as a surprise to me," Kinney said.

"We've been working in-house for months

on that move," Lee said, "and we've played it pretty close to our vests. The attorney general isn't particularly happy about it, of course, but he understands the need to elevate the Bureau to agency status. And, of course, it will give you a freer hand."

The two men shook hands, and Kinney got into his car, reaching for his cell phone.

"There's a better phone in your armrest, sir," the driver said. "And by the way, this is now your official car. We dropped Mr. Heller at his home half an hour ago. I'm Agent Tom Murray."

"Good to meet you, Tom," Kinney said, reaching for the phone. He called his home, and Nancy Kimball answered.

"I saw you on TV," she said immediately.

"Damn, I wanted to tell you myself."

"This is a great day."

"You bet it is. Why don't you work on the details of getting us married as soon as possible, and I'll book us a table somewhere spectacular for dinner tonight."

"Will do," she said.

"I love you."

"I love you, too."

He hung up, and the car continued to the Hoover Building. As Kinney left the car he was appoached by a man in a blue suit, showing an I.D. card.

"Good morning, Director Kinney," he said. "I am Agent Marvin Green of the United States Secret Service, and I will be in charge of your security detail."

Kinney shook the man's hand but was puzzled. "Since when does the director of the FBI get Secret Service protection?" he asked.

"Since right now, sir, by order of the president. Your elevator is waiting."

Kinney was shown to the director's private elevator, and Green and two other agents rode with him. "I need to stop by my office," Kinney said.

"We're going directly to your new office, sir," Green said. "Your secretary has already supervised the removal of your effects from your old office."

Kinney stepped out of the elevator to a round of applause from dozens of agents and clerical workers. He quieted them. "Thank you very much," he said. "Have all you people been watching television when you should have been working?" Everybody laughed. "Get back to work; you'll be hearing from me." Helen, his secretary, was sitting at a desk in his new suite of offices, and Kerry Smith was waiting for him.

The three secretaries stood and applauded, and Kerry shook his hand.

"Come in, Kerry," Kinney said. "I'm appointing you chief assistant to the director."

"Thank you, sir," Smith said.

"You can still call me Bob when nobody's around." Kinney set his briefcase on his new desk and looked around. A large conference table was at the other end of the big office, and it was filled with many objects wrapped in plastic.

"What the hell is all that?" Kinney asked.

"It's the wreckage of Teddy Fay's airplane," Kinney said.

"What's it doing here?"

"I want you to see it personally."

"Why?"

"Because there's something very odd about it."

Kinney didn't like the sound of that.

SEVEN

HOLLY CALMED HERSELF, taking deep, regular breaths. She had taken a polygraph before, in the army. She had even attended a class where she learned to administer them. She forced herself not to think about the money in the Grand Cayman bank account or the credit card in her purse. She was not able to prevent herself thinking about the statement she had signed, under penalty of perjury, that she had divulged all her financial information.

A man opened a door and beckoned her inside a small room. A woman was sitting in a chair next to the machine, and a large mirror was built into one wall. Holly assumed that this was a one-way mirror that allowed others to monitor her performance.

"Please remove your upper body clothing down to your bra and sit down," the woman said.

Holly pulled off the sweatshirt she was wearing and sat down facing the mirror.

"You are here to take a polygraph examination. Have you ever had a polygraph before?"

"Yes, once, in the military."

"This will be different from that experience," the man said. "Much more sensitive. We're going to wire you up now, so just relax and take a few deep breaths."

The man and the woman began attaching devices to her body: a strap around her chest, probes like those used in an EKG to various parts of her torso, clamps on her fingers and something glued to her throat. Both of them sat down behind her.

"All right, we're ready," the man said. "It is very important to your career with the Agency that you not lie on any question, unless instructed to. Periodically, throughout your career, you will undergo polygraph testing as a security measure, but this is the most important one you will take. Is that clear?"

"Yes."

"I'm going to ask you some questions, which will be easy to answer truthfully."

"All right."

"Don't speak, except to answer yes or no."

Holly sat quietly, breathing slowly and evenly.

"Are you sixty-four years old?"

"No."

"Are you a male human being?"

"No." She was breathing rhythmically and answering on her exhales.

"Have you ever served in the military?"

"Yes."

"Do you know how to drive a car?"

"Yes."

"Do you own a pet?"

"Yes."

"All right, now I'm going to ask you some questions, and I want you to lie on each one. This is to help establish a baseline. Do you understand?"

"Yes."

"Is your mother living?"

"Yes."

"Is your father living?"

"No."

"Did you have sex with a man last night?"

"Yes."

"Did you have sex with a woman last night?"

Holly tried not to laugh. "Yes."

"Did you eat steak for lunch today?"

"Yes."

"Did you lie on all these questions?"

"No."

"Very good. Now we will begin. Answer yes or no, and always tell the truth. Some of the questions will be personal, but you must answer them. "Is your name Holly Barker?"

"Yes."

"Is your father's name Hamilton Barker?"

"Yes."

"Is he retired from the military?"

"Yes."

"Are you retired from the military?"

"Yes."

"When you were in the military, did you ever steal anything?"

Holly paused.

"Yes."

"Did you ever steal anything worth more than one thousand dollars?"

"No."

"Do you know how to drive a car?"

"Yes."

"Have you ever fired a weapon?"

"Yes."

"Have you ever had sex with a woman?"

"No."

"Have you ever stolen money entrusted to your care?"

It hadn't been entrusted to her care and, she told herself, it wasn't stealing. "No."

"Have you ever committed murder?"

"No."

"Have you ever killed anybody."

"Yes."

"Was the killing in the line of duty?"

"Yes."

The questioning continued for more than an hour, and Holly became very relaxed, answering the questions easily, hardly thinking about them.

"In the questionaire you answered about your background, did you lie about anything?"

"No," she said easily.

"Anything at all?"

"No."

"When you were younger than twelve years, were you ever sexually molested by anyone, male or female?"

"No."

"As an adult, were you ever sexually molested?"

"Yes." It had eventually caused her to leave the army.

"Were you molested by a superior officer?"

They had read her military record. "Yes."

"Did you testify at his court-martial?"

"Yes."

"During your testimony, did you ever lie?"

"No."

"During the accused's testimony, did he ever lie?"

"Yes."

"Did another female officer testify against him?"

"Yes."

"Did she, during her testimony, ever lie?"

"No."

"Was your superior officer convicted?"

"No."

"Did you feel that justice had been done?"

"No."

"Did you leave the military as a result of his acquittal?"

"Yes."

"Did anyone pressure you to leave the military?"

"No."

"Did you feel that, if you remained in the military, there would be prejudice against you, because of your testimony against a superior officer?"

"Yes."

"Did you feel that it was impossible to advance in the military because of this testimony?"

"Yes."

"Was major your highest rank held?"

"Yes."

"Do you feel that if you had not testified against a superior officer you could have advanced in the military?"

"Yes."

"During your time in the military did you ever have voluntary sex with another officer?"

"Yes."

"During your time in the military did you ever have sex with an enlisted man?"

"Yes."

"Did you ever have sex with an enlisted man while you were an officer?"

"No."

"Did you ever have sex with a female officer?"

"No."

"Did you ever have sex with an enlisted female?"

"No."

"During your time in the military, were you ever insubordinate with a superior officer?"

"Once."

"Answer yes or no. Were you ever insubordinate with a superior officer?"

"Yes."

"Do you have sexual intercourse on a regular basis now?"

"No."

"Are you seeing one man to the exclusion of other men?"

"No."

"Do you consider yourself highly sexed?"

She paused. "Yes."

"Have you ever had sex with a married man?"

"No."

"Do you have any homosexual tendencies?"

"No."

"Have you ever slept with more than one person of either sex at the same time?"

"No." She had thought about it, though. God, they were really interested in her sex life.

"Have you ever had a strong desire to sleep with more than one person at the same time?"

She paused again. "No."

"Is your net worth more than two million dollars?"

"Yes."

"Do you own stocks and bonds worth more than one million dollars?"

"No."

"Is your income more than two hundred thousand dollars a year?"

"No."

"Do you owe any unpaid taxes?"

"No."

"Did you lie on your last income tax return?"

"No." There had been no place on the tax return to list illegally obtained assets.

"Did you recently buy a new car?"

"Yes."

"Did you pay for it with illegally obtained funds?"

"No." Thank God, she thought.

"Did you pay cash for it?"

"Yes."

"Did you obtain the cash legally?"

"Yes."

"Do you have any foreign bank accounts."

She exhaled slowly. "No," she breathed.

"Do you have any overdue debts?"

"No."

"Do you carry any large credit card balances?"

"No."

"Have you ever forged another person's signature to obtain money?"

"No."

"Do you owe any person money?"

"No."

"Do you own a house?"

"Yes."

"Is there a mortgage on the house?"

"No."

"Have you lied about anything during this examination?"

"No," she breathed.

"That concludes the test," the man said. "You are a liar."

EIGHT

KERRY SMITH LED BOB KINNEY over to the conference table in his new office and picked up something the size of his hand, enclosed in bubble wrap. "This is a piece of Teddy Fay's airplane," he said, unwrapping the object.

Kinney took it from him and turned it over in his hands, then handed it back, taking a handkerchief from his pocket and wiping his hands thoroughly. "You're right, these are pretty small pieces," he said.

"Right," Kerry said. "That greasy, gritty black stuff you're wiping off your hands is the residue of a combination of burnt aviation gasoline, saltwater and plastics explosives.

It's on nearly every piece of the airplane we've found." He picked up a larger object, unwrapped it, and read an attached tag. "This is about a quarter of the right-side passenger door of the airplane." He held it up, but Kinney did not touch it.

"It looks pretty much like the other piece you showed me, but larger."

"Yes, and please note that the inside of this part of the door—we can distinguish it from the outside, because the outside has part of a stripe that ran the length of the airplane—is bare metal, with no trace of the upholstered lining of the door."

"Yes, I see that. What are you getting at, Kerry?"

Smith walked around the conference table and picked up a very large chunk of the airplane that was leaning against the wall. He unwrapped it. "Do you recognize this?"

"It's obviously the other door of the airplane," Kinney said.

"The left-side pilot's door," Kerry replied. "Please note its condition. It's bent, on a line from upper left to lower right, but the upholstery is intact, and the Plexiglas window is still in the frame. And it has no gasoline or explosive residue on it anywhere."

Kinney tried to relax the knot in his stomach. "What are you telling me?"

"It would appear that this door was not attached to the airplane when the explosion occurred."

"Well, if Fay was sitting in the pilot's seat at the time, his body would have taken much of the force of the explosion, wouldn't it?"

"Some, perhaps, but compare it to the fragment from the other door. Quite a contrast, isn't it?"

"Well, yes. What do you posit?"

"I posit that Fay opened the door, removed it from its hinges, threw it out of the airplane, set the timer on a bomb, then jumped out."

"Maybe there's another explanation," Kinney said.

"I don't think so. Also, this door was found much closer to the shore than the other fragments of the airplane, indicating that it began its fall sooner."

"I see," Kinney said, feeling a little sick. "And you think Fay was wearing a parachute?"

"Imagine you're about to die," Kerry said. "Do you choose a six-thousand-foot drop into the cold sea as a means of dying or an instantaneous death from the explosion?"

"Apart from the airplane door, what evidence do you have that Fay might have jumped?"

"It's the evidence we *don't* have," Kerry replied. "We don't have any fragment of a corpse, and not only is there no explosive residue on the pilot's door, there's no Teddy residue, either. No blood and guts."

"We both know that a highly fragmented body in the sea would be eaten by some assortment of creatures very quickly."

"True."

"Do you have anything else from shore that might point to Fay's survival?"

"There is one thing," Kerry said, "but it's not much."

"Tell me."

"As part of the shoreside search, we entered and searched a number of houses, most of them closed for the season."

"And?"

"And we found a bicycle in the garage of one of them."

"Huh?"

"I'm sorry, what I mean to say is, we found a woman's bicycle, but we contacted the owner, and he told us there was also a man's bicycle in the garage. It's gone."

"Any other evidence in the house?"

"One anomaly: the water in the hot water heater, which was turned off, was slightly warm, indicating to us that someone might have heated it in order to take a bath or shower. It would take several hours, at least, for it to cool to the same temperature as the inside of the house. The owner of the house is being transported from his home in Boston as we speak, so that he can tell us if anything besides the bicycle is missing or out of place."

"I want to hear about that as soon as you speak to him."

"Of course."

"If you were Teddy Fay and you had escaped from that airplane with your life, what would you do?"

"I'd search for dry clothes and transportation," Kerry said.

"And where would you go?"

"The nearest town was Kennebunkport? From there I'd go to Kennebunkport, then find a ride to Boston. It's a transportation hub, and he could have taken a train, plane or bus anywhere, even overseas. Ireland might be a good guess. We know Fay had access to all sorts of apparently genuine information documents."

"I suppose you're already checking on passengers?"

"I've got a team on the phones right now, checking every mode of transportation."

Helen knocked on the door and opened it. "Kerry, there's a Mr. Taylor on the phone for you from Kennebunkport."

"That's the owner of the house," Kerry said, picking up the phone on the conference table and pressing a button. "Hello? Yes, Mr. Taylor, thanks for calling. Have you had an opportunity to look around the house?" He listened for perhaps two minutes. "Thank you, Mr. Taylor. Our agents will see that you're transported back to Boston, and we're grateful for your help. All right, put him on." Kerry covered the phone with his hand. "The agent in charge there wants to speak to me again." He turned his attention to the phone again. "Yes, I'm here." He listened intently for ten seconds. "Thanks." He hung up.

"Tell me," Kinney said.

"Mr. Taylor is missing some clothing: a couple of shirts and some underwear, a gray suit and a Burberry raincoat, in addition to his bicycle."

Kinney nodded.

"And the agent told me they dug up Mr. Taylor's garden and found a parachute."

Kinney exhaled loudly. "The son of a bitch is alive."

"Yes," Kerry replied.

"And I've just told both the president and the national media that he's dead."

"I tried to stop you on your way out, and I tried to call you, but your cell phone wasn't on."

"I'm never going to turn it off again," Kinney said.

NINE

HOLLY STOOD UP and put on her sweatshirt. "I didn't lie on the polygraph," she said to the examiner.

The man opened a side door, revealing another small room, which held a steel table and some matching chairs. "Go in there and sit down," he said.

Holly went into the room and sat down, and the man closed the door behind her. She found herself facing another mirror. Knowing that she was probably being watched, she sat still and tried to breathe normally. She sat that way for what seemed an hour but was closer to five minutes, then two men walked into the room and took chairs on the opposite side of the table. One of them, Bob, the younger of the two, carried a thick folder.

Bob opened the folder. "You lied on your polygraph," he said.

"No," Holly replied evenly. "I did not."

"The examination you have just taken is the most sensitive and reliable in the world. *Nobody* beats it; certainly not you."

"I didn't lie on the examination."

"I'm giving you an opportunity to come clean, and this is the only opportunity you will have to do so and explain yourself."

"I have nothing to come clean about," Holly replied.

"That's a lie."

"Tell me what, exactly, you think I'm lying about."

"You know, exactly, what you lied about."

"No, I don't. I am baffled by your accusation."

"Tell us right now, or you're out of here."

"Well, I guess I'm out of here," Holly said, standing up.

"Sit down."

ON THE OTHER SIDE of the glass, Lance Cabot sat with the more senior polygraph examiner, watching Holly's responses. "I believe her," he said.

"She lied," the examiner said.

"How certain are you?"

"She said no, and I got a reaction that indicated a lie."

"How big a reaction?"

"A small one, admittedly, but in my professional judgment, she lied."

HOLLY HAD INTERROGATED many prisoners during her careers as a military and civilian police officer, and she was determined to stand her ground.

"Not only did you lie on your polygraph," the man said, "but you have now made yourself liable for criminal charges."

"You, sir," Holly replied, "are full of shit."

The man slammed his fist down on the table top. "Liar!" he shouted. "Do you think we want liars in the CIA?"

The other man, who was older and grayer, spoke up. "Bob, why don't you go get a cup of coffee and let Holly and me chat for a minute?"

Bob stalked out of the room without a word.

The other man gave Holly a rueful grin. "I'm sorry about that, Holly," he said. "Bob is pretty intense about his work, and he sometimes gets a little too excited. My name is Dan, and I want to help you straighten this out, if I can." His tone was fatherly and reassuring.

Ah, the good cop, Holly thought. "I'll be happy to help in any way I can," she said, trying to sound conciliatory.

"That's great, Holly," Dan said, "because we don't want this conversation to be an impediment to your career." He tapped the thick folder on the desk. "I've read your service record, and it's a very fine one. Of course, your C.O. put some stuff in there after he was acquitted at his court-martial, but that's easy to see through. It's clear to me that you were telling the truth, and he was lying."

"Thank you," Holly said, and she meant it. The words made her feel good inside, but she knew that made her vulnerable to what Dan was trying to do.

"Now, why don't you tell me about your questionable answers on your polygraph," he said, "and I'll do whatever I can to fix this."

"Dan," Holly said, "I'd like to help, but I just don't have any idea what you're talking about. I gave truthful answers to all the questions I was asked. Now, it might help if you told me what you think I lied about."

"First of all, Holly, I believe you. I don't think you lied. You seem like an honest person to me. However, Bob is very good at what he does, and he is convinced that you lied."

"Well, why don't you get him in here with his record, and let's go over the answer he's concerned about."

"Unfortunately, that's not how we do things here."

"Well, Dan, I have to tell you that I don't think very much of how you do things here. Not so far, anyway."

"Holly, I think we're both trying to straighten this out, but I have to stick to procedures."

"Is your procedure to accuse me of lying with no evidence of what you think I'm lying about?"

"Of course not. We just have to be very careful here. We don't want this thing to rise up and bite us on the ass, or you either, a few years down the road."

"Well, Dan, in that case, I think you should either reexamine me or launch a full-scale investigation into what you consider my lie."

"I'm trying to avoid those alternatives," Dan said.

"Well, you're not trying hard enough," Holly replied.

BEHIND THE GLASS, Lance was chuckling to himself. "Are you sure you want to go up against this woman?" he asked Bob.

"I still think she lied."

"So, reexamine her. Do it now."

"It doesn't work that way. She knows what she lied about, so she'll be expecting the question, and she may know enough about the polygraph to beat it."

"Well, I'm certainly not going to launch an investigation based on this blip," Lance said. He looked over his shoulder. "Bob, get back in there and tell her what she lied about. Maybe we can elicit some sort of confession, or at least, a concession that she might not have been entirely truthful."

"Whatever you say, Lance," Bob replied, then left the room.

BOB WALKED BACK IN and sat down. "I've got the record, here," he said, opening a file. "You were asked if you had ever stolen anything from the Army."

"And I replied, 'yes,'" Holly said.

"Then you were asked if you had stolen anything worth more than a thousand dollars," Bob said.

"And I replied, 'no.'"

"That's where the problem is, Holly."

"I don't see the problem."

"What did you steal?"

"A Colt .45 pistol. Well, I didn't exactly steal it."

"Tell us about it."

"After shooting on the range one day, I found a .45 that somebody had left on the bench. Rather than turn it over to the range master and get somebody in trouble, I took it with me, planning to find out to whom the gun was assigned. I put it in my safe, then I forgot about it. More than a year later, I found it in the back of the safe, and I took it to the range master and told him what had happened. He told me that he had already done some juggling with the books and reported the gun broken, unrepairable and destroyed. He told me to keep the gun, since it was off the records, so I did. I still have it somewhere."

"How much was the gun worth?" Dan asked.

"I don't know; that was seven or eight years ago. Right now, you could buy a new one for around nine hundred bucks on the Internet and have it shipped to a licensed dealer."

"The army lists the value of a new Colt .45 as a thousand and fifty dollars," Dan said. "Although I doubt that the army owns a new one these days; they switched to the Beretta years ago.

"So when you were asked if you had stolen anything worth more than a thousand dollars, you figured the gun was worth nine hundred?"

"I just thought it was worth less than a thousand. After all, it wasn't new. But during the test, I remember wondering what the value was now. I finally decided to stick with under a thousand, but maybe my momentary indecision caused the blip."

Bob and Dan looked at each other, and Bob shrugged. "What do you want to do?"

"I'll write an addendum to the examination, giving Holly's explanation," Dan said. "I don't think we'll hear any more about it."

"Anything else?" Holly asked.

"No, I think that will do it," Dan replied.

"Thank you, gentlemen," she said, then

shook hands with both men and left the room, looking for Daisy.

It was not until they were outside again that Holly realized she had been sweating profusely under her sweatshirt. She walked slowly to her next class, taking deep breaths to calm herself.

TEN

TEDDY FINISHED INSTALLING the Peg-Board on the walls of his workshop, and he began hanging his tools and outlining them with a Sharpie. Someday they would find this shop, though not before he wanted them to, and he wanted it to be just as well-ordered as the shop at his Virginia home, which the FBI had visited after he had abandoned it. Somehow, it was important to him to impress the FBI.

When he had finished hanging the tools, he uncrated the multipurpose lathe and machine tool he had bought, set it on a thick, rubber pad, then secured it to the floor with lug bolts. Then he set up his computer station and began installing the software he had bought. He connected and tested the DSL connection he had arranged with the phone company, and then he set up a multi-stage connection to a server at CIA head-quarters at Langley, Virginia.

When Teddy had been a highly placed member of the technical services depart-ment, he had had access to the mainframe, and before he retired, he had set up a sys-tem of downloading files and software to an external location, while making it appear that some other member of the agency had done so. Now he began identifying and download-ing every document in the Agency in which his name was mentioned. The process took him most of the day.

Then he began scanning the files, searching for any information that might be of use in finding out more about him. He had done this earlier in his career as an assas-sin, but now he wanted to eliminate anything that had surfaced about him since the Agency's undoubted contact with the FBI to discuss him.

It was past eight in the evening before he finished cleansing the Agency's files of any useful reference to him. He took one more look around his new workshop, found himself pleased, then went back to his apartment and ordered a sumptuous dinner from Restaurant Daniel to be delivered to his apartment.

As he dined, he thought about what the FBI must already know about him, and what they could find out from the trail of evidence he had left. They would certainly have discovered his visit to the cottage north of Kennebunkport and perhaps even have found his parachute. Now they would be checking all modes of transportation to Boston and beyond, and, once they had run down everything, they would know that he had taken the bus to Atlantic City. From there it would be tougher. The only possibility they had of tracking him from Atlantic City would be if they located the concierge who had arranged the limo to New York, and then the driver.

If they, indeed, traced him to New York, they would have to deal with two possibilities: one, that he might have left the city by any number of means for any number of destinations; two, that he had chosen to disappear among the eight million inhabitants of the city. In the first case, they were bound to find at least dozens of men traveling alone to various destinations; in the second, they would start from what they knew about him, that he was a simple man who had always lived simply. It was for that reason that he had chosen an expensive apartment on the Upper East Side of Manhattan. Besides, it was fun not to live simply anymore. He doubted if they had been able to determine the extent of his financial resources, so it was unlikely that they would suspect him of high living.

He finished his dinner, put his tray table outside his door for collection, then turned to the *New York Times,* specifically to the Arts section, where he perused the schedule of the Metropolitan Opera. He had never had enough of the opera and the theater during his working days, and he intended to make up for it. He ordered tickets for half a dozen performances by phone, paying with a credit card, then turned to the book of Winston Churchill's speeches he had been reading.

BOB KINNEY SAT in his first daily national security briefing with the president, the secretary of defense, the chairman of the joint chiefs of staff, the attorney general, the director of Central Intelligence and the national security advisor. The president heard reports from all of them, saving Kinney for last.

"Bob, what do you have for me today?" the president asked.

"Mr. President, following your instructions I have ordered a top-to-bottom survey of the Bureau's security, and I expect to have written reports and recommendations from all the relevant people by the end of the month. As soon as I've had a chance to digest their reports, I'll submit a written report to you outlining what steps I intend to take."

"Excellent. Have you had an opportunity to look for housing yet?"

"The General Services Adminstration has put someone in touch, and my fiancée is screening them for me. I'll let the final decision be hers anyway."

"You're a wise man, Bob. Have you made any personnel changes yet?"

"I've appointed Special Agent Kerry Smith to be my chief of staff, sir, but I intend to make other changes as part of a more sweeping revamping of the Bureau's management. It will be some weeks before I'll be ready to do that."

"I understand. Well, that wraps it up for to-day. Thank you all for coming."

As the group was shuffling out, Kinney stepped up to the president. "Mr. President, may I have a moment alone?"

"Of course, Bob."

"And I'd like for the director of Central Intelligence to stay, as well."

"Kate, hang on a minute, will you?" Lee said.

When the room had been cleared the president invited Bob and Kate Lee to sit down again. "Now, what is it, Bob?"

"Mr. President, I have to tell you that, at the time of my appointment, I inadvertently misinformed you about the disposition of the Theodore Fay case."

"How so?"

"When I returned to the Bureau, after the press conference, I learned that evidence had surfaced, literally, indicating that Fay parachuted from the airplane and survived the explosion."

The president grimaced. "And we've been telling the press that was resolved."

"Yes, sir; I'm very sorry about that."

"Well, if you didn't have the information at

the time, you couldn't give it to me, could you? Tell me why you think Fay is alive."

"There is incontrovertible physical evidence that the pilot's door of the airplane was jettisoned prior to the explosion and that Fay made his way to a disused summer cottage, where he changed clothes, buried his parachute and stole a bicycle. He rode that to Kennebunk, where he ditched the bicycle and got a Greyhound bus to Boston. From there he got another bus to Atlantic City, New Jersey, where he disappeared. We have so far been unable to trace his movements from there."

"Do you think he may still be in Atlantic City?" the president asked.

"I think it's more likely that he made his way to a major city—New York and Philadelphia are easily reached from there, but he could have backtracked and gone anywhere."

"I suppose I'll have to make an announcement to the press," Lee said.

"Sir, I'd rather you didn't, if that's possible."

Kate chimed in. "Bob has a good point, Mr. President. It would be better if we didn't announce to Fay that we're still after him, and even if you made the announcement and Bob made Fay number one on the FBI's most-wanted list, I doubt if that would be of much help. Fay is far too slick to get spotted by an ordinary citizen from a wanted poster."

"I see your point," the president said. "All right, I'll wait until you catch him, and then I'll say I knew all along Fay was alive."

"Mr. President," Kinney said, "I have to be absolutely frank with you. It's very unlikely that we will catch Theodore Fay, unless he commits another murder."

"Bob is right," Kate said. "Fay is an extremely resourceful man, and he knows how to disappear."

"Well," Lee said, "I'm not going to sit around hoping he murders somebody else. We'll keep this knowledge among the three of us and whoever else in both your agencies needs to know." He paused for a moment. "And I think I'd better share it with the ranking members of both parties on the senate intelligence and judiciary committees."

"Thank you, sir," Kinney said, standing up.

"And thank you, Bob, for telling me about this."

As he and Kate Lee walked out to their cars, she tugged at his sleeve. "How can we help, Bob?"

"I think the only thing you can do right now is to comb the Agency's files again for any information about Fay that might be useful to us. I'll assign Kerry Smith to go over what you find."

"I'll give the orders as soon as I'm back in my office," Kate said.

They shook hands and went to their respective cars. Kinney left feeling a little relieved that the president had taken the news as well as he had.

ELEVEN

HOLLY STOOD WITH A DOZEN other trainees in the smaller of the two gymnasiums at the Farm. An instructor with a clipboard walked into the room, counted the names on his clipboard, counted the trainees, then tossed the clipboard aside. Another sergeant, Holly figured, but this one a marine. He was fifty-ish, her height, wiry and had a severe white-wall haircut. At his age, only an ex-marine would walk around with that. What was visible of his hair was black, except for a white streak over his forehead.

"Shut up," he said, though everyone was

already quiet. "You can call me Whitey, and when I talk, you listen."

Holly looked up into the rafters and involuntarily sighed.

"Am I boring you?" Whitey asked.

Holly gazed at him but didn't reply at once.

"No, sergeant," she lied.

"I told you to call me Whitey."

"No, Whitey."

"You're a smartass, aren't you?"

"Possibly."

He glared at her for a moment, then turned back to the group. "This is a fighting class," he said. "It is *not* a self-defense class; it is a hurting class, a maiming class, a killing class. As far as the Agency is concerned, the best opponent is a disabled or dead opponent. Is that clear?"

"Yes, sir," the class replied as one man, except for Holly, who replied, "Yes, Whitey."

Whitey heard this and glared at her again. He walked over and stuck his face in hers. "You don't want to call me 'sir,' huh?"

"You asked me to call you Whitey," Holly replied.

"What's your name?"

"Harry One."

He looked her up and down. "Yeah, 'Harry' is the perfect name for you."

"Was that a reference to my sexual orientation, Whitey?" Holly asked. She tried not to sound annoyed, though she was annoyed. She had put up with that sort of thing in the Army for years.

"Take it that way, if you like."

"I don't like."

"Well, what are you going to do about it?"

"I'm going to demand an apology," Holly said. "Right now."

"Apology for what?"

"I don't suppose you've read the manual we were given, Whitey, but I have. There is a clear prohibition in the manual against personal slurs, particularly of a sexual nature, and there is a prescribed procedure for dealing with them. Now, you can apologize, or I'll subject you to that procedure."

He was back in her face again. "You'd better be careful how you speak to your superiors in this place," he said.

"I hold a field-grade commission in the reserves of a branch of the United States military," Holly said. "What's *your* rank, Whitey?"

"I'll show you what my rank is," Whitey

said. He turned, walked two paces away, then faced her, his hands at his sides. "Come over here and hit me in the face," he said.

Holly walked over and stood loosely and unthreateningly before him. "How hard, Whitey?"

"Just as hard as you can, Harry One."

She knew he expected her to back down. Holly didn't hesitate; she shot a straight left at the middle of his face and felt the satisfying crunch of cartilage. Whitey sat down hard on the mat, blood gushing from his nose, then he was on his feet and coming at her when somebody stepped between them.

"Hold it, Whitey!" the man said. He was in his late fifties, slim and dressed in khaki trousers and a polo shirt. He turned to Holly. "Why did you do that?"

"My instructor instructed me to hit him as hard as I could," she replied. "I'm afraid I partly disobeyed." She looked at Whitey, who was holding a bloody towel to his face. "I hit him, but not as hard as I could."

Whitey started to move toward her, but the man put a hand on his chest and shoved him backward. "Go to the infirmary and get that fixed," he said.

"Whitey glared at Holly again, then turned on his heel and marched out of the gym.

The man turned back to Holly. "What's your name?"

"Harry One," she replied.

The man looked at the group. "This class is dismissed until same time tomorrow."

The group left, but the man crooked a finger at Holly. "You stay."

When everyone had left the gym, and he had watched them do so, he turned back to Holly. "What did he say to provoke you?"

"He insinuated that I was a lesbian."

"Nobody here cares if you're a lesbian," the man said.

"Whitey does," she replied. "He doesn't like lesbians."

"No, I guess he doesn't. Why did that make you so angry?"

"I did twenty years in the Army, and I heard that sort of thing a little too often."

The man nodded. "I apologize, on behalf of the staff here."

"Thank you," Holly said. "And, just for the record, I'm not a lesbian."

"I never thought you were. Your group will have a new instructor tomorrow, and you won't see Whitey here again."

"I didn't want to get the man fired."

"Call it the straw that broke the camel's back."

Holly nodded.

"A word of advice: if you should ever encounter Whitey again outside this establishment, be very careful. He's good at what he does, and he likes doing it a little too much."

"I'll remember that," Holly replied.

"Go get some lunch," the man said, and he turned and walked away from her and out a door.

Holly went to get some lunch.

TWELVE

LANCE CABOT WAS HAVING LUNCH in the Farm's dining room, in the main house, when a woman approached and handed him an envelope. "Thank you," he said to her retreating back. He put down his fork and opened the envelope. Inside was a summons to a meeting of the executive committee at two P.M. He glanced at his watch; he still had twenty minutes, so he ordered dessert and coffee.

THE EXECUTIVE COMMITTEE met in the paneled conference room two floors under the main house. Lance arrived at five minutes before the appointed hour and found no one in the room. He took a seat, rested his head against the back of the high-backed chair and closed his eyes. At one minute before two, half a dozen people filed into the room, among them the director of training, who was the on-site executive officer in charge of the Farm; the director of curriculum, who planned the courses and chose the instructors; and, to his surprise, the deputy director of Central Intelligence for Operations, Hugh English, who was either the number two or the number three man at the Agency, depending on whom you asked.

English nodded at Lance, and Lance nodded back. He and English had never been particularly fond of each other.

"Good afternoon," said the director of training, Tom Harding, who was tall, slim and in his late fifties. "We had an incident this morning, and Jim Willis has called into question whether one of our trainees should remain at the Farm." Willis was the director of curriculum, a short, thick man with a bald head and a perpetual scowl.

Since Lance had no overall duties at the Farm, he realized that Harding must be talking about one of his trainees. He sat up and became alert.

"Jim," Harding said, "why don't you tell us about it?"

"It's the trainee Harry One," Willis said. "I believe her to be unsuited to be in this program."

Lance leaned forward. "Willis, I would be *very* interested to know specifically why you consider her unsuitable."

Willis shrugged. "Background, experience, temperament." He paused for effect. "And she attacked one of my instructors this morning."

That caused a stir in the room, though no one said anything.

"I won't put up with that from *any* trainee," Willis said.

"Circumstances?" Lance asked.

"The circumstances don't matter," Willis said. "It's a rule, and a hard and fast one."

"All right, then, Jim," Lance said, "You mentioned her background, experience, and temperament. Tell us what you find deficient in those areas."

"She was an army MP, for Christ's sake," Willis said, his voice full of scorn. "The lowest kind of cop, in my opinion."

"She commanded a company of MPs and finished as a deputy regimental commander,"

Lance said. "She excelled at everything she did in the army, and she went through two very tough FBI courses at Quantico. Excelled in those, too."

"Then she was a small-town cop," Willis said, as if Lance had not spoken. "Traffic stops, that sort of thing."

"She was chief of a force of three dozen officers and, on two occasions, broke cases the FBI said were of national importance."

"That's open to question," Willis said.

"And temperament?" Lance asked. "What flaws have you detected in her temperament?"

"She doesn't know how to follow orders," Willis said. "Then there's that fucking dog; she won't go anywhere without it. It's disruptive."

Lance sat back. "She got through twenty years as a regular army officer with outstanding fitness reports and with no apparent problem following orders. And I wasn't aware the dog was fucking anybody," he drawled.

Laughs were stifled around the table.

"Then there was the incident of this morning."

"Tell us about that, Jim," Lance said.

Harding spoke up. "That won't be necessary," he said.

"Why not?" Willis demanded.

"Because I was there," Harding said. "And
because we have the incident on videotape."

"We do?" Willis asked, nonplussed.

"We do." Harding picked up a remote control. "I've had some adjustments made in the
lighting, and the audio has been enhanced."
He started the tape.

Lance watched the incident, which ran little
more than a minute. Every word was crisply
reproduced. When Holly made contact with
her instructor's nose, there was a collective
groan of sympathy around the table.

Harding looked at Lance. "She's yours,
Lance; defend her."

"Happy to," Lance replied, resting his el-
bows on the table. "She's an army brat; her
father has a distinguished record of service
in war and peace; she enlisted on gradua-
tion from high school and got her degree
while in the service. She was promoted
quickly, for a woman in the army, holding increasingly responsible posts."

"She accused her superior of attempted
rape," Willis said. "It's all in the record."

"Not quite all of it," Lance said. "The

record doesn't mention that the charges were true. I investigated them thoroughly, and it's a disgrace that the man's buddies acquitted him in the court-martial. He resigned from the service less than six months later."

"She ruined a good man's career," Willis said.

"He was a lousy man, and she did her country a service by exposing a long pattern of behavior unbecoming to an officer and a gentleman."

"That tape is an example of her insubordination," Willis said.

"On the contrary," Lance said. "The tape shows that she acted correctly in every respect and kept her temper. Well, perhaps pulling rank on Whitey wasn't a good idea, but we all heard him *invite* her to hit him. No, *order* her to hit him."

Hugh English spoke up for the first time. "She broke Whitey Thompson's nose; that can't be a bad thing."

Everybody laughed but Willis.

"How do you expect him to continue instructing trainees?" Willis asked. "Word of the incident has already spread throughout the Farm. Whitey is now a laughingstock."

"I don't expect Whitey to continue," Harding said. "I fired him twenty minutes ago."

"Without consulting me?" Willis asked.

"Indeed, yes," Harding said. "I was a witness to the incident, as we now all are. I don't believe you would have had anything to add."

"You fired one of *my* people without consulting me," Willis said. "I should resign."

Harding said nothing, just looked at the man. The room had grown very quiet. "Well, Jim?" Harding said at last.

"It'll be on your desk in half an hour," Willis said. He stood up and stalked out of the room.

Nobody said anything for a long moment, then Hugh English spoke up. "I thought that went rather well," he said. He turned to Lance. "As far as I can see, you're lucky to have the woman."

"Thank you, Hugh," Lance replied.

"See that you hang on to her," English said.

"I'll do that," Lance replied.

THIRTEEN

TEDDY LEFT NEW YORK CITY in a rented car after midnight and drove south. At six A.M. he arrived at a diner not far from McLean, Virginia, where he waited for half an hour in the parking lot until she drove in and parked her SUV near the front door. He gave her a minute to be seated before following her in.

Irene Forster was sitting alone in the same two-seater booth she had occupied for breakfast for at least fifteen years, perhaps longer, certainly during all the time she and Teddy had been sleeping together, sometimes in the motel next door. Teddy slid into the booth opposite her. She looked up at him, preparing to tell him to get lost.

"Good morning, Irene," he said.

She stared at the man in the tweed cap with the gray hair and beard, and slowly comprehension came into her face. "*Teddy?*" she said under her breath.

"Ah, you didn't think you were rid of me, did you?"

"My God," she said, "I thought the *planet* was rid of you."

"Not quite yet. You're looking very beautiful." He wasn't just flattering her. In her late forties, she had ripened perfectly. Her ex-husband was a fool.

"Why aren't you dead?"

"I thought I'd avoid that as long as possible."

"But the announcement from the president and the FBI . . ."

"Somewhat exaggerated. I'm sure they know by now that I'm alive, but they're keeping that quiet." He looked appreciatively at her breasts under the sweater. "You're as beautiful as ever."

She managed a nervous smile. "Good Lord, I'm wet," she said. "I didn't think that could still happen."

"I'm flattered. And I'm hard." He extended his leg until their ankles touched.

"This is very dangerous for you," she said.

"Not unless *you're* dangerous to me."

She shook her head slowly. "Not in the least. I cheered everything you did."

The waitress appeared at their table with a coffee pot and filled both their cups. "What'll it be, Irene?"

"The usual," she said.

"The same for me," Teddy said.

The waitress went away.

"I'm relieved to hear you say that," Teddy said. "I must say, I thought you might approve."

"You always knew me better than anybody else."

"And you, me."

She smiled. "Nobody knows you, Teddy, not down deep."

"Well, I must say, I like being an enigma. By the way, please call me Mike."

"Mike, it is. What on earth are you doing here? Other Agency people come here, you know. What do you want?"

"Immediately, a good breakfast and to make love to you in the motel next door."

"Done," she said. "And then?"

"We can talk about that afterwards."

"Did you know I was promoted?"

"That must be very recent, or I would have known it."

"Last month. I'm special assistant to the deputy director for Operations."

"How is old Hugh?" he asked. "Hasn't Kate Lee found a way to get rid of him, yet?"

"Not yet. I think she's just going to wait him out until retirement. She seems to have found a way to work with him, which I never thought would happen."

Their breakfast arrived, and they dug into it.

"Did you go through the usual vetting for the promotion?" he asked.

"Oh, sure."

"Polygraph and all?"

"The works."

"That's good; they won't test you again for at least a year."

"Probably not, unless I give them cause."

"Don't worry; I'll disappear after this morning, though we can still get together, if you want to."

"You know I'll want to. Finish your breakfast; I'm randy."

THEY LAY BESIDE EACH OTHER, sweating into the motel sheets.

"God, I'd forgotten what it was like," she said.

"I hadn't," Teddy replied.

She turned toward him and rested a cool hand on his belly. "Okay, now that we've fucked each other's brains out, what do you want?"

"Information."

"You're not done, yet?"

"Oh, I'm done with assassinating right-wing politicians," he said. "Now I'm looking for bigger, even more dangerous game."

"What sort of game?"

"My country's enemies," he said.

"I'D BETTER GO FIRST," Teddy said, after they were both dressed.

"How will you contact me?"

"He reached into a pocket and took out a cell phone, wiped it with his handkerchief and laid it on the bed. "It's a throwaway, un-traceable."

She nodded and put the phone into her purse. "Don't call me at work," she said.

"Of course not. Always after hours."

"Now that I know what you're looking for, how do I call you?"

"You don't. That would be dangerous for

both of us. Don't make any calls on that phone at all. If anyone should ever ask, you found it, tossed it in a drawer. It won't make a record of incoming calls, it's a bare-bones device. I'll be in touch in a day or two. In the meantime, start making mental notes, now that you know the sort of thing I'm looking for."

She nodded. "When can we see each other again?"

"Soon, but not here. Do you ever have occasion to travel on business?"

"I'm going to New York with Hugh in a couple of days. There's some sort of meeting."

"Take the cell phone with you," Teddy said. They kissed once more, and he was gone. He could trust her, he thought. He hoped so.

FOURTEEN

HOLLY WAS TOSSING A STICK for Daisy on the lawn in the late afternoon when she looked up and saw Lance coming. She had not seen him for a while.

"Good afternoon," Lance said, strolling up to her and scratching Daisy behind the ears.

"Good afternoon."

"How's your training going?"

"I'm sure you know better than I," she replied.

"Well, yes, I suppose I do. Let me say that I'm very pleased. Your performance on the firing range stunned the training staff; they're unaccustomed to trainees who are dead shots."

"Sarge has been very nice; I've been instructing some of the beginners."

"And to good results, I hear."

She thought she'd broach the subject before he did. "Are they going to throw me out for hitting Whitey?"

"Certainly not," Lance replied. "I watched a videotape of the incident earlier today, and a lot of other people have seen it since and have been greatly entertained. Whitey Thompson was a pain in the ass, and nobody liked him."

"Then my first judgment of him was accurate."

"Whitey has left us, but he lives in the neighborhood, and I would not like you to encounter him out in the world."

"I didn't know I was allowed out in the world."

"This weekend," Lance said. "There's a roadhouse about five miles west of here on the main road called Buster's; some of the trainees sometimes drink there. I want you to avoid it, because Whitey drinks there every night."

"Doesn't sound like my sort of place, anyway," Holly said. "Should I just stay on the reservation, then?"

"It's a free country, more or less, so go wherever you feel comfortable. But you must remember that Whitey is probably as good a street fighter as anyone alive, and he knows lots of ways to maim and kill. If you should come face to face with him, and he looks like making a move, my advice is to shoot him."

Holly laughed, but Lance didn't. "I'll keep that in mind. Am I authorized to go about Virginia armed?"

"Your I.D. card will work with the local and state police. Of course, when your training is over you'll be given I.D. that specifically authorizes you to carry anywhere in the United States and its possessions."

"Can I have my nine-millimeter back?"

"I'll tell Sarge to give it to you, but don't let the other trainees know; they'll feel left out. It's only because I trust your judgment that you're getting the gun back."

"Thank you, Lance."

"Sarge was impressed with the gun."

"My dad built it. You'll have to meet him sometime."

"I've read his army service record and his

record with us in Vietnam. I wish he were working for me."

"Not much chance of that while there are still fish to catch."

Lance looked at his watch. "You must excuse me; I have a meeting. By the way, the deputy director for Operations saw the tape of your interaction with Whitey; he told me to be sure and hang on to you." He gave her a little wave and walked back toward the main house.

Holly was aglow from the praise.

TEDDY DROVE HIS RENTAL CAR down to Manassas Airport, a small Virginia general aviation airfield, and drove slowly along the chain-link fence at its perimeter. He passed a series of hangars and paid particular attention to two of them: one that the FBI had learned about when they were pursuing him and one that they still didn't know about, he hoped. He had kept the ill-fated Cessna there, and when he had flown it away, he'd left his RV there. Now he wanted it back.

There was only one way to find out the status of his second hangar, and that was to drive right up to it. He let himself in through the back gate, using the keypad code, and

drove to the hangar. He took a remote control from his pocket and pressed the button
with one hand while holding a pistol in the
other. The bifold door rose, and the interior
lights came on. The RV was still there, and
the hangar was deserted. He drove inside
and closed the door.

A cursory inspection of the hangar revealed that no one had entered it since he
had left. He unlocked the RV and stepped inside. It was in disarray, since he had loaded
as much of his equipment as possible into it
from the other hangar. He spent an hour
tidying it up, then he hitched the rental car to
the RV and drove out of the hangar, towing
the car, closing the door behind him.

He drove all the way back to New York,
turned in his rental car and found a garage
near his workshop. He would transfer much
of his equipment from the RV to the workshop over the next few days, so as not to at-
tract attention, then he would be fully set up
and ready to go to work. All he needed now
was his first target.

He went back to his apartment and fell
into bed, exhausted. He had some catching
up on his sleep to do.

FIFTEEN

THREE DAYS LATER, Teddy called Irene's cell phone.

"Yes?" she said, sounding businesslike.

"Bad time?"

"Two hours," she said and hung up.

Teddy waited two and a half, then called her back. "Better?"

"Yes, it's all right," she said.

"Where are you?"

"At the Waldorf Towers."

"Are you free for a while?"

"I have another meeting at five."

Teddy checked his watch. Just past one. "Take a cab to Fifth Avenue and Sixty-fourth

Street and enter Central Park there. Turn right at the bottom of the steps, go around the administration building, then turn right again and leave the zoo area. Keep to the path, then sit down on the fifth bench on your right. Take a newspaper, so you can read while you wait. When you're sure nobody has followed you, take off your right shoe and rub your foot. If you think it may not be safe, take off your left shoe."

"Got it."

"Go in fifteen minutes." Teddy hung up. He thought he would entertain Irene; she had always loved the cloak-and-dagger side of Agency work, but she had not been able to become a field agent. He left his workshop, walked down to 64th Street, crossed Park and went into the Plaza Athenee Hotel. At the registration desk he asked for a deluxe double room, paid with a credit card and asked for two keys.

"Where is your luggage, sir?" the woman asked.

"The airline lost it; I'm told it will be delivered this evening."

"Do you require any personal items, toiletries?"

"Thank you, no." Teddy went up to the

room, checked it out, then bought a newspaper and walked toward Fifth Avenue. He walked around the corner, checking everyone on each side of the street, turned East on 65th, waited a moment, then walked back down Fifth to 63rd, checking again. Then he waited near the corner until he saw Irene get out of a taxi.

Since he knew where she was going, he didn't need to follow her closely. He hung a block or so back, looking for suspicious vehicles or persons. He spent a couple of minutes being amused by the seals in the zoo, then walked north away from the zoo. He saw her from a hundred yards, reading a paperback book. When he was fifty yards away, she took off her right shoe and massaged her foot, then put her shoe back on. Teddy walked past her, then sat down on the next bench and opened his newspaper. He read quietly for five minutes, then took the Arts section, folded it to expose the crossword puzzle and began to work it. When he was sure there was no one near the bench, he spoke up.

"When I leave, pick up the newspaper and read for ten minutes. There's a key card for room 710 at the Plaza Athenee Hotel, Sixty-fourth between Madison and Park. Meet me there."

"Got it," she said.

Teddy tucked the crossword under his arm and, leaving the rest of the paper on the bench, left, walking north.

TEDDY WAITED FOR HER in bed, looking forward to her arrival. She let herself into the room, leaving a trail of clothing behind her, then crawled into bed with him, snuggling close and throwing a leg over his. "Hi," she said.

"Hi, yourself."

They played with each other for an hour, exploring every crevice and orifice, then copulated at length. She came twice before they managed it together.

"Wow," she said.

"Wow, indeed."

"I should have joined you when you retired."

"Then you'd be a fugitive. It would be easier to find two of us, instead of one. You wouldn't like the life."

"I like this," she said, snuggling again.

"So do I. How has your visit to New York gone?"

"Very well. We're here to meet with U.N.

officials about providing counterespionage for their security. There's a meeting of heads of state on Monday, and they're nervous."

"And what have you found to report to them?"

"We were asked late to the game, but Hugh came loaded for bear."

"What did he give them?"

"There's a suspected terrorist cell working out of a townhouse near the U.N. owned by an Iranian businessman. Actually, he's an Iranian intelligence officer, and the whole operation is supported by Iranian money. His service is loyal to the mullahs, not the elected government. We've got the place bugged, and a full-time translation team on the tapes."

"What is the group planning?"

"They've been very careful, so we're not sure, but we think they're going to try something during the meeting on Monday. The president is addressing the General Assembly at eleven A.M."

"So the Secret Service will be all over this?"

"You bet they will; already are." She got out of bed. "Oh, I have something for you." She took a small digital camera from her handbag, extracted a card from it and handed it to Teddy, then got back in bed.

"What's on this?" he asked.

"Plans of the building," she said. "I photographed them."

"That was very dangerous."

"Not really. I was left alone with them."

"These should be very interesting," Teddy said. "Do you know anything about their security?"

"It's run by another Iranian." She wrote down a name and the address of the building on a bedside notepad and handed it to Teddy.

"Do you know what their procedure is for accepting deliveries?"

"No one is allowed inside the building. Any deliveries are signed for on the front stoop by an armed guard, then taken down to the outside door of the basement. Presumably, packages are screened there."

"Who delivers?"

"Gristedes grocery store on Third Avenue, FedEx, UPS, messenger services. It's not hot and heavy; they get no more than two or three items a day. We've had some indication that packages addressed to their head of security are not routinely searched. He comes to the basement and opens them himself."

"And his name?"

She wrote it down for him.

He turned and kissed her. "You're a peach."

"Go get 'em!" she said, kissing him back.

Sixteen

On Saturday afternoon, the training class was called into the auditorium, where they were addressed by the director of training.

"Good afternoon," he said. "You may have noticed that your ranks have been noticeably depleted since we last met in this room. Some of your classmates have not met the standards we set here or have failed their polygraphs or have otherwise not survived our security checks. Should you ever encounter any of these people in the outside world, the procedure is to not know them. If you are approached by one of them simply say you're sorry, but they've made a mistake; you have never met. If they persist, disengage them—rudely, if necessary. If they still persist, report the incident to your case officer at the earliest possible moment, giving a full description of the person and the name he or she is using.

"We'd like you to know that those of you who have survived the initial training have all done well, and we are pleased with your performance. As a reward, you'll have a pass to leave the installation tomorrow night, between the hours of six P.M. and twelve midnight. You must have checked in at the front gate by midnight, no exception. Failure to do so will result in appropriate action up to and including expulsion from the training program.

"There are other requirements: you are to travel in pairs or threes, and only with people from your training subgroup—Johns, Harrys, etcetera. Each of you will be given an envelope containing a valid driver's license from one of the fifty states, two credit cards and one or two other forms of identification, along with a written legend. You will memorize the legend and use only that name, even among yourselves, while you are off the installation. Feel free to embroider your legend, but use only those facts that you can remember, in line with the training you have had. If any person on the outside shows too great an interest in your background, you are to report it to my office. When you return to the installation, you are to resume your normal form of address, by subgroup.

"Your movements are restricted to the county, and you will be given a map of the county. You are not to contact any person— even friends or family—during the time off the installation, or to make any phone calls, land line or cell. You may take a cell phone with you, but it is to be used only to contact the duty officer, whose number you will be given, or to call 911 in the event of an emergency. If you receive a call from the duty officer's number, you may answer it or return the call immediately and follow explicitly any instructions you are given.

If you should have an encounter with law enforcement, you are to stick to your legend, unless you are otherwise identified by fingerprints or your identity comes into question and you are unable to talk your way out of the situation. In that case, call the duty officer, and someone will deal with the situation.

"Finally, you are to conduct yourselves as

responsible citizens. You are not to get drunk, commit traffic violations or otherwise break the law. Any questions?" He looked around the room. There were none. "Pick up your envelopes at the rear of the auditorium, and do not leave the installation until you have committed your legends to memory."

The group left their seats and lined up to receive their envelopes. Holly took hers and repaired to her room. She ripped open the fat envelope and spread the contents on her bed. She found a wallet; maps of the county, of Virginia, and of the District of Columbia; a college transcript showing her to have graduated from Georgetown University with a B.A. in elementary education and a typed, six-page document that was a detailed biography of one Helen Bransford.

She opened the wallet and found the promised driver's license and credit cards, along with a voter's registration card for Washington, D.C., and a laminated I.D. card identifying her as a teacher at a private school in D.C. She also found a Virginia license to carry a concealed weapon, giving an address in Floyd, Virginia, the home of Bransford's parents. There was a map of

D.C., with the address of Bransford's apartment in Georgetown marked on it. Holly began reading the legend, memorizing items as she went. She read it three times, then recited all the relevant names aloud.

There was a knock on the door, and Harry Three opened the door. "Hi, you've got a car, haven't you?"

"Yes."

"Can I go out with you tomorrow tonight? I'm without wheels."

"Sure."

The woman walked into the room and stuck out her hand. "I'm Lee Wan," she said, spelling the last name. "I'm from New York. Chinatown, to be exact."

"I'm Helen Bransford," Holly said, shaking her hand.

"I hear there's a hot spot down the road called Buster's," Lee said. "Want to try it?"

Holly shook her head. "I've been warned off the place," she said. "Maybe you'd better ride with somebody else."

"Oh, that's okay," Lee said. "Why don't we try the Holiday Inn? I hear there's a restaurant and a piano bar."

"That sounds good," Holly said. "I'll meet

you in the parking lot tomorrow night at seven?"

"Sounds great."

Holly went back to her legend, going through it twice more.

SEVENTEEN

TEDDY FINISHED putting all his equipment away, then vacuumed the floor of his workshop. He was ready to go to work.

First, he spent an hour on the computer, hacking into the FBI's counterintelligence files and locating the sources of various explosives in the New York City area. He was, in effect, working the Feds' system backward: they would use these files to track down perpetrators in the event of a terrorist attack; he was using them to locate the explosives.

He found many sources for dynamite, mostly construction companies, but only four for plastic explosives, three of them military.

Stealing from the military was too complicated for his current purposes, so Teddy ze-
roed in on the fourth source: the evidence
depository of the New York field office of the
FBI. This would be much simpler.

He hacked into the files of his old department at the CIA, which bore the innocuous
name of Technical Services. From those files
he downloaded templates for an FBI I.D. and
for the Bureau's stationery. He spent another
hour building an I.D., then he inserted the
I.D. into the Bureau's central files. He printed
out several sheets of the stationery, taking
care to get the watermark right.

Then he wrote a letter to the agent in
charge of the New York field office. He made
the letterhead the personal stationery of the
new director of the FBI, Robert Kinney, then
downloaded a copy of Kinney's signature
from the files and affixed it to the letter. As a
final touch, he downloaded the template of a
rubber approval stamp from the Agent in
Charge's office, stamped the letterhead and
affixed a copy of the AIC's signature to the
space provided.

TWO HOURS LATER, Teddy entered the Federal
Building in Foley Square and, following a

plan from the Bureau's files, made his way to the subbasement where the field office's evidence room was located. He presented his I.D. to the clerk, who wiped the card through a reader that checked the bar code against the Bureau's central files, then handed it back to him.

"What can I do for you, Special Agent Curry?" the clerk asked.

Teddy produced the letter from the director ordering the AIC to produce four pounds of C-4 explosive and a box of detonators from the evidence room, to be transported to D.C. as evidence in a trial. The letter was stamped and endorsed by the AIC.

"That's a lot of that stuff to be carrying around," the clerk said.

"Yeah, that's why we're doing it on a Saturday night," Teddy replied. "We've got a secure van outside, and a King Air waiting at Teterboro to take it back and deliver it to the U.S. Attorney."

The clerk disappeared through a door, and Teddy began casing the place for escape, if he needed to. The wait became interminable, and Teddy was starting to worry. Then the clerk appeared, carrying a cheap, leather catalogue case and set it on the counter. "There you are, Mr. Curry," he said. "Four pounds of C-4, complete with detonators. Just get it out of the building before you let it explode." He offered a clipboard. "Sign here, please."

Teddy opened the case and checked the contents, then signed. Ten minutes later he was on a subway, headed uptown.

BACK IN HIS WORKSHOP, Teddy went back into the Agency's files for information on the head of security, Ali Hakim, at the East Side townhouse. He located a fairly complete biography, which yielded the information that Hakim, like many Arabs, was nuts about horses. Excellent, he thought.

Teddy then opened the C-4 and began to knead two pounds of it into a shape, using a craft knife to define its lines until he had what he wanted. When he was satisfied, he sprayed the little sculpture with a gray fixative which both sealed in any detectable fumes from the explosive and caused it to look like stone.

He then built a hollow plinth and assembled the necessary electronics, along with a detonator and a tripwire that could be fastened to a seam in the packaging. He also installed a receiver for a remote control.

Tired from his day's work, Teddy stretched out on his bed, pulled a blanket over himself and got eight hours of untroubled sleep. The following morning Teddy checked his assembly inside the plinth, fixed a lid to a bolt set into the sculpture and set the lid onto the plinth, screwing it into place. He took a moment to admire his handiwork, then he began packaging it in a tightly sealed wooden crate, taking care to boobytrap the lid. He addressed it to Ali Hakim and from the Agency's files downloaded a stencil of the seal of the Royal House of Saud, which he affixed to the crate.

AFTER A GOOD LUNCH from a Chinese restaurant across the street, Teddy dressed in khaki trousers, a white, short-sleeved button-down shirt and a bow tie, then he dug up a black baseball cap. The outfit looked nearly enough like a uniform. On the computer, he made and printed out a delivery log, then signed half a dozen of the blank spaces with fictitious names. He took the subway to 42nd Street, walked crosstown to the address of the townhouse and rang the bell.

Shortly, a tough-looking man in a black suit answered the door. "Yes?"

"Delivery for Mr. . . ." Teddy consulted his log. ". . . Alley Hackim."

"Do you mean Mr. Ali Hakim?" the man asked.

"Yeah, that must be it." Teddy showed him the address on the crate, also displaying the royal seal on the lid.

The man's eyes widened at the sight of the seal. "We don't usually accept deliveries on a weekend," he said.

"Okay, I'll send it back," Teddy said, turning to go.

"Wait!" the man yelled. "Does it have to be signed for by Mr. Hakim himself?"

"No, you can sign," Teddy said.

The man stepped out onto the stoop, and Teddy gave him the clipboard. "Space number seven," he said.

"What is the name of your delivery service?" the man asked.

"I'm from Eastern Freight Forwarders at Kennedy Airport," Teddy replied. "This came in last night and cleared customs this morning. Have a nice day."

"Wait, where is your delivery truck?"

"I took a cab," Teddy said. "This was a high-priority delivery." He gave a little wave and headed off toward the corner. Once there, he looked back. The stoop was empty.

ALI HAKIM WAS DOZING in front of a soccer match on television, when his phone rang. "Hello, Hakim here," he said.

"Mr. Hakim, this is Osama, the security guard on duty at your office."

"Yes? What's happened?"

"Nothing, sir, but we've received a delivery addressed to you that bears the seal of the House of Saud."

"Have you X-rayed it?"

"Yes, sir. It is a small statue of a horse."

Hakim smiled. It must be from a friend of his in Saudi intelligence. "I'll be right over," he said.

Teddy waited patiently for forty-five minutes. He was about to leave when a black sedan pulled up in front of the townhouse and a man got out. Teddy checked the face against the photograph he had downloaded. Hakim himself. Teddy removed the remote control from his pocket, tapped in five minutes and activated it.

It took several minutes to get a cab, and he was about to cancel the code when a taxi finally appeared. "Fifth Avenue and Fifty-seventh Street," he said to the driver. He could walk from there.

The cab pulled away and had driven for a couple of blocks when the detonator did its job.

"What the hell was that?" the cab driver asked.

Teddy looked back at the rising column of smoke and dust. "I don't know," he said, "but let's get the hell out of here."

The driver stomped on the accelerator.

EIGHTEEN

HOLLY AND LEE ARRIVED at the Holiday Inn at seven, had a drink at the half-empty bar, then went into the dining room for dinner.

Lee looked over the menu. "No Chinese noodles," she said.

"Looks like the steak is a safe bet," Holly replied.

"I'm game."

They ordered dinner and another drink. "So, Lee," Holly said, "what brings you to Virginia?"

"Oh, I drove down to see Monticello," Lee said smoothly, "and it was too late to drive back to New York."

"Where do you live in New York?"

"Mott Street, in Chinatown. My parents have a laundry and a restaurant there."

"What do you do?"

"I keep books for my father and do the ordering for the restaurant. What about you? What do you do?"

"I teach second grade in D.C. I came down here to see my parents and thought I'd stay the night before driving back."

"Where'd you go to school?"

"At Georgetown."

The two women continued quizzing each other, running through their legends, until dinner arrived.

"Well, that's enough of that," Lee said. "Who are you, really?"

"I'm Harry One," Holly said, "and you're Harry Three."

Lee grinned. "I thought I might trip you up."

Holly grinned back. "Not as easily as that."

They finished dinner and went back into the bar for a nightcap. Holly looked carefully at every face; she didn't want to run into Whitey Thompson, off his usual beat. She felt for the gun at her waist, too.

"You carrying?" Lee whispered.

"It was suggested that I should," Holly whispered back.

"You worried about running into the instructor guy?"

"Yes."

"Is that why you didn't want to go to Buster's?"

"Yes, it's his regular hangout, I'm told." Holly looked up at the TV over the bar, which was tuned to CNN. Somebody was reporting from a helicopter over New York. The camera panned from a shot of the U.N. to a nearby street, then zoomed in closer to reveal a large gap between two townhouses with a big pile of rubble at the bottom. "Excuse me," she said to the bartender, "can you turn that up for a minute, please?"

"The explosion occurred late this afternoon," the reporter was saying, "and no one has any idea if anyone was inside the house. Firemen can't even start going through the rubble until the houses on either side of the site can be shored up. Although the police are refusing comment, we've heard from sources inside the department that the explosion is thought to be connected with the upcoming meeting of heads of state at the

U.N. We'll keep you posted as details come in. Now back to the studio."

"Thanks," Holly said to the bartender. "You can turn it back down."

"What do you suppose that was about?" Lee asked.

"I don't know any more than you do," Holly said. At that moment, her cell phone vibrated, and she pulled it from her belt. "Hello?"

"Harry One?"

"Yes."

"Is Harry Three with you?"

"Yes."

"Both of you return to base at once. Go to the main house for a meeting in the conference room. Got that?"

"Got it." She hung up.

"What is it?" Lee asked.

Holly put some money on the bar and indicated for Lee to follow her outside. When they were halfway to the car, she said, "They want us back at the Farm right now for a meeting at the conference room in the main house."

"You think this is some sort of drill?"

"Who knows?" Holly asked, but she was

willing to bet it had something to do with the explosion in New York.

As she was getting into her car a shiny new pickup pulled into the parking lot, and a man got out. She didn't recognize him immediately, but then she saw the bandage covering his nose. She breathed a sigh of relief as she left the lot and turned onto the highway.

ALL FIVE OF THE HARRY SUBGROUP were gathered around the conference table when Lance Cabot walked in. "Good evening," he said. "I'm sorry to break into your first night of liberty, but something has come up." He flicked a remote control, and a TV in the room replayed the report that Holly had seen on CNN, then he turned off the TV and turned on a slide projector. A picture came up of the same block before the explosion.

"This is what the house looked like this afternoon," he said, flicking to another photo. "We've had it under surveillance for a couple of weeks, because we learned that the house is owned by an Iranian millionaire with ties to Iranian and Saudi intelligence. We think that the house may have sheltered a terrorist team that was planning an attack during the heads-of-state conference at the U.N., which starts tomorrow.

"In this series of photographs, you see what is apparently a uniformed messenger walk down the street carrying a parcel. He rings the bell, a guard comes to the door, signs for the package, and the messenger walks away." He cut to a series of closeups of the messenger. "He appears to be a middle-aged man of medium height and weight. As you can see, the bill of his baseball cap prevents us from getting a clear shot of his face. It's almost as if he knows he is being photographed. He disappears around the corner and is gone. Fifty minutes later, the house goes up." He switched to a photograph of the house collapsing on itself.

"It would seem that the explosion was larger than one that would have resulted from a bomb in a parcel the size of the one delivered. We speculate that a bomb in the package set off other explosive material already in the house, causing it to collapse." He switched on the TV again. "Here is a statement made by the Iranian ambassador to the U.N. a few minutes ago, from the steps of their embassy."

The ambassador read from a single sheet

of paper in his hand. "The house in the block behind our embassy was used to house embassy employees," he said. "We believe that the CIA is responsible for this act of terrorism, in which a number of embassy employees died."

Lance switched off the TV. "Let me assure you that we were not responsible for the explosion. Either the messenger delivered a bomb or someone inside, while building a bomb, accidentally caused an explosion. We do not routinely commit such actions on our own soil, and the DDO and the DDI are annoyed that we are being accused of doing so.

"All of you are being trained to join a new counterintelligence team that is being assembled in New York to prevent such acts in the city or, if they occur, to work with the FBI to learn the identities of the perpetrators. The attack today has caused the Deputy Director for Operations to believe that it is more important for your subgroup to be moved to New York immediately than to complete the last weeks of your training. Accordingly, your training has been terminated, and arrangements have been made for you to join the team.

"Tomorrow morning you will be issued

with your credentials and reassigned to New York with immediate effect. Two of you have cars and will drive there; the other three will ride with you. You'll be told tomorrow morning where to report. I'm not going to take questions now, because I don't have any answers for you, so return to your quarters, get packed, get a good night's sleep and report here tomorrow morning at seven A.M. That's all, good night." Lance left the room, and the group broke up.

Holly walked back to her room in a state of excitement.

NINETEEN

SHORTLY AFTER DAWN the following morning, Lance Cabot stood on a New York City rooftop with Hugh English, the deputy director for operations, and Robert Kinney, the brand new director of the FBI. They were looking down at all that was left of a townhouse. Lance had choppered up from Langley with the Deputy Director of Intelligence in the middle of the night, and he missed the sleep. He must be getting old, he thought.

The DDIO and the director were grim-faced, and Lance wasn't sure if it was because of what they knew or what they didn't know.

A young agent stepped up to Kinney and whispered something in his ear.

"Excuse me a minute, Hugh, Lance," Kinney said and walked a few steps away with the agent. Lance could see his face as the agent delivered his news, and Kinney looked both astonished and outraged. "That's impossible," Lance heard him say. "I never did that." Kinney came back to English and Lance. "This is Special Agent Kerry Smith," he said, and introduced the two men. "He's brought me some news, and it puts this incident in a whole new light."

"What is it, Bob?" English asked.

"It looks as though the explosive used here was C-4, and that it came from the evidence room in our New York field station downtown."

"How can that be possible?" English asked. "Do you suspect one of your own people?"

Kinney shook his head. "Here's how it went: a man in a suit walked into the evidence room, presented credentials that identified him as an FBI agent and presented a letter, ostensibly signed by me and endorsed by the AIC, authorizing him to remove four pounds of C-4 from the evidence room to transport to D.C. as evidence in a trial. The man's I.D. said his name was Curry. There is no agent by that name, but by God, the name was in the database that confirmed his I.D."

"How could an outsider get hold of a verifiable I.D. card for an agent who doesn't exist?" Lance asked.

"Hugh," Kinney said, "has Kate spoken with you about the Teddy Fay problem?"

"Oh, God," English said, nodding.

Lance was baffled. "Teddy Fay is dead, isn't he?"

"Not anymore," Kinney replied.

HOLLY AND HER FOUR TEAM MEMBERS were in the conference room on time. A man they didn't know came in and put a cardboard box on the table.

"Good morning," he said. "Mr. Cabot couldn't be with you this morning; he's in New York with the DDI." He reached into the box and removed five heavy brown envelopes and distributed them among the group, calling each by name. It was the first time Holly had heard any of their names.

"First, please pass me the I.D. cards you were issued when you arrived at the Farm.

The group turned in their I.D.s.

"Now open your envelopes," the man said. "Inside you'll find a leather wallet with your permanent I.D. card, which bears your photograph, your right index fingerprint and your signature. It also contains, on a magnetic strip, much other information from your service record, including a copy of your DNA profile. The card identifies you as an officer of the CIA and explicitly authorizes you to carry concealed weapons, not just firearms, in the fifty states and the territories of the United States. Should you be sent abroad on duty, you'll be provided with other weapons authorizations.

"Also in the envelope is a copy of your commission, and you will return that to me to be placed in your service record. Also in the envelope is a box of five hundred business cards. Generally speaking, you are not to identify yourself as a CIA officer unless circumstances demand it, but if you must, you'll have these two means of identification. The phone number on your business card is a Washington number, but any calls you receive will be routed to an electronic mailbox or to your local number, upon your instructions.

"Also in the envelope is a card with a New York City address and a street map showing its location. You will present yourselves at that address by three P.M. today. Your car, if you own one, will be garaged in the basement of the building, and you will be temporarily housed there until other arrangements are made. Memorize the address and phone number and the directions, then return the card and map to me.

"Sally Liu," he said to Harry Three, "you will ride with Holly Barker and her dog in her car. William Knox, you will take Harvey Kite and Jennifer Fox in your car.

"We're done here, so now you are to go to the armory, where you will be issued appropriate weapons. Within certain limits, you'll be allowed to choose them. Thank you, good luck and goodbye. Make us proud of you." The man gathered up the envelopes and left the room.

"Sally Liu," Holly said, "I'm Holly Barker." She introduced herself to the other three and memorized their names.

"What kind of piece are you going to ask for?" Sally asked as they left the main house and walked toward the armory.

"I don't know, really; I brought a handgun with me."

They walked into the armory to find Sarge, their firearms instructor, waiting for them.

"I hear you folks are headed for some active duty," he said.

"If you say so, Sarge," Holly said.

"What do you want to pack, Holly?"

"I've already got my nine-millimeter; how about something smaller for backup?"

Sarge went to a drawer and came back with a tiny, black pistol and a metal tube. "Seen one of these?"

"At a gun show once."

"It's a Keltech .380 that has been reworked by Technical Services and fitted with a silencer, which they made for us." He reached into another drawer. "Take an ankle holster and a pocket holster for it. You happy with your gun leather?"

"Yes," Holly said.

"How about a knife?"

Holly grimaced. They had had training with knives, but Holly found them distasteful.

Sarge chucked and handed her a black switchblade. "Take this," he said. "You never know."

Holly dropped the knife into a pocket and signed for her weapons.

"Good luck, kiddo," Sarge said. "I'll miss you."

"I'll miss you, too, Sarge."

"If you ever get tired of fieldwork, we can always use you on the Farm."

"Thanks." She took her weapons and walked slowly toward the car, where Daisy waited for her.

Sally Liu caught up with her in the parking lot. "I can't believe we're out of here," she said, hoisting her bags into the back of the Cayenne, next to Holly's.

"Neither can I," Holly said. "I had been expecting at least a few more weeks of training. I hope we know enough."

She got into the car and started it, and Sally climbed in.

"My pulse is up," Sally said, holding three fingers to her neck.

"So is mine," Holly said. She put the car in gear and headed for the gate.

TWENTY

TEDDY SPENT THE DAY at home, resting after his Herculean efforts to make and deliver the bomb, and flipping from channel to channel on TV, watching the reports that came in. Before dinner, he called Irene on her secret cell phone.

"Yes?"

"It's Mike. Are you indoors?"

"Yes."

"Walk out into your garden before you speak again."

There was a thirty-second pause, then she came back on the line. "I'm outside."

"Have you watched the TV reports?"

"Yes, and there's talk of nothing else at the office."

"I succeeded beyond my dreams, let me tell you. I think there may already have been explosives in the house, and my device set them off."

"That's what they figure at the office, too. There's something else."

"What?"

"They think they know who did it."

"Are they right?"

"Yes."

"Well, I expected they would figure it out."

"They're changing all the entry codes for the computer databases," she said. "It won't be possible to call in and download without them."

"Can you get them for me?"

"I think so; it may take me a few days."

"Be careful. Don't put yourself at risk."

"It's worth a risk, if you can keep doing this sort of thing. Can you imagine the mess if those people had been able to pull off what they were planning?"

"I'm glad to have been able to stop them, but it's equally important to me that you not be found out. Please respect my wishes in that regard."

"Oh, all right. I'll be careful."

"I'll check in with you before or after work in a day or two, to see if you've made any progress."

"Okay. I'll do the best I can."

"It was good talking to you. Goodbye." He hung up. Any doubts he may have had about whether they were onto him had now been resolved. "Okay," he said aloud, "the game is on."

HOLLY PASSED THE FRONT of the building she had been looking for in the east Forties, turned into the steep ramp leading down to the garage and was stopped by what appeared to be a heavy steel door. There was an intercom box with a keypad and a bell button outside her window, so she rolled it down and pressed the button.

"State your name," a metallic-sounding voice said.

"Holly Barker."

"Are you alone?"

"No, Sally Liu is with me, and my dog, Daisy."

"Read aloud the last four digits of your personal serial numbers; they're on the back of your I.D. cards."

Both women got out their cards, and Holly read the numbers.

"Proceed into the garage. You'll be met and directed to a parking space. Step out of the car with your hands away from your body and stand still." The steel door rolled up, and another, steel mesh door behind that rolled up, too.

Holly drove slowly into the garage and saw two men waving her into a parking space. She and Sally got out of the car and the two men searched them with electronic wands and took their firearms. "These will be returned to you upstairs," one of the men said, "and your luggage will be delivered to your rooms. Please take the elevator to the lobby and report to the man at the desk."

Holly, Sally and Daisy rode up two floors in the elevator and got out. They were in what appeared to be the lobby of an apartment building. Ahead of them in the marble-lined lobby was a reception desk, and two men in doormen's uniforms were behind the chest-high counter.

"Good afternoon," one of the men said. "Ms. Barker and Ms. Liu and, I believe, Daisy?"

"That's right," Holly said.

The man placed a clipboard on the counter. "Please sign in."

Holly and Sally signed and noted the time of their arrival.

The man handed them keys. "Your rooms are on the sixth floor, and your luggage and weapons will be delivered there shortly, after your bags have been searched. There will be a meeting in the twelfth-floor conference room at five P.M. Please do not leave the building before that time."

"I'll need to take my dog outside for a couple of minutes," Holly said.

"Very well, but stay within a hundred feet of the building and within sight of the doorman."

They took the elevator to the sixth floor, which was like that of an ordinary apartment building, and found their rooms next door to each other. Holly's room was a small studio apartment. She had a bedroom with a sitting area, a kitchenette and a bathroom with a shower. It was much like a medium-priced hotel room. The windows looked out onto Second Avenue, and she was impressed that she heard zero traffic noise.

She took Daisy downstairs and allowed her to relieve herself near the building, and when she came back, her bags had been delivered and her weapons were on the bed. She unpacked, then switched on the TV and watched reports of the bombing on the news channels until five o'clock. Then she collected Sally, and they rode up to the twelfth floor and were directed to the conference room, which contained a large table and two dozen chairs. The other three members of their team were there, and a moment later, looking tired, Lance Cabot walked into the room.

"Please be seated," he said, "and we'll begin the briefing."

TWENTY-ONE

LANCE SAT DOWN WEARILY at the head of the conference table.

"Good morning," he said. "Those of you who have just arrived, welcome to New York. Ladies and gentlemen of the FBI, welcome to the CIA.

"This building is the new headquarters of the New York City station of the recently formed counterterrorist arm of the directorate of operations of the Central Intelligence Agency. We bought the building when it was under construction and added many, ah, improvements. For instance, the exterior walls are clad with two half-inch layers of armor, one of steel, one of Kevlar. The exterior cladding and the interior drywall are installed over that; the windows facing the streets are two-inch-thick armored glass, so that you may feel safe in your beds. Those of you who do not already live in New York are being housed here temporarily, until you learn something of the city and are ready to move into quarters of your own choosing, which you may not choose until the location and other attributes have been approved by our chief of security.

"There is no smoking anywhere in this installation. Meals are served continuously in our own restaurant on the penthouse floor, one above us. Laundry and dry cleaning may be left at the front desk; there is a laundry room in subbasement one, and a garage in subbasement two. Communications, technical services and the armory are in subbasement three, well underground.

"The building is as secure as we can possibly make it, with cameras and audio pickups practically everywhere. You will be admitted to the building only after you have properly identified yourselves, and you are not to have visitors without a written pass from the chief of security's office, which will not be given lightly.

"Each of you will be issued a rather special personal telephone which operates on both cell and satellite systems and which has a GPS capability, so that you can be tracked, when necessary. You are to carry it on your person at all times, set to vibrate, and you are never to turn it off, so carry at least two backup batteries. You are not to lose it; I hope that is perfectly clear."

Lance took a deep breath. "Now, let me tell you why you are here. Last year a man retired from the Technical Services Department of the Agency. I expect you've heard of him: his name was Theodore Fay."

Everyone shifted expectantly in their seats.

"Teddy Fay was a genius at his work. At one time or another in a career of forty years or so, he worked in every division of Tech Services—documents, communications, weapons, electronic surveillance—and he excelled in each one of them. For the last ten years of his career, he served as a Tech Services coordinator—an outfitter, as the field agents call them. It was his job to equip a field agent with clothing, documents, weapons, communications devices, maps—everything he or she could possibly need.

"When Teddy retired, he kept busy by faking his own death and disappearing from the face of the earth. At the same time, he caused to disappear every photograph and every record of his employment by the agency that ever existed. After he dematerialized, he began killing people whose politics he disagreed with—all right-wing political figures. You've read about those killings, of course, and seen the TV news reports.

"Finally, or almost finally, he retreated to a well-prepared hideout on a Maine island, but the FBI tracked him there and surrounded the place. But Teddy also had a well-prepared escape route. He got out, walked to the little airfield on the island and flew himself out. At the behest of the FBI the president ordered two navy jets into the air to pursue him and force him down or shoot him down. Before they could accomplish their mission, Teddy exploded his own aircraft and himself with it.

"There the story was thought to have ended, but a search turned up fragments of the airplane that indicated that he had escaped. He stole some things from a vacant beach house, made his way first to Boston, then to Atlantic City, then he disappeared.

The news of his survival has been kept secret from the public and most of the Congress, to avoid tipping Teddy off that he's being pursued again.

"Yesterday, as you know, there was an explosion in a townhouse not far from here. Our people had the building under surveillance, and they photographed this man delivering a package and departing." He pressed a remote control, and a series of photographs appeared on the screen. "We believe him to be Teddy Fay. He is about five feet, ten inches tall and weighs about a hundred and sixty pounds. He is balding, but often wears wigs, along with false beards and mustaches. He is otherwise hirsute, if his forearms are any indication. That's all we've got. The photographs you are looking at are the only ones of him that exist, if indeed, they are of him.

"The president has ordered the director of the FBI and the director of Central Intelligence to create a combined task force to find and arrest Teddy Fay. The people in this room are the task force, along with all the support personnel you require. The task force has two leaders: me, representing the

CIA, and Special Agent Kerry White—stand up, Kerry—representing the FBI."

Kerry White, at the other end of the table, stood briefly, waved and sat down again.

"I expect you've heard a lot about how American intelligence and American law enforcement need to be working more closely together," Lance continued. "This task force is the result of that need. Each CIA officer will be paired with an FBI special agent, and you will work as coequal partners. You will both report to both Kerry and me. No CIA officer is to withhold any information from his partner or from Kerry. Does anyone here question that?"

Nobody said anything.

"Any of my people question that?" Kerry Smith asked.

Nobody did.

"Kerry is going to bring us up to date on the latest information on Teddy Fay," Lance said. "Kerry?"

Kerry pushed back from the table. "The story of this bombing, as far as we know it, will give you a nutshell description of how Teddy is able to operate," he said. "He somehow learned that the CIA was surveiling a townhouse where, it was suspected, a terrorist team was being sheltered, before a planned attack on the U.N. head-of-state conference that begins tomorrow morning and lasts two days. Teddy understood that, since most or all of the people in the townhouse had the diplomatic protection of Iran's U.N. embassy, there was not much that could be done except to surveil them and hope to catch them in the act, so he took it upon himself to remove the threat. He did an outstanding job, though he was probably helped by the presence of explosives already in the building.

"First, though, Teddy had to obtain the explosives. This is how we think he did it: he hacked into the FBI's computer databases to learn the locations of C-4 in New York City, then he hacked into CIA computers and created for himself FBI identification and letterheads, then created a letter from the director to the New York City agent in charge, directing that four pounds of C-4 be surrendered to an agent named Curry—this was Teddy, himself—for delivery to Washington as evidence in a federal trial. I've seen the letter, and it is perfect in every respect.

"He then built his bomb and hand-delivered it to the building. We don't know why they accepted delivery or what they did to inspect the package before it exploded, but the thing worked. Everything Teddy does seems to work.

"The CIA has since changed the access codes to their computers, and so has the Bureau, so we will at least have robbed him of those resources. We have also been back and reinterviewed every person we first talked to when Teddy was killing right-wing political figures, and we have come up with one shred of information that might have some small importance: Teddy Fay loves the theater and the opera. That's it. That's all we have.

"I need hardly tell you that we are at a disadvantage; we are up against an opponent who is smarter than all of us, with the possible exception of Lance and me." Kerry permitted himself a smile. "We cannot rely on him to make a mistake, because, to the best of our knowledge, he has never made a mistake."

A man in a suit spoke up. "If he didn't make any mistakes, how did you find him in Maine?"

Kerry sighed. "A federal prisoner, a former CIA officer, read about the murders and offered information in exchange for a pardon. The prisoner had a summer home on the Maine island that Teddy chose for his hideout, and several years ago saw him at the post office and recognized him. So, the prisoner got his pardon and the reward, and we got Teddy's hideout. Unfortunately, we didn't get Teddy. So, you see, Teddy didn't make a mistake. We found him because of a coincidence."

"Who here knows something about the opera?" Lance asked. Nobody moved. "Oh, come on. Somebody must know *something* about the opera. You're not all philistines, are you?"

Holly slowly raised her hand. "I sometimes listen to the Saturday afternoon broadcasts from the Metropolitan Opera," she said. "I *like* the opera; I just don't *know* a lot about it."

An FBI agent in a suit across the table from her raised his hand. "I sometimes listen to those broadcasts, too, and I'll watch PBS if an opera is televised. I've been to the opera a couple of times. That's about it for me."

"Okay," Lance said, "you two are partners; you're the Opera Patrol. Teddy likes the theater, too, but there are too many theaters in New York for us to cover. The opera is pretty much contained in the New York City Opera company and the Metropolitan Opera company. Get on it."

After the meeting broke up, the FBI agent approached Holly. "I'm Tyler Morrow," he said, extending his hand. "How do you do?"

"Hi, Tyler," she said, looking him up and down, at the sharply pressed blue suit and the shiny shoes. She judged him to be in his late twenties. "I'm Holly Barker. You're going to fit right in at the opera."

"Thank you," he replied. "I hope you will, too."

He didn't crack a smile, but Holly thought she had just been speared.

TWENTY-TWO

AT EIGHT O'CLOCK on Monday morning, prior to his daily intelligence briefing, President Will Lee convened a meeting of the congressional leadership of both parties in the Oval Office, along with the director of Central Intelligence and the director of the FBI. When they had all been served coffee and pastries he welcomed them.

"Good morning, ladies and gentlemen," Will said. "I've asked you here this morning to impart to you some news that you will not like, as I do not. You will recall that recently, at a White House press conference, I announced that the aircraft flown by Theodore Fay during his escape from Maine had exploded and that Mr. Fay was presumed dead. Not long after that announcement an examination of the wreckage of that aircraft revealed that Fay had probably parachuted from the airplane on the coast of Maine. Later, it was discovered that someone had broken into a nearby beach cottage and stolen some items, and still later, a parachute was discovered buried in the garden of that cottage. So it now seems clear that Mr. Fay is alive."

"Why haven't we heard about this on the news?" the speaker of the House asked.

"That's why we're here today," the president said. "The directors of the FBI and the CIA have asked that we not announce that Fay is still alive."

"Why not?" the speaker asked.

"Bob, you want to explain that?" the president asked Kinney.

"Mr. Speaker, we feel that, because of the lack of photographs of Fay, along with his ability to disguise himself, it is unlikely in the extreme that an ordinary citizen could identify him, and we do not want to be flooded with false sightings by the public."

"I concur in that opinion," Kate Lee interjected.

"So why are we here?" the speaker asked.

"Mr. Speaker," Will said, "I didn't want you to think that I was withholding information from you."

The majority leader of the Senate raised his hand. "Question for Director Kinney," he said. "Does this mean that we can expect Fay to resume killing people in Washington?"

"I am not ready to draw that conclusion," Kinney replied.

"Do we have to wait until one of us is murdered before you draw that conclusion?" the majority leader asked.

"It appears that Mr. Fay has taken up residence somewhere in the New York City area," Kinney said. "We believe he was responsible for the bombing of the Iranian townhouse in New York yesterday."

"I hope you're right," the majority leader said.

Will spoke up again. "Another reason for this meeting is to offer you all additional security, should you feel you need it. I'm prepared to go back to the security level we maintained before Fay was thought dead, if that's what you want."

"The previous security level didn't help the previous speaker much," the speaker of the house said.

"What would you like me to do, Mr. Speaker? Call out the National Guard?"

The group emitted a low chuckle.

"It occurred to me," the president said, "that some or all of you might feel that the appearance of additional security might be noticed and difficult to explain."

"It wouldn't be difficult to explain if you announced that Fay was still alive," the speaker said.

"You've already heard the disadvantages of that," Will replied. "However, if it's the sense of this meeting that it is preferable to announce Fay's resurrection, I'll do so this morning. You can all come with me to the White House press room right now, and we'll do it together. I'm sure the FBI will find a way to handle the resulting phone traffic."

Nobody said anything for a long moment.

"No," the speaker said, finally. "Perhaps it's better to follow the director's advice. Of course, Mr. Director, you've got confirmation hearings coming up, and it might reflect badly on you if that turns out to be the wrong advice."

"I can only advise you to do what I think is best, Mr. Speaker," Kinney said, "and not concern myself with the hearings."

"Let the chips fall where they may?" the speaker asked, grinning.

"Yes, sir," Kinney replied. "I expect I can find another job, if I have to."

"Any questions, gentlemen?"

"You going to keep us posted, Mr. President?"

"I'm not going to issue bulletins, at least not until Fay is caught, but feel free to call either Bob Kinney or Kate Lee for an update, whenever you like. If that's all, gentlemen?"

A lot of handshaking took place, and the group filed out, leaving Will alone with Kate and Kinney.

"Anything else, before we bring the others in for the security briefing?" he asked.

"Mr. President, there's something I should mention," Kinney said.

"Go ahead, Bob."

"I was *very* surprised to learn that the CIA had in their computers templates of FBI I.D. cards and letterheads, allowing them to create convincing but bogus FBI agents and correspondence at will."

Kate spoke up. "Bob, surely you can imagine that sometimes our field officers need to impersonate FBI personnel in order to further their work."

"Quite frankly, Kate," Kinney replied, "I *can't* imagine that that would ever be necessary. However, should the need ever arise I think it would be best if you made a request for I.D.s directly to me, instead of printing your own."

"Kate?" Will asked, when she hesitated.

"I would much prefer to keep things as they are," Kate replied.

"Well, in that case, I'm sure you won't mind furnishing us with templates of CIA I.D.s and letterheads, so that my agents can impersonate Agency personnel at will."

Will was amused but tried not to show it. "Is that unreasonable, Kate?"

"All right, Bob, I'll have the templates removed from our databases and destroyed, and I'll come to you, if we need the I.D.s."

"Thank you, Kate," Kinney said, beaming.

TWENTY-THREE

HOLLY SAT AT HER LAPTOP at the desk in her room while Tyler Morrow looked over her shoulder.

"This is nuts," Holly said.

"What do you mean, nuts?"

"There's no way we can begin to cover opera in New York. You've got the Metropolitan and the New York City Operas, both at Lincoln Center, both running five days a week. What's more, the same opera often plays more than one night during a week. Look at this: *Carmen* on Thursday night and Saturday night. Even if we knew that Teddy loved *Carmen,* which performance would we cover? And *Carmen* is on the following week, too. And we don't know that Teddy loves *Carmen.* We can't go to two operas five nights a week, either."

"I see your point," Morrow said. "After all, there are only two of us."

"You don't have to attend the opera to find out if Teddy does," said a voice from the hallway.

Holly and Tyler turned to find Lance standing in the door.

"You just said that both the opera houses are at Lincoln Center. Why don't you stake out both houses, one each, every night before the performance and watch the audiences go in? Look for men alone, fifty or older; Teddy is said to look at least ten years younger than his sixty-seven years."

"Good idea," Holly said, embarrassed that she hadn't thought of that herself.

"And how about record stores specializing in opera?"

"I've spent half the morning going through those already," Holly said, pleased to have anticipated him. "Most record stores carry opera, and the specialty stores don't get much narrower than classical, which includes opera."

"There's a shop I visited once with a girl,

years ago," Lance said. "I can't think of the name, but it's something related to opera. It's in the West Forties, between Fifth and Sixth Avenues, as I recall. Small place, but it had everything, even some quite obscure recordings. You might try that."

"You can't remember the name?" Holly asked.

"Do I have to think of everything?" Lance disappeared down the hall.

Holly went back to the laptop and had Google search for "opera record stores." "Dammit," she said, "I can't get the search narrowed enough. It keeps giving me all kinds of record stores."

Tyler opened Holly's bottom desk drawer and took out the New York City Yellow Pages. "Let's try the old-fashioned way," he said.

"You do that. I'll try Yahoo," Holly said.

Tyler opened the Yellow Pages and flipped through a few pages. "How about this?" he said, pointing.

Holly followed his finger and saw a small ad:

ARIA
Opera, opera and more opera
LPs, CDs and DVDs

"It's on West Forty-third Street, between Fifth and Sixth."

"That took about a second," Holly said, disgusted. "So much for computers."

"We can't go to Lincoln Center until tonight," Tyler said. "Why don't we go check out Aria?"

"Why not," Holly said, grabbing her coat.

They took a cab to the corner of Fifth and 43rd, and got out and started down the block.

"Where are you from, Tyler?" Holly asked.

"Call me Ty."

"Is that what folks back home call you?"

"No, nobody has ever called me anything but Tyler, and I'm sick of it."

"Where are you from?" she asked again.

"Little town in Georgia, Delano, forty-five hundred people."

"And they wouldn't call you Ty?"

"Never. Just Tyler."

"How old are you, Ty?"

"Thirty-one."

"You look like twenty-one and dress like fifty-one."

"You're not the first to point that out."

"The contrast is a little jarring."

"Women usually say that."

"You actually know women?"

"Not . . . exactly."

"Why not? You're a pretty good-looking kid, uh, guy."

"Listen, if I knew . . ."

Holly stopped walking. "It's across the street," she said, nodding toward the shop.

"You mind if I do this alone?" Ty asked.

"Why?"

"I don't know; there doesn't seem to be any advantage in double-teaming them."

"Okay, sure, go ahead. I'll wait here. Holly turned and began looking in a shop window.

TY WALKED INTO THE SHOP, which was not very large but packed to the ceiling with recordings, and approached a girl at the sales counter. She was dressed entirely in black, had long, black hair and wore black spectacles. "Excuse me," he said.

"Yes?" she asked pleasantly, smiling at him.

Ty produced his I.D. "I'm Special Agent Morrow, with the FBI, and I'm looking for someone who may be one of your customers."

Her face fell, and her brow furrowed. "FBI? You think I would rat out a customer for you federal pigs? You made a friend of mine's life hell for two years, and I wouldn't give you the time of day. Now, unless you've got a search warrant or something, get out!"

Ty took a step back, stunned by the reception he'd received. "I'm very sorry," he said. He turned and left the shop.

HOLLY SAW HIM COMING. "That didn't take long," she said. "Did you have a look around?"

"Not exactly," Ty replied.

"You're all red in the face. What happened?"

"The lady in the shop wasn't exactly receptive to a visit from the FBI," he said.

"What did she say?"

"You don't want to know. Apparently, a friend of hers was once hassled by the Bureau."

"You flashed your I.D.?"

"Of course; we're trained to . . ."

Holly burst out laughing. "What have you been doing since you got out of the FBI Academy?"

"Working in Washington, coordinating bank robbery investigations."

"In an office?"

"Well, yes, kind of."

"You need to get out into the world more, Ty. *Everybody* hates the FBI. Didn't you know that?"

"Well, no, I didn't. Why would they hate us?"

Holly sighed. "Come on, Ty, let's get some lunch; this is going to take a while."

Twenty-four

Teddy waited a couple of days, then phoned
Irene.

"Hello?"

"Outside," he said.

There was a pause, and then she said,
"I'm outside, and I'm glad you called. Something's come up."

"What?"

"They've figured out how you got into the
FBI evidence room in New York and got the
explosives."

"I thought they might," he replied calmly.

"But they're changing all the log-in codes,

so you won't be able to get into our computers again."

"That's not good," Teddy said. It was worse than not good. "Can you get the new codes?"

"I've already got them. I burned them onto a CD this afternoon, and I've got it at home. Where can I send it to you?"

That brought Teddy up short. He wasn't about to give her an address in New York. "Send the disk to John Quinn, care of General Delivery, Fort Lee, New Jersey," he said. Fort Lee was just across the George Washington Bridge. It wasn't far enough away, but it would have to do.

"No, that won't work."

"Why not?"

"Because you have to log on before midnight tomorrow, or you won't get in, and we'll have to start over. And I can't keep burning disks for you."

"No, you can't."

"Also, the disk I have is the DDO's, and when you log in it will automatically identify you as Hugh. You're going to have to hack into the codes on the disk and change them. Can you do that?"

"Probably, but it will be a bitch. I may have

to log in as the DDO once, to get at the codes in the mainframe."

"That would be very dangerous for me, Mike. They could put me under surveillance, maybe even polygraph me."

"You're right; I'll have to think of something." He made a decision. "I'll come and get the disk tonight. Meet me at the motel? I'm dying to see you, anyway."

"What time?"

"I've got to make some stops on the way," he lied, "but I can be there by midnight."

"I'll get the room," she said. "Call me on this phone when you're a few minutes away."

"Will do. See you then."

He had told her he had stops to make in order to account for the five hours it would take for him to get there. He got his RV out of the garage. It already had good Maryland plates and a registration certificate, and he had an I.D. to match, so he felt safe. But then, as he drove, paranoia began to creep in. Suppose Irene had had second thoughts and told Hugh English about him? Suppose the new codes on the CD were just a ruse to flush him out?

Irene wouldn't rat him out; of that he was certain. But what if they were onto her and had created this situation to entrap him? He worried about it all the way to Virginia.

He got to the motel at midnight and drove past it at moderate speed, looking for signs of a setup. Finally, he turned around and drove back, parking in the lot of the diner next door. He went in and ordered some scrambled eggs and coffee, constantly checking the arrivals and departures in the parking lot. Just before midnight, he saw Irene's car turn in and park. She got out and hurried to the motel office.

He called her cell phone.

"Yes?"

"Are you in the clear?"

"Yes, I'm certain of it. I made sure there was no tail. There's not much traffic around here this time of night."

"No vans or RVs in sight?" he asked getting up from the table while continuing to talk. He put a twenty-dollar bill on the table and left.

"There's an RV in the restaurant side of the lot," she said.

"That one's all right; I checked it out. What's your room number?"

"Ten, all the way at the end."

He kept walking. "Leave the door ajar."

"All right."

He stepped up to the door and opened it.

"Jesus!" she said, pocketing her phone. "You scared me; I didn't expect you so quickly."

"I couldn't wait," he said, putting his arms around her waist.

"I wanted to be naked and in bed when you walked in," she said.

"We can fix that right now." In a moment they were making love.

When they had finished, Teddy had relaxed a little. If they were out there, they wouldn't have waited this long to break in. "Where's the disk?" he asked.

"In my handbag, on the desk," she said.

Teddy retrieved the disk. "I've got to get going," he said, sitting on the side of the bed and kissing her. "I'd love to stay and do it all again, but I really have to go and get to work on this disk."

"I understand; it's all right."

"It's better if I go first."

She kissed him again. "You go ahead. Call me when you can."

Teddy got into his clothes, slipped the disk into his jacket pocket, kissed her and checked outside. All quiet. He stepped out the door and walked slowly toward the parking lot, checking for trouble. His was the only vehicle in the restaurant's lot; they had closed, and it was dark around the RV. His heart pounding, he got into the RV, started it and drove off. Nobody followed. After a few minutes, he settled down and drove on toward New York.

He had to stop these all nighters; they were wearing. And he had the opera the following evening.

TWENTY-FIVE

HOLLY STOOD OUTSIDE the Metropolitan Opera House at Lincoln Center and watched the flow of people as they arrived for the performance. It was cold, and she snugged her muffler tighter and turned up her coat collar.

She had seen two or three men alone who might have fit the description of Teddy Fay, but they had all met women and had gone in as couples. Ty was over at the New York City Opera, doing the same thing, and she wondered if this was a productive use of their time.

She spotted another candidate for Teddy, a man in a tuxedo who appeared and began loitering around the door, just as she was doing. Too athletic-looking, she decided finally. Probably around fifty.

"Excuse me," a man's voice said from behind her.

Holly turned to find an elderly gentleman standing there, and she sized him up quickly. Mid-seventies, slim, carrying an aluminum cane and wearing an obvious toupee. Too old.

"Yes?" she asked.

"You've been standing here for some time, and I wondered if you were looking for a ticket." Reedy voice, New York accent. "I have an extra ticket, and I'd be pleased if you'd join me as my guest."

Why not? Holly thought. Might as well have a look around inside. "Why thank you; that would be very nice."

He beamed. "Good! Do you mind if I take your arm? I'm a little lame."

"Please do," she said.

He took her arm, and they walked slowly into the building. "I had a knee replacement four months ago, and it's taking hell's own time to get over it," he said.

"I'm sorry."

"I swear, if my doctor had told me about

the recovery, I don't think I'd have done it. I couldn't play tennis anymore, you see. By the way, my name is Hyman Baum."

"I'm Holly Barker."

They made their way into the huge auditorium, and Holly was delighted to find their seats in row H, on the aisle. "What wonderful seats," she said.

"Oh, yes, it took me a long time to get them. I've been coming to the Met since the late sixties; I started in the second balcony, and each year I improved my seats a little. I've had these for four years," he said, "every Friday night."

"You're a lucky man, Mr. Baum."

"Please call me Hy," he said. "Everybody does."

They settled into their seats and put their coats in their laps.

"I never check my coat," Hy said. "Takes too long to get it back."

Holly was checking everyone within sight for someone who fit Teddy's description.

"What sort of work do you do, Holly?"

"I'm sort of retired," Holly said. "I was widowed a couple of years ago, and I sold my little shop and decided to travel."

"Is that what brings you to New York?"

"Yes."

"Where are you staying?"

"With friends. What do you do, Hy?"

"I'm retired from the dress business. My father had the business before me, and now my son is running it."

The lights dimmed, and the curtain came up. *La Boheme* was beginning. In moments, Holly was entranced.

THE FIRST ACT WAS ENDING when Holly's cell phone began vibrating. As the curtain came down she turned to Hy. "I've got to run to the ladies'," she said, and she raced up the aisle ahead of the crowd.

She stood in a quiet corner of the lobby and opened the phone. "Yes?"

"It's Ty, where are you?"

"I'm inside the Met."

"You bought a ticket?"

"I got an invitation."

"You got picked up?"

"Sort of. An elderly gentleman."

"Is it Teddy?"

"I don't think so," she said drily. "Too old, too frail. He's had a knee replacement. He's wearing an obvious toupee, and I don't think Teddy would be obvious. How did you do?"

"Nothing," he said. "You want to get something to eat?"

"No, I'm enjoying the opera; I'll see you tomorrow."

"Okay, good night."

"Good night." She closed the phone, found the ladies' room, then returned to her seat.

THE OPERA ENDED, and Holly was in tears. She hadn't expected this.

"Had you seen *La Boheme* before?" Hy asked, as they made their way up the aisle.

"No, I haven't been to the opera before."

"Were you waiting for someone?" he asked.

"Yes, a girlfriend; we were going to try to get last-minute seats, but she didn't show, and you made me a better offer."

"How about some dinner?" he asked.

"If you'll forgive me, I'm pretty tired. I think I'd better get home."

"Can I drop you?" They were outside now.

"No, it's not far; I'll walk." That should ditch him, with his knee. "Thank you so much for the seat. I loved the opera, and I appreciate it very much."

"Perhaps again next Friday night?"

"I'm afraid I'll be in London by then." He was sweet, but boring and way too old for her.

"Then I wish you a happy trip."

"Thank you, goodbye."

He turned and made his way down the steps toward the street, and she used the moment to check out the departing crowd. No Teddy.

Then, as she was turning to go, she saw Hyman Baum jogging toward the curb rather athletically, waving his cane at a taxi. He jumped in, and the cab drove away.

Holly was halfway home in her own cab before the penny dropped.

TWENTY-SIX

HOLLY FOUND LANCE the following morning in the twelfth-floor dining room having breakfast. "Good morning," she said, "do you mind if I join you? There's something I'd like to talk to you about."

"Please sit down," Lance said, handing her a menu. She gave the waitress her breakfast order, then turned back to Lance. She was very uncomfortable with this.

"How are you and Ty working out as partners?" he asked.

"I like him," she said. "He's bright and willing, even if he is a little stiff."

"FBI men are often stiffs," Lance said.

"The difference in our ages bothers me a little," she said.

"Holly, I didn't ask you to sleep with him."

"That's not what I mean. You see, we can't work pretending to be a couple, and we don't look like sister and younger brother, either; we just don't look right together, and it complicates things a little."

"I see your point, but I'm sure you'll find ways around that. What did you want to talk to me about?"

Holly's breakfast arrived, and she played with it a little, dreading what she had to say. "I think I might have met Teddy last night at the opera."

Lance set down his coffee cup and stared at her. "You *met* him?"

"I was standing outside the Met, looking for Teddy, and this elderly man with a bad toupee and a cane walked up to me and asked if I'd like to be his guest for the opera."

"Teddy's supposed to be quite a makeup artist," Lance said. "I should think that if he wanted hair, he'd make it look real."

"That was my thought, too. He leaned on me going into the hall, said he'd had a knee replacement, and the recovery was taking longer than he'd thought. He said his name was Hyman Baum and he was a retired garment center businessman, a dress manufacturer. He said his father had had the firm before him, and his son had it now. He said he'd been going to the opera there since the sixties, and that's why his seats were so good."

"Where were the seats?"

"Row H, two and four."

"That would take some doing at the Met; the best seats are held by long-time subscribers. What about him made you think he might be Teddy, and if you thought so, why didn't you call for backup?"

"Once we were inside, it never crossed my mind that he might be Teddy, but after we left the building, after I'd declined dinner or a drink with him, I saw him running after a taxi, waving his cane."

"Running after a taxi with a new knee replacement? I don't think so."

"Neither do I. But I didn't think of that until ten minutes later, when I was on the way home in a cab."

"Any idea which way his taxi went?"

"No, it could have gone anywhere—the East Side, the Village, the Bronx."

"Describe him as accurately as you can," Lance said, taking out a notebook.

"Blue eyes, close to six feet—I'm five-nine, and I was wearing three-inch heels, and we were eye to eye—fairly slender, maybe one-sixty; pale complexion, bags under his eyes, good teeth (too good for his age, maybe dentures, maybe prosthetic, part of the makeup); curved nose; fastidiously dressed but off-the-rack clothes, I think; liver spots on the back of his hands, and his hands looked strong. And, as I said, bad toupee: too low on the forehead, too thick, and the gray on top didn't quite match the gray over his ears."

"We could put you with a sketch artist, but I don't think it would do us any good. If he wasn't Teddy, it will just be a distraction; if he was, then the nose, the liver spots, the bags under the eyes could be makeup."

"Maybe Hyman Baum is the identity he's using; shall we check it out?"

"I'll talk to Kerry and get some of his FBI agents on that; they're more accustomed to background checks than we are. Did he say where he lived?"

"No, though he asked me."

"What did you tell him?"

"I told him I was a widow, and I was staying with friends, before continuing to London. He also asked me to go to the opera with him the following week; he has seats every Friday night, apparently the same seats."

"Well," said Lance, "we'll certainly be going to the opera next Friday night, and we'll have seats H two and four surrounded. You were right to tell me about this, Holly. How did you do with the record store . . . what's it called?"

"It's called Aria, on East Forty-third."

"That's the one."

"Ty went in, but I'm afraid the woman in charge reacted poorly to having an FBI agent in her store. I'm planning to go back and see what I can do with her."

"See if you can soften Tyler up a little, will you? I'm afraid he's the sort of young agent J. Edgar Hoover would have loved."

"I'm trying."

"Anything else you can remember about Mr. Baum?"

Holly thought hard. "That's it, I think." She felt humiliated and angry to have come so close to the man and to have let him walk so easily. She was beginning to really want him.

TWENTY-SEVEN

TEDDY HAD WORKED HARD on the new log-in codes for the CIA computers, but he had had to first log on as DDO Hugh English; it was unavoidable. Now, though, he once again had free rein to romp through the mainframe and the various servers and to go from there into other government computers, state and federal, all over the country and in many places abroad.

It made him laugh. He could now register a car in Bulgaria or obtain an Idaho driver's license; he could upload a Florida license to carry a concealed weapon, which worked in twenty-six states. Access to the Agency's computers was a license to be anybody or to simply vanish into America. And nobody knew he could do it. He spent until early afternoon creating half a dozen new identities for himself, complete with credit reports, licenses and passports and uploading them into state and federal computers. Now he could enter the country or depart through any airport, and his I.D. would hold up.

After lunch he took a cab to the corner of Fifth Avenue and 43rd Street and walked down the block toward Aria. He was a few feet short of the shop when a woman got out of a cab and walked across the sidewalk to the shop's front door, passing no more than six feet ahead of him. He felt a physical shock; it was the woman he had taken to the opera the night before—Holly something. He kept walking.

She had not so much as given him a glance, of course, since he looked very different today from last night. He crossed the street and stood behind a parked truck, trying not to tremble, watching the reflection of Aria's shopfront in a store window. What was she doing in Aria? Had they somehow traced his interest in the shop? Of course, she liked the opera, or she wouldn't have been there last night, but still, this was too much of a coincidence. He fought the urge to run, to go directly to the bus station and leave New York. But no, he had worked too hard to create this existence to simply walk away from it before he was sure how much trouble he was in.

HOLLY WALKED INTO ARIA and stopped when she saw the woman behind the counter. Ty had found her a tough nut to crack, and she looked just as tough now.

"May I help you?" the woman asked.

"Oh, I'd like to find a good recording on CD of *La Boheme,*" she said.

The woman got down off her stool and led her to a bin of CDs. "My favorite is the Pavarotti," she said pleasantly. "Did you have a preference as to cast?"

"The Pavarotti sounds perfect," Holly said. As she waited for the sale to be rung up she started to ask about anyone resembling Teddy, then thought better of it. She'd come back in a day or two and ask then. The woman might be more open if she recognized her as a previous customer.

"There you are," the woman said, handing

her a bag and her change. "Please come back."

"I'd like to," Holly said. "I went to see *La Boheme* last night at the Met. It was my first time at the opera, and I loved it."

"We'll always be happy to help you find recordings," the woman said. "We have synopses and scores, too."

"Thanks very much," Holly said, smiling. She left the shop and walked toward Sixth Avenue.

TEN MINUTES LATER, the woman came out of the shop, and Teddy watched her back as she walked toward Sixth Avenue. Should he follow her or find out what she had done inside? Both, he decided. He ran across the street and walked into the shop. "Hi, Esmerelda," he said to the clerk who was always behind the counter.

"Hi, there," she replied, smiling at him.

"I thought I just saw someone I know just leave the shop. Was there a woman in here?"

"Yes, just a moment ago," Esmerelda replied. "She bought a copy of the Pavarotti *La Boheme.* Said she'd seen the performance at the Met last night and loved it. Everybody loves *La Boheme.*"

"Did she ask about me?" Teddy asked.

"No."

"Esmerelda, I have to ask you a favor. I knew her a couple of years ago. We had a relationship that ended badly, and since then she's stalked me, done everything she can to make my life miserable. If she comes back and asks about me, I'd really appreciate it if you could deny all knowledge of me."

"Sure, I can do that."

"She might even send private detectives, and those guys use false I.D.s, say they're cops."

"Now that you mention it, a guy came in and flashed an FBI I.D., said he wanted to ask me some questions. I threw him out; I hate those guys."

"You did the right thing," Teddy said. He glanced at his wristwatch. "Oh, my, I'm late for an appointment. I'll have to come back."

He left the shop and hurried toward Sixth Avenue. As he turned the corner, he saw the woman getting into a cab. He hailed another and got in. "Not to sound too dramatic," he said to the driver, "but would you follow that cab, please?" He pointed to the taxi ahead.

"Sure, brother," the cab driver said, sounding bored. "Whatever you want."

"Not too closely," Teddy said, "just keep it in sight."

The cab made its way to an address in the East Forties, an apartment building. As Teddy waited in traffic, he saw her get out of the taxi and go into the building. The doorman touched his cap bill and opened the door for her. She was known there.

"Okay, now what?" the driver asked.

"Take me to Sixty-fourth and Madison, please." He took out a notebook and jotted down the address of the building. What was the woman's name? Holly something. He couldn't remember the last name, though he tried all the way home.

Back in his apartment he went to the computer and logged onto the CIA server. What was her last name, dammit? He could check the Agency and FBI records for a file. He couldn't think of the name.

Instead, he did a search for the address of the building she had gone into. The computer found three references to the address. He clicked on the first and found himself in a long, boring budget file. He checked the second reference. It was a memo: purchase of the building at that address was recommended, through a front real estate company.

He clicked on the third reference to the address and found a copy of a memo to the director from the head of purchasing, reporting on the appraisal of a building under construction and suggesting that it could be bought, approximately half-finished, for fifteen million dollars and finished to Agency specifications for another twenty million.

The building that the woman had entered was, at the very least, a CIA safe house, and, given the costs involved, more likely a center of some sort.

He slapped his forehead: he had sat through a performance of *La Boheme* next to a CIA officer.

"Jesus Christ," he said under his breath. How had this happened? Were they that close to him? Impossible, he thought. If she'd realized who she was sitting with, she would have called in support, and yet she had let him walk. A coincidence? He hated coincidences.

TWENTY-EIGHT

HOLLY WAS CALLED into a meeting with Lance and Kerry Smith in the twelfth-floor conference room. Ty was there, and several other people who looked like FBI.

"Sit down, Holly," Kerry said. "We've run a thorough check on your Hyman Baum character. There are several in the New York phone book, but none matching your description, and there is nobody recently in the garment industry by that name."

"We think you've scored, Holly," Lance said, "and I want to compliment you on your observation of this man. If he's not Teddy Fay, then he's someone else of the same description who goes around impersonating elderly dress manufacturers."

Holly didn't warm to the praise. "I didn't score; I just stood there outside the opera and let him walk away. Or rather, run."

"Don't beat up on yourself," Kerry said. "What's important is that we now have a location and a target date for Teddy. We know he may be at the Metropolitan Opera next Friday night in seats H two or three. If he shows, then, for the first time since Maine, we've got a real shot at taking this guy off the street, and it's all because of your good work."

"Thank you," Holly said.

"What we've got to do now is to formulate a plan for taking him in a crowded concert hall without anybody getting hurt," Kerry said. "What I think we should do is put our people in seats all around him, and take him before the opera starts, the moment he sits down."

"I'm not sure that would work," Holly said.

"Why not?"

"Because Teddy has these same seats every week, and so do all the people who're sitting around him. If he walks in and sees a lot of strange faces around his seat, he's going to bolt. I think it would be better to take him either as he enters the building or as he leaves."

"You have a point," Kerry admitted.

"Holly," Lance said, "you met him outside the hall, right?"

"Right."

"Well, then, let's have you meet him at the same place again."

"He invited me for next Friday night, but I told him I would be in London by then."

"So, your plans changed, and you went back to the opera in the hope of being able to accept his invitation after all. At the very least, if he sees you, he'll come over to ask why you aren't in London."

"It could work," Holly said.

"We'll arrange a visual signal: you'll change your handbag from one shoulder to the other when you see him, and as soon as you start to talk, we'll be all over him."

"I'm game," Holly said.

TEDDY CALLED IRENE at home and had her walk out into her garden.

"How are you?" she asked.

"I'm well. I got in with the new codes, but I had to log in as Hugh English the first time."

"I thought that might happen," she replied.

"If anybody notices, can you tell them that you logged on using his codes, just to be sure they were working?"

"Yes, I can do that; it might work."

"Let's hope nobody notices. Do you know a CIA officer based in New York with the first name of Holly?"

"No, I don't, but that doesn't mean there isn't one."

"I sat next to this woman at the opera, and later, when I saw her on the street, I followed her to an address on the East Side." He gave her the address. "Does that ring a bell?"

"Yes, it's a new, joint CIA-FBI counterintelligence operations center. If she got past the doorman, it's because she's authorized to enter. Do you have a last name for the woman? I can check her out."

"No, I can't remember it, and even if I could, she was probably using a cover name."

"Well, if she was that close to you, why didn't she call in the cavalry?"

"Because she didn't know who I was. She may have figured it out later, though."

"Mike, if you're in New York, maybe it's time to go somewhere else."

Teddy was not going to confirm this to her, so he ignored the question. "I need a new target," he said. "What do you have?"

"Well, if you want one in New York, the U.N. embassies make for a target-rich environment."

"Who's running intelligence operations out of U.N. embassies besides the Iranians?"

"Who isn't? How about the Syrians or the Israelis?"

"I'm not interested in the Israelis, but the Syrians sound good. What's going on in their embassy?"

"They're spying on the Israelis, of course. They've rented an apartment across the street from the Israeli embassy, and they're doing everything they can to listen to their conversations or read their mail. So far, the Israelis' counterintelligence has kept them at bay. But if you attack the Syrians, they're going to blame the Israelis. Do you want that?"

"I don't much care," Teddy said. "Since they blame everything on the Israelis, nobody will pay any attention to what they say. I might take a look at their rented apartment."

"I don't think that's a good idea, Mike," Irene said.

"Why not?"

"Because if you start showing an interest in that particular street, the Israelis are going to notice you, and that would not be good. They might think you were casing them instead of the Syrians."

"You have a point. Who is the head of Syrian intelligence in New York?"

"A very nasty character named Omar Said, or that's the name he uses. We've been keeping an eye on him for at least a year."

"Maybe he's my target," Teddy said.

"Same problem as with the Israelis: you start following him around, and our people are going to notice you."

"Well, then," Teddy said, "I'm just going to have to be unnoticeable. Where is the Syrian U.N. embassy?" He wrote down the address: three blocks from the Iranian house he had destroyed. "I've got to run, Irene; we'll talk later." He hung up.

Teddy went back into the Agency's computers and did a search for Omar Said. Soon he had a photograph of a tall, balding Arab in a London bespoke suit and shirt getting out of a black Cadillac. A couple of more clicks, and he got a license plate number: a New York City diplomatic plate, SY 4.

At least the guy didn't ride in a Lincoln Town Car, like half the other people in New York. He went carefully over the available pictures of the car. Nothing that he could see indicated that it was armored. Said's only protection in the rear seat was blackened windows. He didn't even appear to travel with a guard, other than his driver.

Teddy began to formulate the rough outlines of a plan for taking the Syrian. He wasn't quite sure where, just yet, but he had a very good idea about when.

TWENTY-NINE

WILL LEE WAS WORKING in his private study off the Oval Office when his secretary buzzed him.

"The director of Central Intelligence for you, Mr. President."

Will picked up the phone. "Good morning, Madame Director."

"Mr. President. You asked for any news on the Teddy Fay hunt."

"Yes."

"Mr. Fay apparently went to the Metropolitan Opera last Friday night and picked up a lady. Unbeknownst to him, she was a CIA officer."

"Did they take him? Why wasn't I told sooner?"

"They did not take him, because she didn't realize who he was, even though she was looking for him. He's that good at disguise. The good news is, he told her he has the same seats for every Friday night performance, so they're planning an operation for that night."

"I have to wait until Friday?"

"I'm afraid you'll have to be patient, as will we, Mr. President."

"I'm getting worse at being patient as I get older," Will said.

"I've noticed."

"How did Fay get the tickets? Were they mailed to him, maybe?"

"An excellent question, Mr. President. He went to the box office and bought season tickets with cash, then he hung around until somebody showed up to collect tickets for better seats than his, and negotiated a swap. The ticket seller remembers him, but, of course, his description was different from last Friday's."

"A slippery fellow," Will said.

"We trained him well," Kate replied. "Unfortunately, we're sometimes not as good at catching our own people when they go bad as we are at finding outsiders."

"Is this the only lead you have?"

"There's a record shop specializing in opera that we think he might go to now and then, so we're keeping that under surveillance, but we have no hard evidence of that."

"Did you question the staff?"

"An FBI agent blundered in there and alienated the only person who seems to work there. We're trying to tread more lightly now."

"Good idea. How is it working out, your people and the FBI?"

"The team has made a good start," she said. "They're trying very hard to work together, and it's my hope that gradually, their institutional attachments will be superseded by their loyalty to the team. It's not an easy transition for any of them."

"Bob Kinney starts his confirmation hearings this week, and I expect he'll be asked for his views on that subject."

"I'll be watching, Mr. President. I'll be interested in hearing his views."

"Is Bob being helpful?"

"Yes, when he's not finding things to complain about in the way the Agency works."

Will laughed. "You left yourself wide open on the question of FBI I.D. cards," he said.

"Don't rub it in. Please."

"I'll do my rubbing when you get home."

"I'm shocked, Mr. President, that you would indulge in sexual harassment. On a White House telephone line, anyway."

"See you later."

"You betcha, Mr. President."

TEDDY CONTINUED to pore over the CIA's file on Omar Said. The most interesting item he found was that, while Said had a wife ensconced in an apartment in the U.N. Towers, he also had two girlfriends kept in apartments located on the East Side. He spent his weekdays with the wife, and the weekends with the girlfriends.

One of the girls, in particular, interested him. She was a belly dancer in a Middle Eastern restaurant a few blocks south of the U.N., and Said frequently began his weekends with her, dining at the restaurant and watching her performance, then taking her to her apartment later to express his appreciation for her work. The transcripts of their recorded conversations were disgustingly vivid, involving imagery that included references to various desert animals. Said was usually with her until the wee hours. Then, the following night, he would be with the other girlfriend. A busy man, Omar.

Teddy began to formulate a plan.

THIRTY

ROBERT KINNEY ARRIVED at the office of the chairman of the Senate Judiciary Committee promptly on time, then was required to wait for half an hour while the chairman tended to whatever chores he considered to be more important than seeing the director of the FBI.

Finally, the senator emerged from his office and heartily shook Kinney's hand. "Good morning, Bob," he said cheerfully. "Good to see you. Looking forward to your hearing."

"Good to see you, Senator."

"Come, let's walk over to the hearing

room together," the senator said, striding out the door, leading the way.

Kinney, with his long legs, had no trouble keeping up with the shorter man.

"My committee staff tells me you were unhelpful during the staff interview period, Bob. Why was that?"

"I'm sorry, Senator, but as you can imagine, we're going through a very busy time at the Bureau, and I didn't really have time to answer questions twice, when once ought to do." Kinney had infuriated the committee staff by refusing to schedule meetings with them. He was aware that the members of their committee used their report to formulate their questions, and he was happier answering original questions from members without being crawled over by an army of staff ants.

"It's how we do things, Bob."

"Senator, this isn't a talk show, where guests get pre-interviewed by staff before being questioned by the host, is it?"

"Some might say it is, Bob."

"I'm sorry, I never looked at a Senate hearing as a talk show."

"Welcome to showbiz, Bob."

The senator led Kinney into the huge

hearing room, which was packed with spectators and press, shook his hand for the cameras and deposited him at the witness table, where he endured a barrage of strobe flashes from the photographers. Kinney had chosen to be seated at the table alone, against the advice of a Bureau lawyer, who was sitting in the first row of seats, looking nervous.

After five minutes of idle chatter and back-slapping among the committee members the chairman called them to order, and Kinney was sworn.

"Good morning," the chairman said. "We sit today for hearings on the president's appointment of Robert Kinney as director of the Federal Bureau of Investigation. Mr. Kinney, welcome."

"Thank you, Mr. Chairman."

"Let's begin with your education and experience in law enforcement, Mr. Kinney."

"I grew up in the Greenwich Village neighborhood of New York City and attended New York University and the NYU law school," Kinney said. "After that I joined the New York City Police Department as a patrolman, was promoted to detective three years later and spent, in all, twenty-one years in the department, rising to the rank of lieutenant. Then . . ."

"Excuse me, Mr. Kinney, did you say that you rose only to the rank of lieutenant during your twenty-one years' service?"

"That's correct, Mr. Chairman. Lieutenant was the highest rank I could hold and still conduct investigations, which I felt was my strong suit, so I did not seek promotion beyond that level. Captains and above are primarily concerned with administrative matters."

"I see," the chairman muttered. "Please go on."

"I was recruited from the NYPD by the FBI twelve years ago, when the director at that time felt that the Bureau's investigative techniques needed strengthening. In short, he needed new people who could actually solve crimes. I led investigations into criminal activity designated by the director as special, among them investigations into bank robbery, financial wrongdoing and serial killers. Four years ago I was appointed deputy director for investigations, and after that I oversaw all the criminal investigations conducted by the Bureau."

"Well, that's fascinating, Mr. Kinney," the

chairman said drily. "I understand that you and the most recent director had different opinions about one or two things."

"The most recent director and I disagreed about almost everything," Kinney replied.

"Can you think of any instance when you felt able to give your director your full support for his actions?"

Kinney thought for a moment. "No, Mr. Chairman. I cannot."

There was a roar of laughter from the audience in the big hearing room, and the chairman angrily gaveled them into silence. "Did you mean to be funny, Mr. Kinney?"

"No, sir, simply candid."

"Did you think that your disloyalty to your director made you a better FBI man?"

"Mr. Chairman, my loyalty was to the quality of the investigations conducted by the Bureau. The director's actions often infringed on that quality, and when that happened, I opposed him."

"That's your opinion, is it not?"

"It's a fact, sir."

The chairman, looking thoroughly unhappy, passed the questioning on to another senator.

"Mr. Kinney," the senator began, "the president has proposed that the FBI be severed from the Justice Department and operate as an independent entity. Do you support this recommendation?"

"Yes, Senator, I do, unreservedly."

"Why don't you want the supervision of the attorney general?"

"I think we have a fine attorney general, Senator, but I believe the Bureau can operate more effectively if it is independent. In the past, some attorneys general have used the Bureau for political ends, and that is not the Bureau's purpose."

"Would you care to be specific about that?"

"No, sir, I would not. I'm not here to criticize former officeholders."

"Except the former director."

Kinney simply shrugged. "I answered the questions I was asked."

"When you were with the New York City Police Department you worked in conjunction with the district attorney's office, did you not? They prosecuted the cases you investigated. Is that so different from the way the Bureau has worked with the justice department in the past?"

"Yes, Senator, it is. The NYPD is an independent police organization, and it does not report to the district attorney or follow his orders."

The questioning continued for another two hours. Kinney was, by turns, blunt and charming. Some committee members seemed miffed, but the audience loved him.

When the hearing ended, Kinney was surrounded by reporters and cameras and besieged with questions, which he declined to answer.

ON THE WAY BACK to the Hoover Building, Kinney called Kerry Smith. "Are you all set for tonight at the Met?" he asked.

"Yes, sir, we are," Smith replied. "We've pulled everybody off everything else in order to saturate Lincoln Center with our people. If he shows, he'll be ours."

"Don't fuck it up," Kinney said, then hung up.

THIRTY-ONE

HOLLY STOOD IN FRONT of the Metropolitan Opera House, shivering in the cold and occasionally stamping her feet to keep them warm. Her eyes raked the giant plaza of Lincoln Center, searching for Hyman Baum. All she saw were CIA and FBI agents. She hoped to God they were not as visible to Teddy Fay as they were to her.

She stood near the door where she had met him on the previous Friday night and hoped he would arrive before she froze to death. She had spent the last four winters in Florida, and she had forgotten what cold weather was. New York was reminding her.

A young man approached her. "Looking for opera tickets, ma'am?"

"No, thanks. I already have mine." She felt old, being called "ma'am."

"Want to sell them?"

"No, thanks." She watched him wade back into the crowd, then continued her search. Not even Teddy Fay could turn himself into a twenty-one-year-old black kid.

Gradually, the crowd thinned, as people moved into the opera house and found their seats. She could now see every person left in the plaza, and not one of them could possibly be Teddy Fay. Her phone vibrated. "Yes?"

"There's an elderly man and woman sitting in seats H two and three," Lance's voice said. "Get inside and cover the entrance to that aisle."

She showed the pass she had been issued to the ticket taker and ran toward the door, stepping inside just as an usher was closing it and the first strains of the overture to *Le Nozze de Figaro* rose. She could see two agents standing in the aisle next to row H, hands in their coat pockets, talking to a man in the first seat. Gesticulating, he got out of his seat and started up the aisle.

He was different, but he could be Teddy, she decided. Then, as the three men reached where she was standing, she decided he was not.

"I'm telling you, I traded my tickets for these seats," the man was saying.

"Where were your original seats?" an agent asked.

"At the rear of the parterre level," he said.

"Where's that?"

"One level up." He pointed and gave the agents the seat numbers.

Holly followed the two men, who were sprinting across the lobby for the stairs while one of them spoke into the microphone in his fist. They arrived at the entrance to the parterre level and brushed aside an usher who tried to stop them. They found the proper row and began wading down it, stepping on peoples' toes, and a moment later they were back with a boy of about nineteen. They hustled him out the door.

"What the fuck is going on?" the boy asked, clearly scared.

"How did you get your seats?" an agent asked.

"I traded some in the dress circle for them," he said.

A moment later the agents were running up more stairs, but Holly did not follow them. She called Lance. "We've been had; Teddy has traded seats at least twice. He's probably not here."

She could hear Lance speaking into his radio. "Everybody hold your positions and check out anybody who leaves by any exit." He came back to his phone. "Holly, wait in the lobby and keep an eye out for anybody who might be Teddy."

"Right," she said, then started down the stairs.

TEDDY SAT in a stolen 1988 Oldsmobile, parked halfway down the block from the Middle Eastern restaurant. Omar Said's car was double-parked out front, its engine running to keep the driver warm. Teddy's eyes ran up and down the block, building by building, looking for surveillance. For the life of him, he could not spot anybody.

Suddenly, to his surprise, Said and a woman left the restaurant and got into his car. Apparently, urgent loins precluded dinner. Teddy waited until the Cadillac turned the corner, then drove to the end of the block and, just to throw off any undetected surveillance, turned in the opposite direction and drove around the block, before continuing. After all, he knew where they were going.

He got there in time to see the door to the brownstone closing behind them. He had already cased the building, top to bottom. The downstairs door had not even required lock picking, just a credit card. Said's Cadillac was idling outside, and the driver had settled in for the duration. Teddy parked his stolen car in front of a fireplug and got out. No need to wipe anything down, since he had been wearing gloves all evening.

He trotted up the front steps of the building and quickly let himself in. The apartment was two floors up, and he listened to be sure they were not still in the hallway, then walked slowly and silently up the stairs.

He stood outside her apartment door and placed one end of a listening device of his own construction in an ear and the other, microphone end, on the door. The two pieces were connected by a wire. The first thing he heard was ice cubes striking glass; they were mixing drinks. There was a minimum of conversation, then they moved out of the living room. No doubt where they were headed.

Teddy waited three minutes, leaning against the wall next to the door, then produced a set of lock picks from a little wallet and in thirty seconds had the door open. He pulled down the knitted cap he was wearing, and it became a ski mask. He took his little Agency Keltec .380 from his overcoat pocket and screwed the silencer into the barrel. Then he stepped inside and very quietly closed the door behind him.

He could hear the bed squeaking, and he knew that it took two people to make the other noises he was hearing. As long as they were vocal, he need not worry about being detected. He stepped to the bedroom door.

Omar Said was in the saddle, pumping away. The girl's face was turned toward Teddy, and her eyes were squeezed tightly shut. Then, as he approached the bed, she opened them.

Teddy pointed the pistol at her and brought a finger to his lips. She now had to decide whether to sacrifice her life for her lover's. She made her decision; she closed her eyes again. Teddy took another step and put one round into the back of Said's head.

The Syrian rolled off the girl and onto the floor on the other side of the bed. Teddy walked around the bed and put another round through his forehead. He looked back at the girl, who lay rigid on the bed, her eyes screwed shut.

"Wait ten minutes before you call anyone," Teddy said in Arabic. He didn't speak or understand the language, but he had memorized a number of handy phrases. The girl nodded.

Teddy left the apartment, listened for others in the hallway, then, hearing no one, walked downstairs, rolling his ski mask back into a cap. He took a look through the glass of the front door and saw Said's chauffeur's head laid on the headrest of his seat. He was asleep; no need to kill him.

Teddy left the building and checked the block for surveillance. Nothing. He walked three blocks, checking, before he took a cab back to his own neighborhood.

HOLLY STOOD OUTSIDE the Metropolitan, watching the last of the operagoers leaving the building. Lance, elegant in a cashmere topcoat and soft hat, came over and stood beside her.

"He didn't show," she said.

"He showed, but not here," Lance replied.

"I just got a call from Dino Bacchetti at the 19th precinct. A Syrian diplomat named Omar Said, who is an intelligence operative, was shot twice in the head while in the throes of passion at his girlfriend's apartment."

"I don't think Teddy will go to the opera next Friday night, either," Holly said.

Thirty-two

Will and Kate Lee were in bed, reading, when her private line rang. "Yes? Say again? This doesn't make any sense; how long have we been watching him? That's what I thought. Fay had already left the Agency when we started watching him. All right, we'll meet in the morning and talk about it then. Good night." She hung up.

Will looked at her sideways but said nothing. She looked back at him.

"Oh, all right, I'll tell you. Teddy Fay didn't show up at the opera tonight. While all our agents were enjoying *Le Nozze de Figaro* . . ."

"I love that overture," Will said.

"Don't interrupt. While they had the opera house staked out, Teddy killed a Syrian spy named Omar Said, who we've been surveilling for about four months, ever since he arrived in New York. He is . . . *was* attached to the Syrian mission to the U.N., and he had diplomatic immunity."

"Is Mr. Said a great loss to the U.N., the Agency or the human race?" Will asked.

"Certainly not; he was a goatish, murderous son of a bitch, and the planet Earth is a better place without him."

"Then I take it we have no complaints?"

"It's an embarrassment to the Agency that a diplomat who was under our constant surveillance was murdered while we were lured away."

"You weren't providing him with any sort of protection, were you?"

"No, we were trying to catch him hobnobbing with terrorists, so we could arrest them and kick him out of the country."

"Does anybody know you were surveilling him?"

"Just the FBI. They were helping us."

"Then, if he wasn't your charge and nobody knows you cared, why is it an embarrassment?"

"It just is," she said. She turned out her light, fluffed her pillow and turned away from him.

"I suppose this terrible news means you're not in the mood for . . ."

"I didn't say that," she said, turning back to him.

Late the following morning, Kate convened a meeting in her conference room. Attending were Hugh English, the DDO; his deputy, Irene Foster; Ian Thrush, the DDI; his deputy, George Weaver and, by television conference hookup from New York, Lance Cabot.

"All right, Lance," Kate said, "give us the whole thing."

"Good morning, Director," Lance said.

"Good morning from all of us."

"One of my officers, a new one named Holly Barker, while looking for Teddy Fay at the opera a week ago yesterday, found him, quite by accident. He walked up to her and invited her to join him for *La Boheme.* He was heavily disguised, and she didn't recognize him, and she thought it might be a good idea to look around inside, so she accepted. He told her his name was Hyman Baum and that he was the retired owner of a dress business in the garment district.

"After the opera, he invited her to join him. She declined, saying she would be traveling, and they said good night. Part of his disguise was a cane, ostensibly because he had had a recent knee replacement, but after they parted, Holly saw him sprinting for a cab. On the way home, she realized that she might have spent the evening with Teddy. Her suspicions were reinforced by the fact that our investigation determined that Mr. Baum did not exist.

"He told her that he had the same seats every week; accordingly, last night we staked out the Met in large numbers, pulling people off other assignments. Teddy had exchanged his tickets three times with other operagoers, leading us on a wild goose chase around the hall. While we were chasing Teddy at the Met, he was dispatching Mr. Said, at the apartment of his girlfriend. We questioned her, and she said all she saw was a man in a ski mask with a small gun. She phoned the police, and one of our consultants, Lieutenant Dino Bacchetti, of the NYPD, called me. That's it."

"There are two things that concern me here," Kate said. "One: if Teddy didn't show and went to the trouble of exchanging his tickets three times, he must have made Ms. Barker as one of us. How?"

"Holly introduced herself, using her own name, but that would have meant nothing to Teddy, and she cannot think of any other reason he would know who she was. Neither can I or anybody else who has addressed the issue."

"Two," Kate said. "Said has only been in the country for four months, and we have only been interested in him for that long. Since Teddy retired from the Agency more than a year ago, how would he have been aware of Said's existence, let alone his presence in New York?"

"I think that is an issue best addressed at your end of this hookup," Lance said.

Irene Foster half-raised a hand. "That information had to have come from inside," she said, glad to be the one to point it out.

"Or from someone on the New York task force," Kate said. "Lance, question everyone there who knew about Said. While you're at it, I want you to wring out Ms. Barker and figure out how he made her."

"Will do," Lance said.

"Hugh," she said, addressing her DDO, "I want your people to make a list of everyone in this building who knew we were sur-veilling Omar Said and put every one of them through the ringer—polygraphs, the works."

"Yes, Kate," English said. He turned to his deputy. "Irene, this will be your baby; get on it as soon as we're out of this meeting."

"Certainly, Hugh," Irene replied.

"Director," Lance said from New York.

"Yes, Lance?"

"Holly Barker is with me, and she may have figured out how she was made." Lance introduced an attractive woman to the group. "Tell them, please."

"Good morning," Holly said. "A couple of days before I first met Teddy at the opera, my FBI partner and I checked out a record store called Aria, on the West Side, at Lance's suggestion. My partner went in alone, and when he identified himself as an FBI agent, the clerk behind the counter re-fused to talk to him and told him to get out. The day after I met Teddy, I went back to the shop, looked around and bought a CD. I mentioned to the clerk that I had seen *La*

Boheme the night before and that I wanted the recording, and she suggested a version."

"Did you identify yourself, Holly?" Kate asked.

"No, ma'am, not in light of my partner's experience. I thought I would go back after establishing myself as a customer and see what I could learn. My point is, at the opera I gave Teddy absolutely no reason to think I was Agency, and the only other point of contact could have been at the record shop."

"Do you think he might have been in the shop?"

"No, I was the only customer, but I think it's quite possible that he saw me either enter or leave the shop, or both."

"But why would seeing you there make him think you were Agency? You were just a woman buying a copy of *La Boheme,* for all he knew."

"Unless he followed me from the shop," Holly said. "From there, I walked to Sixth Avenue and took a cab back to the Barn. If he followed me, he would know where the building is."

"But Holly, we've only been in the building for a couple of weeks; it's brand new. How could he associate it with us?"

"Maybe he saw someone he knew at the Agency going in or out," Holly said.

"Or," Lance said, interrupting, "maybe he researched the address on the Agency's computers."

"But we've locked him out of the computers," Irene Foster said. "We've changed all the log-in codes."

"Then I think that puts the ball back in your court at Langley," Lance said. "Maybe the codes should be changed again."

"Thank you, Lance," Kate said, "and thank you, too, Holly; you've been a great help."

"Thank you, Director," Holly said.

Kate turned back to the group. "Call Technical Services and change the codes again. Irene, there are still a lot of people down there who knew Teddy. That would seem a logical place to start your internal investigation."

"Yes, Director," Irene said.

THIRTY-THREE

LANCE CABOT AND KERRY SMITH were in a meeting in the twelfth-floor conference room when a call came in. Lance picked up the phone. "Yes?"

"Director Robert Kinney for you or Agent Smith," the operator said.

Lance pressed the speaker button. "Director, this is Lance Cabot; I'm here with Agent Smith."

"Afternoon," Kerry said. "Something has come up. Kerry, you remember the hangar at Manassas Airport where Teddy Fay had his workshop." It wasn't a question.

"Yes, sir," Kerry replied.

"This morning we had a call from the airport manager down there. Apparently, Fay had a second hangar, where he kept the Cessna he blew up, and the manager found it on a routine check this morning. There's a lot of stuff in the hangar, but the man says he didn't touch anything. I'd like you—and Lance, if he likes—to take a couple of people, fly down there and process the scene, see what you can come up with."

"All right," Kerry said. "I'm on my way. Will you send a tech team from there to meet us? I suppose it will be about . . . three hours, before I can get there."

"Director," Lance said, "if it's all right, I'm going to let Kerry handle this; I have a lot on my plate here."

"Yeah, I heard about the Said thing," Kinney said. "Send whoever you like."

"Thank you, sir." Lance punched off the call. "Kerry, why don't you take Holly and Ty with you?"

"Okay. Do we have a chopper yet?"

"Not our own; we have a service that operates out of the East Side Heliport. I'll have someone call and book one."

* * *

HOLLY LOOKED OUT the window of the helicopter and saw Manassas Airport as they approached. It was a quiet little field nestled in the Virginia countryside. "Teddy had a workshop here?" she asked Kerry.

"Yeah. He also kept an RV and a souped-up Mercedes sedan there, too. He crashed the Mercedes, running from the scene after he killed the speaker of the house and abandoned the car in a parking lot nearby. We don't know what happened to the RV, and we didn't know he had a second hangar. Apparently, he kept his airplane there. I should have ordered a search of all the hangars on the field."

The chopper settled onto a taxiway on the side of the field opposite Dulles Aviation, the FBO that serviced local and visiting aircraft. Two rows of hangars took up most of the space there. A man in a warm coat met them and introduced himself as the airport manager.

"Your other people are waiting in a big van over by the hangar," he said. "Come on, I'll walk you over there."

At the hangar, Kerry met the head of the tech team. "Are we worried about booby traps?" the man asked.

"I don't think so," Kerry said. "The manager has already been in there today, and
he's still with us. You take your people in first
and establish a perimeter around whatever
evidence is there, so we can get out of this
cold."

The man nodded and signaled for his three
assistants to follow him. He opened the door
of the hangar and looked around, then turned
back to Kerry. "You can come in," he said;
"everything is down at the other end."

Holly followed Kerry into the hangar,
which was brightly lit. She stood just inside
the door and waited for the head of the tech
team to do a quick survey of the items in the
hangar. He came back after a few minutes.

"Okay, we've got tire tracks of an airplane,
Michelin tires, tricycle gear. That's consistent
with the Cessna 182 RG Fay was flying, until he blew it up. We've also got a set of
Goodyear Wrangler tracks. That's a truck tire
often used on SUVs and RVs, and the width
of the vehicle is consistent with an RV or a
rental truck. When we have precise mea-
surements, we should know which. There
are also a lot of miscellaneous tools and
scraps of materials."

"Check everything for prints," Kerry said.

"To this day, we don't have Fay's prints, not even from his house in Maine."

"How does somebody not leave prints in his own house?" Holly asked.

"We think he cleaned up the place before he left the last time. He had only been back for a few minutes when we went in. His house in the Virginia suburbs was also clean of prints, the first time I'd ever seen a house with no prints at all."

"Yeah, I was the tech team leader on that one," the tech guy said, "and I'd never seen that either. This guy is really something. By the way, I won't put this in writing, but it's my guess that the truck or RV was driven out of here some time after the airplane left."

"Any idea how recently?"

"Days, is my guess. Why don't you folks get a cup of coffee or something and come back in, say, two hours?"

Kerry nodded and led them out of the building. The airport manager drove them to the terminal, and they got sandwiches from the machines in the pilots' lounge.

TWO HOURS LATER, they were back in the hangar. "Tell me about it," Kerry said.

The tech team leader laughed. "Teddy's

done it again: not a print anywhere, and believe me, we've looked *everywhere.* The guy is a neat freak, paranoid to a turn."

"Is there anything at all interesting here?" Kerry asked.

"We've determined that the vehicle was an RV, consistent in size with one manufactured by Winnebago. If you find it, we can match it to the tracks in here. One other thing, we found this." He held up a small plastic bag with an object inside.

"Looks like a computer chip," Kerry said.

"It is; automotive. It's from the central computer of an SUV, a stock-standard chip, no alterations. Can you associate that with anything?"

Kerry thought for a minute. "Yes," he said. "The Supreme Court justice killed in the automobile accident."

"Right. The chip we recovered from that vehicle had been altered to reverse the commands sent from the onboard computer to operate the automatic stability control. If the car went into a skid, for instance, the ASC would cause one or more wheels to brake in order to correct the skid. The replacement chip did the opposite, causing it to skid even more. Fucking ingenious."

"Well, anyway," Kerry said, "it lets us tie Teddy to the death of Mr. Justice What's-his-name."

"It would, if we had found any material evidence that Teddy had ever been in this hangar," the tech guy said. "Without prints or other evidence, we can't prove he was here."

"Better circumstantial evidence than no evidence at all," Kerry said.

"If you say so," the tech guy replied. "But this Teddy is really something, you know?"

"I know," Kerry replied.

Holly knew, too.

THIRTY-FOUR

HOLLY GOT BACK SHORTLY before dark and took Daisy for a run, cutting over to Park Avenue. She liked the broad boulevard, with its garden down the center and its elegant apartment buildings. She wondered what a small apartment on Park cost, and if there were any small apartments. She could afford to buy something, if it wasn't too outrageous, and she was getting tired of living in what amounted to a dormitory. There was almost no privacy, unless she locked her door, and if she did that, she felt claustrophobic in her small room.

Back at the Barn, she picked up a *New*

York Times at the front desk and took it upstairs with her. After feeding Daisy, she took a shower and stretched out on her bed with the paper. She came to the classifieds and, on a whim, turned to the real estate section. Almost immediately, an ad caught her eye:

> *Park Ave. 60's, est. sale, Lg 1 BR w/wbf,*
> *sep. dr. fur. avbl. 650K.*

She called the number, got a woman immediately and made an appointment for the following morning.

HOLLY ARRIVED AT THE BUILDING, which turned out to be a large, limestone-fronted edifice with a uniformed doorman who found a cookie for Daisy. He called the apartment and told Holly to take the elevator to the twelfth floor, apartment A. She was met by a well-dressed woman in her forties, whom she assumed was the real estate agent.

"I'm Clarissa Bonner," she said, offering a hand. "Oh, what a handsome dog!" She stroked Daisy's head. "I grew up with a Doberman, and they're just lovely. Come and see the apartment."

Holly followed her around the rooms,

which were surprisingly large, with high ceilings. The place was furnished in a rudimentary way, but didn't look lived-in. When they had seen the whole place and talked about the building, Mrs. Bonner offered her coffee, and they sat down in the living room in front of the *wbf*, which was blazing cheerfully away.

"Let me tell you what's happened," Mrs. Bonner said. "My mother had an eighteen-room apartment covering this whole floor, and when she died last year, we divided it, selling the larger one and keeping this one as a pièd-a-terre, just a place to sleep when we drive in from Connecticut for the theater. We kept some of her furniture, too. Then my husband was transferred to San Francisco, so we put it on the market and found a buyer almost immediately. Unfortunately, when she went through the application process, the co-op board turned her down. Her mother, a wealthy woman, was going to cosign the lease with her, but she declined to show the board her tax returns, so that was it. This happened forty-eight hours ago, and we have to be in San Francisco next week. We contacted the two other people who had made offers, but they had both bought other properties, so it's back on the market, and you're the first to see it."

"I'm afraid I don't know anything about how a co-op works," Holly said.

"It's like this: the building is incorporated, the corporation owns the building and leases the apartments. Each lessee owns a number of shares in the corporation, corresponding to the square footage of his apartment. Co-op boards can be very picky, but ours is generally all right. You would have to demonstrate a net worth and income that would show that you could pay the monthly maintenance, and you'd have to meet with the board."

"How do they feel about pets?"

"No problem with that, as long as your dog is well-behaved, and Daisy certainly appears to be."

Holly's mind was racing. She loved the apartment, and she had a feeling Mrs. Bonner was desperate to sell, given her circumstances.

"Mrs. Bonner," she said. "I believe I could demonstrate to the board that I'm qualified, and I'd like to make an offer right now, if we can agree. What is the lowest price you would accept for the apartment, furnished, as is?"

Mrs. Bonner didn't bat an eye. "Six hundred thousand dollars," she said, "if you can pay cash; I can't wait for a mortgage to be approved. I have to tell you that if the place had a second bedroom we'd get a million dollars more for it; that was our mistake when we divided."

Holly offered her hand. "Done," she said. "What do I do now?"

Mrs. Bonner went to a desk, opened a drawer and pulled out a manila file. "Here is the application. I urge you to answer every question fully and to supply copies of your bank and brokerage statements and your tax returns. The board is meeting again the day after tomorrow, for the last time before Christmas, and I think it would be a good idea if you brought Daisy along to your interview."

"Is there a broker involved?" Holly asked.

"No, you can give me a check for ten percent as earnest money, and there is a standard purchase contract in the folder."

Holly wrote the check. Mrs. Bonner filled in the blanks in the contract, and Holly signed. "I'll have the application and the other documentation to you by the end of the day." She stood up and offered her hand again.

"It's a pleasure doing business with you," Mrs. Bonner said. "Oh, I forgot to tell you: the monthly maintenance is twelve hundred and fifty dollars, and fifty percent is tax deductible. Oh, and another benefit is that the building owns a garage around the corner, and your monthly rate will only be two hundred dollars, if you have a car. That's less than half what you would pay if you had to use a commercial garage."

Holly hit the street, practically at a run. As she left the building she collided with a man in a sheepskin coat, a tweed hat and big sunglasses. "Oh, excuse me," she said.

"Quite all right," the man replied. He gave Daisy a pat. "Beautiful dog."

"Thank you." She got a cab back to her building and went looking for Lance. She had the money, all right, but she couldn't list all the cash in the Caymans account on her financial statement.

HOLLY EXPLAINED EVERYTHING to Lance. "So, do I use my own name? Do I tell them who I work for? Is my two-million-dollar net worth going to be enough to satisfy the co-op board?"

"Yes, use your own name, but not the name of your employer," Lance said. "We have a front outfit that is, ostensibly, in a private investment firm at this address. We'll make you a senior vice president. How much are you paying for the apartment?"

"Six hundred thousand."

"I don't know whether or not two million will do it with the board, so we'll set up a paper account in your name with the firm and show a list of stocks and a balance of, say, six million? We'll produce a monthly statement for you, and you can include that with your application, and we can supply you with three years' tax returns, too, federal and state. When you're questioned by the board about your job, say that the firm manages the money of one extended family, whose name you may not divulge. I'll get you some letters of recommendation from real people, too. Our security people will have to vet the building, of course, but I don't anticipate a problem with that; it's the kind of building they like."

"Thank you so much, Lance; I really appreciate this."

"Take some time off and get all the paperwork together and make your financial arrangements. I'll set up everything else and get your letters of recommendation before the day is out."

TWO DAYS LATER, Holly, dressed in a black Armani suit, rang a doorbell on the top floor of the apartment building, and was escorted into the living room by a maid. There were a dozen men in the room, all in business suits. Holly shook their hands and allowed Daisy to say hello.

"Ms. Barker," the president of the board said, "we've reviewed your application, and we thank you for completing it so quickly. Your financial qualifications are excellent and your recommendations are impressive."

"Thank you."

Many of our shareholders have dogs, but I'm sure you can understand that we insist on their being well-behaved." He glanced at Daisy, lying quietly at Holly's feet. "Your dog doesn't seem to be a problem."

"Daisy is very well trained."

"Does she bark much?"

"Never, unless asked to."

"Dobermans have a reputation as rather

dangerous guard dogs. Is there any of that in Daisy?"

"If I were attacked, Daisy would take serious exception, but she would never harm any person or animal, except in those circumstances." That was not entirely true. Daisy would be happy to rip the man's throat out if commanded.

"Very good. What sort of work is it, exactly, that you do?"

"I'm a senior vice president of Morgan and Bailey, a private investment firm."

"And what sort of clients do you work with?"

"We handle the investments for one extended family—a couple of dozen members—and we advise them both as a group and individually."

"The family name?"

"I'm afraid that must remain confidential," she said. "It's a condition of my employment."

"I understand."

Twenty minutes later she was out of there, and an hour after that she received a phone call from Mrs. Bonner.

"I'm delighted to tell you the board has approved your application," she said. "I must say, you got everything together breathtakingly fast. I've never seen anything like it."

Neither had Holly. "I'm ready to close whenever you like," she said.

"Tomorrow, ten A.M. at my lawyer's office." She gave Holly the address.

"Can you give me the firm's trust account number? I'll wire the funds today."

"Yes, I have it right here." Mrs. Bonner read out the number.

"I'll see you tomorrow morning then," she said. She hung up and hugged Daisy. "We have a home, baby!" Daisy approved, wagging all over. Holly called her broker, told him to sell five hundred and forty thousand dollars of her investments and wire the money to New York.

THIRTY-FIVE

TEDDY WALKED INTO HIS APARTMENT, took off his coat and leaned against the wall. He was sweating. He went into the kitchen and got himself a glass of ice water and sat down. He was seeing way too much of this Holly woman, and the string of coincidences was driving him crazy.

First, the opera, then the record shop, now coming out of an apartment building a block and a half away. He habitually maintained a high level of paranoia, as a means of survival, and alarm bells were ringing all over the place.

He waited until evening and called Irene Foster.

"Hello?"

"Are you inside?"

"I'm in New York, at the Waldorf again. We must meet."

"Central Park, in an hour?"

"Where in the park?"

"Outside the boathouse restaurant, find a bench; I'll find you."

"All right." She hung up.

TEDDY ENTERED THE PARK only after walking around the block twice, checking for tails. He was going to have to relocate to another city immediately, that was clear. He walked up to the boathouse, past it, then back by another route, before he sat down on the bench where Irene was reading the *Post*.

"I don't know how you read that trash," he said, not looking at her.

"I never miss Page Six," she said. "Can I pass you something?"

"Put it inside the paper and hand it to me," he said. She did so, and he found two CDs.

"They've changed the codes again," she said. "They suspect someone inside the Agency is helping you. In fact, I suggested that myself, in order to avoid suspicion, and Hugh English has put me in charge of the internal investigation."

"How very convenient."

"Yes, but it's a pain in the ass. What I suggest you do is create a file for a fictional employee, give him all the proper clearances, then use his name when you log on. Can you do that?"

"Sounds like a good idea; I wish I'd thought of it earlier."

"How's it going, in general?"

"I've been living in New York, but I'm going to have to leave immediately," he said.

"Why?"

"That agent I told you about, Holly something; I've run into her again. It can't be an accident."

"Holly Barker," Irene said. "She did a teleconference yesterday, with Lance Cabot. Why are you worried about her?"

"I saw her at the opera, at a record store and coming out of an apartment building a block and a half from my apartment. That's too many coincidences."

"Take it easy," Irene said. "I've read her report: the first time, at the opera, she was looking for you, but she didn't figure out that she met you until you ran for a cab with your 'new knee.' The second time, she went to the record shop looking for you, because they were covering everything they could think of to do with the opera. That's it. If you saw her coming out of a building, then that was a co-incidence. She doesn't know where you are or what you look like."

"You're sure?"

"Absolutely. I read everything that comes through from Lance's group."

"I met Lance once, a long time ago, in Tech Services."

"He doesn't remember it, so you're okay. You've got to change your log-in codes to-day, though. I've already gone into Hugh's computer to make it possible, ostensibly as a test."

"That's good; thank you."

"Listen, Teddy, this is going to have to be-come a two-way street, if I'm going to con-tinue to help you. I have to know how to get in touch with you. If you're using a phone like mine, it can't be dangerous."

"It makes me nervous, though."

"Well, you've got to make a choice," she said. "If I were going to give you up, you'd be surrounded right now."

Teddy sighed and gave her the phone number. "I want you to know that it was not because I don't trust you implicitly; I was just being as careful as I could."

"I understand, but you're going to have to trust somebody if you're going to continue to do this sucessfully."

"What do they know about me?"

"They think you're in New York, and that's it. And they know you've made Holly. That was very funny, the thing with the opera seats; it drove them crazy, but you've got to drop everything to do with the opera, except watching it on TV. That's their big, new piece of information, that you love the opera."

"Oh, all right," Teddy said, "though it was my chief pleasure in New York."

"Find another pleasure," she said, "and make it something you've never done before."

"My new pleasure is going to be Holly Barker," Teddy said. "I'm going to read her file, but what can you tell me about her?"

"She's an ex-Army MP commander, and for four years she was chief of police in a little town in Florida called Orchid Beach, where she broke a couple of big federal cases, much to the embarrassment of the FBI. Lance met her in New York earlier this year and recruited her as part of his new group. She was in training at the Farm when they suddenly moved most of her class to New York to start looking for you."

"So she's green?"

"Yes, but she's smart, or Lance wouldn't have recruited her. He's the best judge of talent I've ever seen, and she's his fair-haired girl. Oh, and I've got to tell you, she broke Whitey Thompson's nose in her self-defense class; it was the talk of the training command, and Whitey got fired as a result of it."

"That's the funniest thing I ever heard," Teddy said, laughing. "I always hated that guy."

"Everybody did. Well, he's gone, now."

"How are you coming with your internal investigation?"

"Oh, I'll wring out the whole place, everybody but myself."

"They'll polygraph you before it's over. Can you handle it?"

She nodded. "I have some pills that will do the trick."

"Good. Let me give you a code: if you ever learn that I'm about to be busted and I should run, call the number I gave you and say, 'Is this Bloomingdale's?' then hang up. If I hear that, I'll drop everything and go."

"Got it."

"Shall I find a hotel room?"

"Can't this trip; we're too busy. Hugh thinks I'm running an errand for him, so I've got to get back."

"Thanks for the new codes, Babe. I'll talk to you soon."

"Bye-bye." She got up and left.

Teddy sat on the bench, feeling greatly relieved. He was glad he wasn't going to have to leave New York, after all the trouble he'd gone to to set himself up here. He was sorry about the opera, though.

THIRTY-SIX

HOLLY CLEANED OUT her room and, with the help of the two security men in the lobby, loaded everything into her Cayenne Turbo and drove over to 868 Park Avenue. With the help of the doormen there, she got everything unloaded and upstairs into her new apartment, then she went back downstairs. The Cayenne was gone.

The super approached and introduced himself. "I'm Danny," he said. "I put your car in our garage. Just call the doorman when you want it, and someone will bring it around for you. They need about fifteen minutes' notice."

Holly thanked him and went back upstairs

to her apartment. She unpacked and put everything away, then she sat down on the living room sofa and called her father on her cell phone.

"Ham?"

"Hey, Baby, how are you? I haven't heard from you for a couple of weeks, and I thought maybe they killed you during training."

"I'm just fine," she said. "I'm in New York."

"You finished at the Farm already?"

"They cut the training short so that my class could join the New York team for a special project."

"And what is the project?"

"If I told you I'd have to dispatch somebody down there to dispatch you. How's Ginny?"

"She's just great; she's hired two more instructors for her flight school, and business is humming."

"Ham, I bought an apartment in New York."

"Yeah, where?"

"On Park Avenue. Can you believe it?"

"Well, you're a woman of some means," Ham said. "It's probably a good investment."

"I think it is. And you and Ginny can come visit. There's only one bedroom, but I'll get a pullout sofa."

"Thanks, but I can afford a hotel. We're not bunking in with you; we screw too much, and Ginny is noisy."

"Oh, Ham, stop it. You'd be perfectly welcome."

"I know we would, but we'd prefer a hotel."

"Give me a little time to get my feet on the ground, then come visit."

"Okay. How's the work going?"

"It's good but frustrating. We've got a tough assignment, and it isn't going as well as I'd like."

"Well, if you're willing to say that, things must be going pretty badly."

"Now you're getting the picture."

"Tell me about the apartment."

"I'll wait and let you see it. Your daughter has come up in the world."

"I've been tempted to open that envelope you gave me."

"Don't you dare, unless you hear I'm dead." The envelope contained a copy of her will and the second credit card that would give Ham access to the Cayman bank account, plus a letter explaining everything.

"Okay, it's in my safe until the day. But you better not die before me; I'll kick your ass."

"I know that. Listen, I've got to run; I've got

a ton of work about to fall on me. I'll call you next week. Love to Ginny."

"Bye-bye." Ham hung up.

"Come on, Daisy," Holly said. "Let's go shopping."

TEDDY FAY WAS WALKING to his workshop when he saw Holly Barker and her dog on the other side of the street. He watched her out of the corner of his eye without turning his head; it still made him nervous to see her around. She must live nearby, he figured.

Once locked into his workshop, he fired up his computer and used the disks Irene Foster had given him to log into the CIA mainframe. He spent two hours constructing a file for a fictitious officer, Charles Lockwood, supplying Lockwood with a biography, an educational background, a service record, a financial history and the proper security clearances. To entertain himself, he had Lockwood reporting directly to Hugh English, the deputy director for operations. Now he could safely log into the mainframe at any time.

When he was finished, he went into the personnel records and pulled up Holly Barker's file. He read through it carefully, then read the Agency's investigation report on her background and the record of her training at the Farm. She sounded like a good one, he thought. He read the account of the incident with Whitey Thompson, which the director of training himself had apparently witnessed, and was much amused by it. He had outfitted Whitey, once, for a mission in East Germany, and from what he had heard later, the man had turned out to be a disaster in the field, blowing the whole operation and almost getting two of his colleagues killed. After that, he had been banished to the Farm, where the Agency had figured he couldn't get into too much trouble teaching trainees to kill people.

HOLLY WENT TO A HARDWARE STORE called Gracious Home, which also had a furnishings shop, across the street. Lance had given her the name of the place, and it turned out to be a gold mine for what she needed for her apartment. She shopped for an hour, then filled out a charge account application, giving Morgan & Bailey as her employer. The front operation was turning out to be a very convenient thing to have as support. She felt almost like a real New Yorker, now, with an apartment and a conventional job and the business cards Lance had given her. She asked the store to deliver her purchases to her apartment building, then she walked the few blocks to Central Park and made her way downtown, sometimes jogging alongside Daisy to give her some exercise. She enjoyed herself. Tomorrow she would be back at work, looking for Teddy Fay.

TEDDY SPENT THE AFTERNOON going through the operations directorate's files on terrorist suspects attached to foreign embassies and with diplomatic immunity. He'd let the Agency take care of the clandestine individuals and groups who had no immunity. He'd deal with the ones the Agency and the FBI couldn't touch, because of their diplomatic status.

There were a surprisingly large number of them. He selected three and began downloading their dossiers from the CIA mainframe.

HOLLY ARRIVED BACK at her apartment, where her purchases from Gracious Home were waiting for her. She put everything away, then ran a hot bath and slipped into the big, old-fashioned tub, while Daisy curled up on the mat next to her.

There was something still missing in her life; she had been able to put it out of her mind while she was in training and after her arrival in New York, but now it was creeping back into her brain, and into other places, as well.

She needed a man.

THIRTY-SEVEN

HOLLY SAT IN THE LITTLE THEATER on the eleventh floor of her headquarters, which the agents had begun calling the Barn. Kerry Smith, her FBI co-boss, was at the lectern; the screen behind held a sketch that Holly had worked on with an Agency artist.

"This is a drawing of the man Holly Barker sat with at the Metropolitan Opera," Kerry was saying, "minus the hat, the glasses, the nose and the bad toupee. This is the man we now know to be Teddy Fay."

It looked sort of like him, Holly thought, but he was so ordinary that he could qualify as the wallflower at any dance.

"As you can see, there is nothing whatever distinctive about him," Kerry was saying, confirming her judgment. "A description of him would probably match that of a hundred thousand other men in this city."

"He looks sort of like Larry David," somebody said.

"Who?" Kerry asked.

"The guy who's on 'Curb Your Enthusiasm,' on HBO."

"I've never seen it."

"He does look a little like Larry David," somebody else agreed. "But less distinctive."

"Swell," Kerry said. "We also know that Fay likes the opera and that he has hairy forearms."

"How do we know he has hairy forearms?" somebody asked.

"We had a frame of him from a security video at a church in Atlanta a few months ago, when he was trying to kill a TV preacher," Kerry said. "He was disguised beyond all recognition, but he was wearing a short-sleeved shirt, and he had hairy forearms—gray hair."

"Do we have fingerprints?" somebody asked.

"No, and we don't have photographs, either," Kerry said. "Fay went to great lengths to obliterate photographs of himself from the record of his life, such as it is. And when we got into his house in Virginia, every surface in it had been wiped down with Windex, so we don't have any prints. None in his Maine house, either."

"What Kerry is saying," Lance interjected, "is that everything we know about Teddy Fay adds up to just about zero, and that is remarkable. The man worked for the federal government, for the Agency, no less, for forty years, and when he retired, he vanished like a wisp of smoke. He's faked his death twice: once after his retirement, when he managed to insert a death certificate into his home county records, and once when he jumped out of that Cessna on the Maine coast. We could legitimately consider him dead, except that he keeps killing people."

There was an uncomfortable stir in the room.

"We need ideas," Kerry said, "and I don't care how crazy they are; Lance and I will listen to any suggestion."

Holly raised her hand. "Why don't we pretend to be him?" she asked.

"How would that help?" Kerry asked.

"Well, could we say, after the fact, anyway, that the victims he chose were predictable?"

"I suppose so," Kerry said. "After the fact."

"So why don't we make up a victim list, using Teddy's criteria? Maybe we could get to one of them first, or at least, at the same time Teddy does."

"That is a very good suggestion," Kerry said. "How would you go about it, Holly?"

"Teddy is an Agency man; how would the Agency go about making a list of potential threats in New York City?"

Lance stood up and walked to the podium, standing next to Kerry. "We have a watch list," he said, "of threats working in United Nations embassies in New York, both people with and without diplomatic immunity."

"How many people are on that list?" Kerry asked.

"Probably between two and three dozen," Lance replied. "Surely, the New York field office of the Bureau must have a similar list." He looked at Kerry.

"I'll find out," Kerry said.

"Probably there's a lot of overlap in our two lists," Lance said. "What criteria should we use to assess these people, from Teddy's point of view?" He posed the question to the room at large.

Holly raised her hand again. "I think he would go after the ones the Agency and the Bureau can't touch," she said. "The ones with diplomatic immunity."

"Why?" Kerry asked.

"Because he doesn't care if they have diplomatic immunity, and he knows we have to care. The way Teddy sees things, he's helping us, and in a weird kind of way, I suppose he is."

Lance broke into a broad smile. "Don't ever let anybody outside this room hear you say that. Okay, Holly, you and your partner assemble a list of probable targets, using both Agency and Bureau recommendations. Anybody else have any ideas?"

No one spoke.

"All right, that's it for the moment. Go back to your previously assigned duties."

Ty fell into step with Holly as they left the room. "That was brilliant," he said.

"No, just logical," she replied.

"I'm going to start thinking of you as Spock."

"I don't have the ears for it," she said, "but

putting together this list ought to be more fun than keeping surveillance on that record store."

"I'll second that," Ty said.

Holly looked her partner up and down. He was wearing a new tweed jacket, cavalry twill trousers and a yellow-striped shirt with a knit tie. "Ty, you're looking pretty swift these days."

"I took your advice," he said, "and bought some new clothes. I hope I look less like an FBI agent."

"Let your hair grow a bit," she said. "Then you'll look less like an agent." He was a nice boy, but he wasn't going to solve her man problem. "Excuse me a minute," she said. "I forgot to ask Lance something." She went back into the room and found Lance still in his seat.

"Something I can do for you?"

"I just wanted to thank you for setting up what I needed for the co-op board application," she said. "I moved in yesterday, and the place is great."

"Glad to be of help," Lance said. He went back to the pad in his lap, then looked up again. "Something else?"

"Well, yes. I wonder if it would be okay if

I . . . got in touch with Stone Barrington. I mean, if it would be okay from a security standpoint."

Lance seemed to suppress a smile. "Sure, why not? After all, he's under contract to the Agency, so he's one of us, in a way."

"Thanks, Lance." Holly turned and walked out of the room again, happy.

THIRTY-EIGHT

THE PRESIDENT OF THE UNITED STATES and the director of Central Intelligence were sitting on the floor of the White House residence living room, eating pizza, drinking beer and watching "The West Wing." A commercial break arrived.

"You know," Will said, "Jed Bartlet has an easier time being president than I do."

"What? With his getting shot in an assassination attempt and his daughter getting drugged by her boyfriend and kidnapped and having to let John Goodman be president and throw him out of the Oval Office? You think that's easier?"

"Well, not that stuff, maybe, but he seems to have an easier time being right than I do. And Leo, his chief of staff, seems to do all the hard work, too. My chief of staff doesn't do all the hard work."

"You don't have the slightest idea what she does when she's out of your sight," she said. "She probably works three times as hard as you do."

"Are you questioning my work ethic?" Will asked. "You wound me."

"Oh, horseshit! Sure, you work hard, well, pretty hard anyway. And anyway, there are compensations when you're president."

"What compensations?" Will demanded. "I don't see any compensations. I mean, you could say I get driven everywhere, but I'd really rather drive myself, but the Secret Service won't let me, except on the farm, and even then they get all nervous."

"Poor baby," she cooed, patting his knee.

"And why can't I ever get a pizza through security while it's still hot? I hate cold pizza, except at breakfast, and why won't Domino's leave the green peppers off the Extravaganza special, like I ask them to?"

"Well, maybe if they knew the Extravaganza was for the president instead of the guard at the main gate, they'd pay more attention."

"I thought of that, but the Secret Service won't let me tell them it's for me; I guess they're afraid there's somebody at Domino's who would poison me if they knew. And why can't I own a Porsche instead of a Suburban? I always wanted a Porsche."

"Then why didn't you have one before you were president? I like Porsches."

"Because I was a senator, and I had to drive a Suburban, because it was built in Georgia—at least, I think it was. And even if it wasn't, I couldn't be seen driving a foreign car. Can you imagine what the Republicans could make of that? 'A white wine–drinking, quiche-eating, "West Wing"–watching, Porsche-driving president?' They'd go nuts."

"I think the American people might like a pizza-eating, beer-drinking, Porsche-driving president," she said, handing him another beer. "Wouldn't the NASCAR dads like that, if they knew?"

"A Heineken-drinking president who wouldn't eat good American green peppers on his pizza? I doubt it. They'd barbecue me at a tailgate party, or something."

"Poor baby," she said, patting his knee again.

"And another thing: why can't I just let Teddy Fay run amok? He's doing a better job of killing America's enemies than a certain intelligence agency I could name. Why do I have to sic the law on him?"

"Tell you what," she said. "You give me a written authorization to kill America's enemies, regardless of their diplomatic status or location, and *I'll* run amok *for* you. I'd like nothing better than machine-gunning fake diplomats in sidewalk cafes in Paris or planting bombs in the cars of the terrorists' Swiss bankers."

"You would, wouldn't you?" Will laughed. "You'd be out there shooting them yourself, wouldn't you?"

"Damn straight, I would!"

"Would you settle for heating up this pizza? It's getting pretty clammy."

Kate got to her feet and grabbed the box. "Oh, all right. I guess heating pizza will have to do," she said as she disappeared into the kitchen.

The commercials ended, and Will went back to watching "The West Wing." He resolved to try to be more like Jed Bartlet.

THIRTY-NINE

TEDDY FAY TACKED THE PHOTOGRAPHS of five men and one woman on his bulletin board and sat back to read each of their files. For some reason—it may have been the man's face—he strongly wanted to go after one Hadji Asaam who, under another name, was listed as a chauffeur at the Iranian embassy. Asaam was an assassin, pure and simple, and he had already been in the country for eight days. How long before he would be instructed to ply his real trade? Of course, there would be Agency or FBI surveillance on him, but he would find a way to lose them when he wanted to work. In the meantime, he was driving an attaché around New York, probably learning the streets.

His decision made, Teddy went to a news-stand and bought several newspapers. Back in his shop, he went carefully through the classifieds, until he found something that suited him in the *Village Voice:*

Vespa 180, only 1200 mi., pristine, $3K for quick sale.

He called the number. "I'm interested in your Vespa," he said. "If it's as described in the paper, I'll buy it for cash today."

"It's exactly as I described it," the young man said. "You'll love it."

"You have the registration and the insurance card?"

"Yep."

"You have the title? It doesn't have a loan on it, does it?"

"Nope, I have the title."

"Can you meet me at the Twenty-third Street Lexington subway stop at two o'clock? We can do the deal right there; I'll bring cash."

"Sure, I'll be there. What's your name?"

"Jeff Snyder. Yours?"

"Bernie Taylor."

"See you at two, Bernie." Teddy hung up.

He went through his makeup kit and selected a prominent nose and a large mustache. Half an hour later he was somebody else. At one-thirty, he walked down the street to the subway stop at 63rd and Lex, and took the train downtown. At street level, Bernie was sitting on the scooter, waiting.

"Let's go for a ride," Teddy said, indicating that Bernie should take the passenger seat. Teddy hadn't driven a Vespa for years, but how much could have changed? He drove quickly around the block; the engine ran as it should, and the gears shifted smoothly. Teddy stopped.

"You'll throw in the helmet for three grand?"

"Sure," Bernie said.

Teddy handed him an envelope containing thirty one-hundred-dollar bills. He waited while Bernie counted the money carefully without actually salivating.

"Here's the registration and title," he said. "And the insurance card, but you'll have to change it to your name. Oh, and it has a full tank of gas."

"A pleasure doing business with you,"

Teddy said. He pocketed the papers and drove away. Back at his workshop, he parked the scooter in the downstairs hallway and went upstairs to start planning his surveillance, based on the daily schedule of the attaché Asaam would be driving. He would not have long to wait, since the attaché was picked up daily at precisely six P.M. and driven to his apartment twenty blocks away. Teddy liked the idea that it would be at rush hour.

At five o'clock, Teddy dressed in black coveralls over his clothes, checked his makeup and went downstairs for the scooter. With the helmet and goggles, plus the makeup, he would be unidentifiable. He wiped the scooter for prints, then put on his driving gloves and pushed it into the street.

Twenty minutes later he was driving past the Iranian embassy to the U.N. and checking out the block. No doubt the embassy was under surveillance, and the second time around the block, he spotted two bored-looking men in a green Chevrolet sedan. They were dressed too neatly for NYPD detectives, so he reckoned they were FBI.

He went around the block again, then parked at the end of the street, some distance behind the surveillance vehicle, and waited. At five minutes before six, a black Lincoln with diplomatic plates drove up and double-parked in front of the embassy. At exactly six o'clock, the front door of the building opened and a middle-aged man in a pin-striped suit came down the front steps and got into the car. While the driver was holding open the door, Teddy checked his face against the photograph Irene had e-mailed him. A moment later, the driver was behind the wheel, and the car was moving. The FBI guys were moving, too.

Teddy stayed behind the two cars waiting for rush-hour traffic to do half his job for him. This took less than five minutes. Everything came to a halt because of some obstruction ahead. And Teddy saw the head of the diplomat's driver come out the window, checking out the traffic.

Driving between lanes, Teddy accelerated around the FBI car and kept moving forward, his feet occasionally touching the pavement to help with his balance. The driver's window was still open as he pulled alongside.

AT THE BARN, Holly and Ty were making their presentation to Lance and Kerry.

"There are a dozen candidates," Holly said, "but we've narrowed the field to three for our purposes."

"What criteria did you use for narrowing?" Kerry asked.

"Nothing more than a gut feeling," Holly said, "because that's what we think Teddy will use to make his choice."

"Why?"

"We think this process is emotional for Teddy. He's doing this out of hatred for people he believes are enemies of his country."

"Okay, let's hear the three candidates," Kerry said.

"Two men and a woman," Holly said. First there's Ali Tarik, who is a thug whose specialty is tracking down Syrian defectors to the States and beating them up or killing them. Then there's Carla Mujarik, who is in charge of buying materials for the Iranian nuclear weapons program. She buys what she can get, either in the U.S. or abroad. It's a tough job, but she's had some success. We haven't cut her off yet, in the hope of catching some big rats among the sellers." She held up another picture. "This is Hadji Asaam, an assassin, pure and simple, who's only been in the country for a week or so, but who we think has been brought in to kill some specific person as yet unknown to us. As you know, we've got this heads-of-state meeting at the U.N. coming up, and that makes him worrying to us."

"Ugly bastard, isn't he?" Lance said.

"That's why he's our number-one candidate," Holly said. "We think Teddy will have the same reaction you did when he sees his picture."

"You're operating on the premise that Teddy still has access to Agency files?"

"Yes."

"But all the codes have been changed, and there's a big internal investigation run by Irene Foster in Hugh English's office underway. How could he possibly get into the mainframe again?"

"We don't know, but we have to operate on the premise that Teddy is smart enough to figure out a way to know what we know."

Lance shook his head. "That's a mighty big assumption," he said.

"Why?" Holly asked. "He was at the Agency long enough to figure out ways into the computers, and he may even have inside help among the people he knew and worked with before he retired. Some of them may feel some sympathy with what he's doing. To be perfectly frank, *I* feel some sympathy with what he's doing. Don't you?"

"I'm not answering *that*," Lance said. "All right, let's follow your hunch and see where it leads us."

"God knows," Kerry said, "we don't have anything else to go on." He opened a file and looked through it. "Looks like the New York field office of the Bureau has round-the-clock surveillance of Asaam."

"How much surveillance?" Lance asked.

"Two men."

"All right, let's triple that," Lance said. "Let's put Holly and Ty on him, and we'll assign another team, as well."

A secretary knocked and opened the door. "Lance, there's a Lieutenant Bacchetti on the phone for you; he says it's important."

Lance picked up the phone and pushed the blinking button. "Dino? What's up?" He listened for a moment. "How long ago?" He listened again, then thanked the caller and hung up, shaking his head.

"What?" Kerry asked.

"A man on a motor scooter shot Hadji Asaam fifteen minutes ago, while your two agents watched. He got away in the rush-hour traffic."

Holly and Ty exchanged a glance.

"Well, Holly," Kerry said, "it looks like your theory of how Teddy chooses targets might be pretty good."

Holly felt a warm glow inside. "If it is, then we'd better beef up surveillance on Ali Tarik and Carla Mujarik."

"Done," Kerry said.

FORTY

HOLLY STOOD AND WATCHED the young man through the one-way mirror of the interrogation room. He looked worried and baffled; the contents of his pockets lay on the table before him. She opened the door, walked into the room and sat down, opening a thin file folder and regarding it for half a minute before speaking.

"Your name is Bernard Taylor?" she asked.

"That's right."

"Bernard, you own a Vespa motor scooter with the New York State tag number 1059, is that correct?"

"Yeah, uh, or at least it was until earlier today."

Holly tried to look disgusted. "Come on, Bernard, you're not going to tell me it was stolen earlier today."

"No. Uh, I sold it. Earlier today."

Holly shook her head. "Let me put you straight, Bernard."

"You can call me Bernie; everybody does."

"Listen to me, Bernard. You're about to be arrested as an accessory to a murder. Do you know what sentence you could get as an accessory?"

"No. Uh, I mean, I didn't commit any murder."

"We're not saying you pulled the trigger, Bernard, just that you supplied the motor scooter. As an accessory, you get the same sentence the murderer does, and in New York, that's the death penalty."

"All I did was sell my motor scooter!" Bernie wailed.

Holly poked among the pile of his pocket contents on the table and her finger stopped on an envelope. "What does this envelope contain?" she asked, though she already knew.

"The money from the sale of the scooter," Bernie replied.

Holly opened the envelope, removed the contents and quickly counted thirty one-hundred-dollar bills. "Three thousand dollars," she said. "Bernard, is that your price for participation in a cold-blooded murder? You came cheap."

"No, ma'am," Bernie said, "It's my price for my scooter. That's what the guy paid me."

"All right," Holly sighed. "Tell me your story for the record. Just for your information, you're being recorded."

Bernie related the details of the sale of his motor scooter, while Holly took notes.

"His name was Jeff Snyder?" Holly asked.

"That's what he said."

"What I.D. did he show you?"

"Nothing. I didn't ask for nothing. He had the money; that was all the I.D. I cared about."

"Describe this Jeff Snyder."

"About my height, with a big nose and a handlebar mustache. On the thin side."

"The mustache?"

"No, that was thick. His build was on the thin side."

"What was he wearing?"

"A kind of car coat and a cap, you know, like golfers wear? Like Ben Hogan?"

"Where did you meet?"

"At the entrance to the subway station at Twenty-third and Lex. He came out of the subway, I think."

"What do you mean, you think?"

"Well, I didn't exactly see him come out of the subway; I just assumed that's how he got to the corner. I didn't see him get out of a cab or a car."

"And he paid you three thousand dollars in hundred-dollar bills for your scooter?"

"It was a fair price; the scooter had only twelve hundred miles on it. Not a scratch. Pristine."

"And you're sticking to this story?"

"Lady, it's the only story I got," Bernie said heatedly. "It's what happened."

Holly got up and walked out the door. Lance and Kerry were waiting for her on the other side of the mirror.

"What do you think?" Lance asked.

"I think he's telling the truth. It was a slick way for Teddy to get the scooter he needed without stealing it and running the risk of getting pulled over. Obviously, the big nose and the handlebar mustache were a disguise. A witness would concentrate on features like that. I'm surprised that Bernie, here, gave us as good a description as he did."

"Cut him loose?" Lance asked Kerry.

"Sure," Kerry replied. "We'll know where to find him, if we need him again."

"Oh," Lance said, "the NYPD found the scooter, and they're processing it for prints."

"They won't find any," Holly said. "Where did they locate the scooter?"

"Parked between two cars on East Twenty-fourth Street, off Lexington."

"It's the subway," Holly said.

"What?"

"Bernie said he met Teddy at the subway entrance at Twenty-third and Lex. That's how Teddy got there, and it's how he went home. I'll bet you he lives within a block or two of the Lexington Avenue subway."

"Possibly," Lance said. "How is that going to help us?"

"Let's put somebody on the subway eight hours a day and have him photograph every possible person who fits Teddy's description as to height, weight and age."

"You're talking about thousands of people," Kerry said.

"All right," Holly said, "skip rush hour at both ends; Teddy probably would, since he doesn't have to be at work anywhere. Photograph all the sixtyish, tallish, slenderish men between, say, ten and four, every day for a week, then run . . . no, we don't have any photographs to compare them to . . . show the photographs to people who worked with Teddy at the agency. Maybe somebody will give us a positive I.D., and if we get that, then we'll have a photograph to circulate."

"That's a lot of work for a slim hope," Lance said.

"It would be, if we weren't so desperate," Kerry replied. "Even with a new murder every few days, this investigation is drying up. We don't really have all that much for our people to do."

"All right, Holly, you set it up," Lance said. "We're probably going to need more than one body on each train."

"I'd suggest picking up every train at Ninety-sixth Street and riding it to Twenty-third," Holly said. "I don't know how many trains there are, but I'll find out. When our people get to Twenty-third, they'll turn around and go back to Ninety-sixth Street, and we'll do it for five days."

"Sounds good," Lance said. "I'll call a meeting and assign you everybody who isn't already following another lead. But I warn you, if we get something new, I'll pull off as many people as it takes to run it down."

THE NEW ASSIGNMENT was received in stony silence by the group of eighteen unassigned agents in the conference room. Lance made his little speech, then turned the meeting over to Holly and left.

"Questions?" Holly asked.

"Yeah, just one," an agent said, raising his hand. "Are you nuts?"

"Have you got a better idea?" Holly asked. "Have you got another lead? Are you too busy for this?"

The agent looked at the ceiling, and nobody else spoke.

"All right, listen up," Holly said, and she began reading a list of names from a clipboard. "You're being issued concealed cameras; the lens can be worn in a lapel or on the brim of a baseball cap. We're looking for full-frontal shots, here, folks, no backs of heads or pulled-down hat brims. We need faces, got it? Isn't intelligence work fun?"

She got back a collection of grumblings she was glad she couldn't quite hear.

FORTY-ONE

WILL LEE, AT THE END of his daily national intelligence briefing, dismissed everyone but
Kate Rule of the CIA and Bob Kinney of the
FBI, then he held up a copy of the *New York
Times* and pointed to a story in the lower
left-hand corner of the front page. "I suppose
you've seen this?"

MIDEAST U.N. EMBASSIES CLAIM CIA
IS MURDERING THEIR DIPLOMATS

Both nodded.
"Just for the record," the president said,

"tell me the CIA is *not* murdering Mideast diplomats."

"The CIA is not murdering Mideast diplomats," Kate said. "I believe you know who is murdering them."

"I believe I do," Will said, "and I'm getting very uncomfortable about knowing it. If this continues, we're going to have to announce that Teddy Fay is still alive and working."

Bob Kinney spoke up. "I hope you won't feel that is necessary right now, Mr. President."

"Well, Bob, you can always hope, but I've dug myself a hole, here, based on the advice of the two of you, and nobody's getting me out of it. How close are we to arresting Fay?"

"About as close as we were when we thought he was dead," Kate said glumly.

"All right, Madam Director," Will said, "I want you to issue a statement, through your spokesperson, saying, as dryly as possible, that the CIA is not murdering Mideast U.N. diplomats. Let's have that denial on the record, and be sure this guy at the *Times* gets the message. But I have to tell you both, I don't know how much longer we can continue keeping a lid on the Teddy Fay story.

I've had two calls from congressional leaders this morning, and they're squirming in their seats, believe me. As much as I dread doing it myself, I don't want one of *them* to be the one to break this to the press."

"Yes, sir," both directors said in unison.

LATER THAT MORNING, Kate Rule sat in a meeting in her conference room with the deputy directors for Intelligence and Operations and their deputies.

"All right," Kate said, "let me have your reports on your internal investigation into who might be helping Teddy Fay with his little crusade."

Hugh English, deputy director for Operations, spoke up. "Director, I'm going to let Irene Foster, who personally conducted the investigation, bring you up to date."

Kate turned and looked at the handsome, middle-aged woman across the table from her. "Irene?"

"Director, under my supervision, every department head in the building has conducted an in-depth investigation of every channel of communication in and out of the Agency that could be a means of passing information to Teddy Fay. In addition, our Computer Services division has audited the computer time of every employee with level-one access to the mainframe, which is the only level at which this information could be accessed. Finally, two hundred and twelve employees who possibly could have had access or gained access to this information have been given class-one polygraphs, and every single one of them has passed. The only possible conclusion that we can draw from all this work is that the source of the information that Teddy Fay is getting is *not* inside the Agency." She paused. "That's my report, and I'll stand by it."

"Director," Hugh English said, "I've reviewed every aspect of Irene's investigation and I've found it to be thorough and complete. I'll stand by it, too."

Kate stared at English and Foster. "You are absolutely certain about your conclusions?"

"To a great deal more than a reasonable certainty," English replied.

"Then where is Teddy Fay getting his information?" Kate asked.

"Director," Irene said, "Fay could be compiling this information from multiple sources—half a dozen agencies have bits and pieces of what he is learning—but the only other agency that has it all is the FBI. My reluctant conclusion is that the Bureau is the source of Teddy Fay's information, and my report so states."

"Great," Kate said. "Bob Kinney is going to love that."

"You want me to put it to Kinney?" English asked.

Kate sighed. "No, Hugh, I'll save that treat for myself."

Irene Foster stood and handed Kate a thick document. "Director, here is my written report. There's an eight-page summary of the work up front, detailing the steps I took; the rest is substantiation: copies of interviews and polygraph tapes."

"Thank you, Irene," Kate said. "That will be all, everybody."

The group shuffled out of the conference room, and Kate walked back into her office, picked up her phone and spoke to her secretary. "Please get me Director Kinney at the FBI."

A moment later her phone buzzed and she heard a male voice. "Kate? It's Bob."

"Bob," Kate said, trying not to sound weary, "can I buy you lunch over here today?"

"What's up, Kate?"

"Something I'd rather tell you about when you've got half a bottle of wine in you. I'll even send a chopper; you'd like that, wouldn't you?"

"I don't fit very well in helicopters, Kate," Kinney said. "If it's bad news, I'd rather hear it right now."

Kate sighed. "There's good news and bad, Bob. The good news is we've conducted an extraordinary, in-depth internal investigation, involving thousands of employees and hundreds of polygraphs, plus an audit of everybody's computer time, and the only conclusion we can come to is that Teddy Fay is not getting his information from the CIA."

There was a long silence on the other end of the phone.

"Bob?"

"I'm still here, Kate. I take it that what you're telling me is that Fay has somebody in the Bureau who's feeding him stuff?"

"I'm afraid that's the best conclusion we could come to, based on the evidence. You can go ahead and blow, now."

"Kate, I've just come from a meeting with all my deputy and assistant directors who've been investigating this matter Bureau-wide. They've handed me a thick report on their investigation, and to give you the short version, they have determined that Fay's information could not possibly be coming from anyone at the Bureau or from our computers. Their best recommendation is that it's coming from the Central Intelligence Agency."

There was a short silence, then both of them burst out laughing.

TEDDY FAY RODE DOWN the escalator into the East 63rd Street subway station and stood on the platform with twenty other people, waiting for the next train. A minute and a half later, there was a rush of cool air and a rumble as the train squealed to a slow halt.

As the last moving car trundled past where Teddy waited, he caught a glimpse of a familiar face and figure aboard the car. The next car stopped where he stood, and the doors opened.

Teddy hesitated, and people were surging around him.

"C'mon, Mac," a man said. "Get on or step aside."

Teddy stepped aside. The doors closed, and the train departed the station. The person he had seen in the previous car was the

CIA operative Holly Barker, and she was with a younger, neatly dressed man, who had to be her partner.

This was one coincidence too many, he thought. As he took the up escalator to the street, Teddy replayed his memory of the past few days, of his actions. He had made a mistake. He had met the scooter guy at the 23rd Street subway stop, and he had abandoned the scooter a block from that entrance. They were looking for him on the Lexington Avenue subway.

They must be desperate, he thought, to spend manpower that way. At street level he hailed a cab. He'd stay off the subway for a while.

FORTY-TWO

A WEEK PASSED, and Holly and Ty went to Lance's office to present their report. Lance and Kerry Smith waved them to a seat.

Holly set a flat-screen monitor on Lance's desk and placed the wireless laptop associated with it at a corner where she could easily access the keyboard.

"Here's what we've done," she said, tapping some keys. The screen filled with passport-sized photographs of men in their late middle years. "We took eight hundred and forty-one digital photographs of men on the Lexington Avenue subway between the apparent ages of fifty-five and seventy-five.

We eliminated slightly more than half, because they weighed too much and their faces were too full. Then I personally went through all the remaining photographs and eliminated all the men I felt could not possibly be our guy. I know this is subjective, but I'm the only one who's actually set eyes on the man, even if he was disguised. We finished up with two hundred and ninety-two possible Teddy Fays, and we transmitted their photographs to Langley, specifically to the Technical Services division, where they were reviewed by a couple of dozen employees who had worked with Teddy or, at least, had seen him several times a week. The result is that not one of them identified a single photograph as Teddy Fay."

Kerry looked at the ceiling, and Lance sighed.

"I took the additional step of ordering another sketch of Teddy, which was seen and commented on by all the people who had looked at the photographs, and here is the result." She placed a sketch on Lance's desk.

Lance and Kerry looked at the sketch for a long time.

"It's Larry David," Lance said, finally.

"We've heard about the resemblance before," Ty said.

"It's useless," Kerry said. "Unless we were looking for Larry David."

"He's too bland," Lance said, "too devoid of distinguishing features: no prominent nose, no beetle brows, no scars, no buck teeth."

"What can I tell you?" Holly said. "Teddy Fay is the Sir Alec Guinness of serial murderers. He's a nearly blank canvas upon which he can stick prosthetics and hair and become somebody else."

"So we can't post him on the ten-most-wanted list," Kerry said. "We can't call up 'America's Most Wanted' and nail him that way. It would never work, and we'd get thirty thousand phone calls from all over the country from people who think it's their Uncle Harry. Or Larry David."

"This is why I'm not a police officer," Lance said glumly. "Or why I wasn't until now. Being a spy was a lot more fun." He turned and looked at Holly. "I don't want you to feel badly about this," he said. "It was a good idea, and it was worth the manpower; it just didn't pan out; we weren't lucky enough."

"Any more ideas?" Kerry asked hopefully.

Holly looked at her feet. "Well . . ."

"What?" Lance asked. "Say it."

"There was this one thing that happened in the subway, at the Sixty-third Street Station."

"What?" Kerry demanded.

"As the train pulled into the station, I caught a glimpse of a man I've seen in my neighborhood. I don't know his name, but I've sort of bumped into him a couple of times, and he fits the description. What makes me think of him is that he was standing on the platform when the car I was on passed, but he didn't get on the train. I looked through all the other cars for him, but he wasn't on the train."

"Why do you think he didn't get on?" Lance asked.

"I think he may have seen me," Holly replied. "I didn't make eye contact with him, but if he's Teddy Fay, he knows me from the opera. Maybe he saw me on the train and balked."

"That makes sense," Kerry said. "God knows the guy has good instincts. If he saw someone on the train whom he knew to be CIA or FBI, that would be enough to keep him off it."

"Maybe he even guessed what we were

doing," Lance said. "Does he know where you live, Holly?"

"The first time I saw him was when I was coming out of my building," Holly said.

"Well, if he saw you arriving at the Sixty-third Street station on the train, and he knows that's the one nearest your building, and you didn't get on there or get off, maybe he put it together."

"I guess I shouldn't have gotten onto the trains myself," Holly admitted. "It was such shitty duty that I thought I ought to share it with the others."

"The first thing you have to get used to when you're supervising people, Holly, is handing people shitty assignments without pity," Lance said. "From now on, I don't want you on any surveillance detail of any of the potential victims we're watching. I don't want Teddy to spot you in a car or on a street, except where you live."

"All right," Holly said. "But what can I do around here?"

"Consider yourself reassigned as my assistant. Ty, we'll find you another partner."

Ty nodded. "Yes, sir."

"The only time I want you to be seen by Teddy is in your own neighborhood—at your building, walking Daisy in the park, shopping, that sort of thing. Clear?"

"Yes, Lance."

"We should have Holly followed at those times," Kerry said.

"Right," Lance agreed. "I want a team of four on Holly every time she leaves her apartment building. I want them well back from her, constantly changing places, and I want the team changed twice a day. Holly, I want you to carry your cell phone with an earpiece in your head at all times. Program the team number into it so that you can call them if you spot your man. I don't want you to be seen using the cell phone, and don't move your lips when you talk. This guy spooks easily, and we don't want to cause him the slightest anxiety."

"Okay," Holly said.

Kerry spoke up. "And if you literally run into him, be nice, let him pet Daisy, but don't attempt to engage him in more than perfunctory conversation; don't be *interested* in him, got it?"

"Got it," Holly said.

"On the other hand," Lance said, "if he appears to have an interest in *you*, don't put him off. Behave the way you did at the opera; just don't go overboard or appear too curious about him. Is he someone who, in the normal course of your life, you might find attractive?"

"No, not really, though I liked him at the opera. I wouldn't want to fuck him, if that's what you mean."

Lance looked chastened. "I wasn't suggesting that you should. What I meant was, if a mutual attraction seemed natural, you might exploit that to your advantage, but if not, don't fake it."

"I understand."

"Can I be on the team?" Ty asked.

"No," Kerry said. "If he saw Holly on the train, he might have seen you, too, and your presence would spook him immediately. We have this little advantage that he's seen Holly on the street before, so it won't alarm him to see her on the street again."

"Will you bust him immediately, if I see him?" Holly asked.

"No. We'll have the team get in touch with Kerry or me for that decision. They'll tail him from a distance and report it if he goes into a building. I want to know where he lives and where he does his work. He has to have some sort of workshop somewhere, either in his home or nearby, and the equipment, weapons, disguises, etcetera, that we might find there would be very useful in prosecuting him. This guy might have an identity so tight that we might have trouble breaking it in court. We're going to need all the ammunition we can get. Remember, we don't have photographs, fingerprints or DNA to work with."

"Right," Holly said. "How do you want me to proceed?"

"Do you bring Daisy to work with you every day?"

"No, just sometimes."

"On the occasions when you don't, you go home to walk her?"

"Yes, I go home at lunchtime. She only needs walking once after I go to work, then when I come home again."

"Start having lunch at home and walking Daisy then. When you're off duty, take her with you when you leave the house. We want it to be easy for Teddy to spot you."

"All right." Holly groped for words.

"What?"

"What about my . . . personal life?"

Lance looked sympathetic. "If there are times when you don't want a team on you, let me know, and I'll pull them. If you should run into Teddy then, you can always call it in."

"Thank you, Lance." Not that she had a personal life, but she was still thinking about Stone Barrington.

Lance looked at his watch. "Give me fifteen minutes to get a team together, then go home to lunch."

FORTY-THREE

Two days after the incident in the subway, Teddy saw Holly Barker again. She was leaving her building and, apparently, headed for the park, since she had her dog with her.

Since seeing her on the train, Teddy had gone back and read her file from the Agency again, and this time he had Googled her and read the newspaper accounts of the big cases she had been involved in when she had been chief of police in Orchid Beach, Florida. It made amazing reading, since it concerned a small-town police officer, and Teddy was intrigued. He thought he would like to get to know her personally, but the business on the train bothered him.

He followed Holly at a distance of more than a block, then, as she entered the park at 64th Street, he turned down Fifth Avenue and simply walked away. He hadn't spotted a tail, but he wasn't taking any chances. He got on the Fifth Avenue bus and watched to see if anyone got on behind him, or if a car were following the bus. Seeing nothing, he got off in the Fifties, walked over to Madison and took the bus back uptown, constantly watching for a tail.

As he got off the bus at 63rd Street, he saw Holly cross the street a block ahead, apparently headed back to her apartment building. He turned down 63rd, walked to Park and crossed the street, looking back in time to see her enter her building. He glanced at his watch. Lunch time. She must have come home from her office just to walk the dog. He loitered around the corner long enough to watch her leave the building, then he walked to Lexington, took a cab and got out a block from the CIA building. Ten minutes later Holly appeared on foot and walked into the building.

Once again checking for tails, Teddy walked to Third Avenue, took the bus uptown, and, after walking around the block a couple of times, went into the building that housed his workshop.

He hung up his coat and sat down at the computer, logged on to the Agency mainframe and ran a non-Agency search on her name. This time a new reference appeared: a website for some sort of financial management firm, Morgan & Bailey. Holly was listed on the site as a senior vice president. Obviously, the firm was an Agency front, and they had gone to the trouble to create the website to lend verisimilitude to the legend.

It occurred to him that Holly was living above her means, if her Agency salary was all she had. Perhaps she was taking a salary from Morgan & Bailey, to help her establish credentials in the city, or perhaps the firm was paying for the apartment.

He went back to the news clippings and read the story reporting the death of her fiancé, who was an innocent bystander at a bank robbery and got in the way. He ran a search on the fiancé, Jackson Oxenhandler, and discovered that he had been a prosperous lawyer in Orchid Beach. Maybe she had inherited his estate. That would make her, perhaps, prosperous enough to afford an apartment on Park Avenue.

It was clear to Teddy that, based on her career in the military, plus her very successful career as a police chief, Holly Barker was a very smart and motivated woman. If he had needed further evidence of that, her training report from the Farm showed plenty of guts and initiative. He would have to be careful to limit his contact with her in the neighborhood, and if she showed any interest in him, he would have to pull up stakes and find a new place to live.

THERE WAS A NOTE on Holly's new desk: "See me—Lance." She went and knocked on the door that connected their offices.

"Come in," he said.

She found him at his desk, looking at photographs. "You wanted to see me?"

"The team had a sighting of a man who may have been following you for a couple of blocks."

"When?"

"In the last hour. He went in your direction until you entered the park, then he got on a bus downtown." He beckoned her to his side of the desk.

Holly looked at the photographs; they were taken from more than a block away with a low-resolution digital camera. "He's a blur," she said.

"That's as much as we could enhance it," Lance said. "Don't believe everything about surveillance you see on TV."

"I can't make him from these," she said, shuffling through the prints. "Did anybody follow him when he broke from me?"

"The team lost him when he got on the bus. We're going to have to add vehicles, obviously."

"I feel guilty about soaking up this much manpower," Holly said.

"Have a seat," Lance said, walking around the desk and sitting next to her on his sofa. "I'm concerned about you."

"Why?"

"You look depressed."

Holly laughed. "So do you."

"I guess we're all a little depressed about how this is going."

"Has it ever occurred to you that we may be the wrong people for this work?" Holly asked. "I mean, my class's training was cut short, and not much of it has been useful to me on this assignment. A few years as a cop in Florida was better training for this."

"It occurs to me every day," Lance said, "but what can I do? I can't call Langley and tell them to shut us down. That would be admitting failure, and the failure would go into the personnel file of everybody in this station. The Agency culture can tolerate a certain amount of failure, because operations frequently don't pan out, but the culture would look askance at *admitted* failure, especially of a project and a unit commissioned directly by the president of the United States. We don't really have a choice; we're going to have to catch Teddy Fay or die trying. If we can do that, praise will rain down upon us, good things will be said about us in our fitness reports and we will be princes in our realm."

"Well, I guess that's better than *admitted* failure," Holly said.

FORTY-FOUR

On a Thursday night Holly called the duty officer and asked him to pull the team off her for the night. Then, she dressed in a cashmere sweater and slacks that showed off her ass in a favorable light, put on her coat and got a cab to 88th Street and Second Avenue. She got out, took a deep breath and walked into Elaine's.

Thursday was the busiest night of the week, she knew, and she reckoned it was her best chance to "bump into" Stone Barrington. She hoped to God he wasn't with someone else.

Gianni, the headwaiter, spotted her and

came and kissed her on the cheek. "Holly! Long time! You meeting Stone?"

"Well, no, but if he's here, I'll say hello."

Gianni turned and pointed at a table along the wall. Stone and Dino Bacchetti, his former partner on the NYPD, were having drinks and arguing about something. "Let's break this up now," Gianni said, taking her arm and walking her back to the table. "Look who's here," he said to Stone.

Stone was on his feet, looking surprised, and so was Dino. Everybody hugged and kissed. "Join us?" Stone asked.

"Sure," Holly replied

"Gianni, bring Holly a Knob Creek on the rocks," Stone said, and Gianni departed for the bar. Stone was a lawyer who was counselor to a prestigious New York law firm, Woodman & Weld, and his specialty was handling the cases Woodman & Weld did not want to be seen to be handling. He was also one of Lance's recuits as a consultant to the Agency. So was Dino.

"Excuse me a minute," Dino said, apparently giving them a moment. "Be right back." He walked toward the men's room.

"So, you and Dino were really going at it when I came in. What's going on?"

"Oh, Dino and Mary Ann have been having some problems, and I was just counseling him."

"Counseling him? It looked more like you were yelling at him."

"He needed yelling at."

"You aren't exactly qualified to be a marriage counselor."

"All right, all right. What are you doing in New York? I thought Lance had shipped you off to some place in Virginia to be remolded by the Agency."

"I was already a deadly weapon and performed brilliantly, so they graduated me early and assigned me to New York."

"How'd the rest of the class do?" Stone asked suspiciously.

"Well, they did brilliantly, too," she said.

"So he brought your whole training class to New York?"

"Everybody who survived the training." Her drink arrived, and they clinked glasses.

Stone leaned in close. "You're on that Teddy Fay thing, aren't you?"

She was surprised he knew. "Sorry, that's classified." She took a deep sip of her drink.

"Come on, Dino's been reporting to Lance about a bunch of murders around the U.N.,"

Stone said. "And I think Lance let something slip."

"That doesn't sound like Lance," she said, keeping her guard up. "But if anybody lets anything slip about anything, it ain't going to be me."

"Okay, okay. God, it's good to see you; it's been months."

"Has it?" she asked, feigning indifference.

"You know very well how long it's been. I tried to call you in Orchid Beach, and I got some young lady who's house-sitting for you. That's when I knew you must be in Virginia."

"You're so clever, Stone; how could I ever hide anything from you?" she said, batting her eyes theatrically.

"So, how's life as a spy?"

She looked around to be sure nobody could hear. "Actually, I appear to be still a cop, the way things are going. I'm looking forward to this thing being over."

"He's a very smart guy," Stone said. "It may never end."

"I don't know who you're talking about," she said, "but the thought of it never ending is more than I can bear. Let's talk about something else."

Dino came back to the table and sat

down. "So," he said, sipping his drink, "how's it going on the Teddy Fay thing?"

Holly sighed. "Dino, I don't know what you're talking about, and even if I did, I wouldn't know what you were talking about."

"I get your drift," Dino said, "but I still want to know what's going on."

"Then you'd better have dinner with Lance," she said, "and you'd better not tell him you even mentioned the subject to me."

A waiter brought them menus.

"Shouldn't you be getting home to your *wife*?" Stone asked Dino pointedly.

"I haven't had dinner yet," Dino said indignantly. "You want me to starve?"

"As I recall, Mary Ann is a very fine cook."

"Yeah, well the last time she cooked for me was so long ago that I can't put a date on it."

"If you weren't in here every night, maybe she'd cook for you more often," Stone said.

"All right, you two," Holly interjected. "Cool it; let's order dinner."

"You have any idea what a pain in the ass Stone can be?" Dino asked.

"Dino, I am not going to spend the evening refereeing, so if you and Stone can't just remember what good friends you are and talk pleasantly to each other, then I'm having dinner elsewhere." She put down her menu.

"All right, all right," Dino said, patting her arm. "I'll be nice if he will."

"Stone?"

Stone nodded.

The waiter came back. "Is there any osso bucco left over from last night?" Holly asked. Wednesday was osso bucco night.

"I'll check," the waiter said. He left and returned. "Yep."

"I'll have that, too," Stone said, and Dino joined the movement.

"Sorry, there's only one order left," the waiter said, "and the lady gets it."

The two men grumbled and ordered something else.

MUCH LATER, as they finished their coffee, Dino stood up. "Well," he said, "I guess I'd better go home and face the music."

"You make home sound like a horrible place, Dino," Holly said.

"Sometimes it is," he replied. He gave her a kiss, put on his coat, gave Stone a wave and walked out.

"Well, now," Stone said. "We're finally rid of him; what are we going to do now?"

Holly laughed. "I take it you have a suggestion?"

"I have several suggestions," Stone said.

"And what are they?"

"They are better transmitted by nonverbal communication," Stone said. "Can we communicate at my house?"

"I've got a better idea," Holly said. "Why don't we talk about it at my house?"

"You have a house?"

"I have an apartment, thank you. Anyway, I have to walk Daisy."

"How is Daisy?" Stone asked, getting up and retrieving their coats.

"You'll see shortly," Holly said, slipping into her coat and buttoning up.

THE CAB PULLED UP in front of Holly's building, and they got out.

"You're moving up in the world," Stone said.

"Onward and upward."

They took the elevator to the twelfth floor, and Holly opened her front door.

"You don't lock your door?" Stone asked.

"The security is good here," Holly said, "and here it comes."

Daisy made a fool of herself over Stone.

"We'll be right back," Holly said, reaching for Daisy's leash. "Don't go away."

"I'm not going anywhere."

MUCH LATER, Holly rolled over in bed and encountered the sleeping Stone. This was much better than sleeping alone, she thought, even better than sleeping with Daisy.

FORTY-FIVE

TEDDY WAS HALF A BLOCK from Holly's building when he saw a man come out with a Doberman on a leash. The two stopped when the dog wanted to inspect a street lamp.

Teddy continued past but spoke. "Good morning, Daisy," he said. Daisy interrupted her business and came over to say hello. Teddy scratched her behind the ear and talked to her for a moment. "She's very popular in the neighborhood," he said to the man.

"I'm not surprised," the man replied.

Teddy gave him a quick once-over: six-two, a hundred and ninety, blond hair, stubble. He had the look of a man who had just gotten out of bed and hadn't had his coffee yet. Teddy felt a pang of something he recognized as jealousy. "Bye-bye, Daisy," he said. "Good morning to you," he said to the man, then continued down the street. Jealousy? That was something he hadn't felt for many, many years, but it was real, and it was disturbing.

HOLLY WAS PUTTING BREAKFAST ON the table when Stone and Daisy returned. "Thanks for taking her out," she said.

"Glad to. Daisy seems to be very popular in the neighborhood."

Holly turned and looked at him. "Why do you say that?"

"Oh, a passerby stopped and chatted with her, knew her name. She reacted as if they'd met before."

"What did he look like?"

"I don't know," Stone said. "Maybe six feet, slender, graying, mid-fifties. He looked sort of like Larry David."

"Holy shit," Holly said, rushing to her windows overlooking Park Avenue and opening the blinds. She looked up and down the street. "Only one neighbor has made friends with Daisy. Come over here, Stone." Stone came. "Do you see him anywhere?"

Stone looked up and down Park. "Nope."

"Which way was he headed?"

"North to south. He may have turned a corner toward Madison a block down. I wasn't really paying attention. Why are you interested in him?"

"Because I think you just met Teddy Fay."

Stone blinked. "You're kidding."

"No, I'm not." Holly was on the phone. "It's Holly Barker; just had a Teddy sighting in front of my building; he was headed south on Park, west side of the street. Right." She hung up the phone. "Damn," she said, "and I had the team pulled last night."

"Team?"

"The team that's been following me, trying to get a shot at Teddy."

"You're planning to shoot him?"

"No, I mean a shot at capturing him. We think he may live or work in the neighborhood. What was he wearing?"

"A tweed overcoat and one of those Irish tweed hats with the brim turned down all the way around; sunglasses."

"Did he speak to you?"

"After he spoke to Daisy and petted her,

he said she was very popular in the neighborhood. Then he said good morning and continued on his way."

Holly waved Stone to a seat and sat down in front of her bacon and eggs. She stared into the plate. "He said Daisy was very popular in the neighborhood?"

"Yes."

"Then he *must* live in the neighborhood."

LANCE LISTENED TO HER REPORT quietly and waited until she had finished before he spoke. "Someone else was walking Daisy this morning?"

"A friend," she said.

Lance nodded. "And you pulled the team last night. Of course."

"Of course, what?"

"Of course Teddy would turn up just when the team wasn't there. He knows Daisy?"

"Yes, the first time I saw him outside the building, he petted her and asked her name."

"Maybe Teddy is following *you*," Lance said. "Why else would he be camped outside your building?"

"I don't think he was *camped*," Holly said. "I really think he lives in the neighborhood."

"Or works in the neighborhood."

"There aren't any workshops on Park Avenue," she said.

"Holly, I want you to put some people on visiting all the realty firms in the neighborhoods that handle rentals, especially short-term rentals, a year or less. Find out if anyone answering Teddy's description has rented something on Park Avenue or in the immediate environs during the past month. Don't go yourself; I don't want Teddy to see you in a real estate office. And tell them to go singly, not in pairs, and use FBI agents. They have a more instant authority with the general public than we do."

"I'll get right on it," Holly said, and returned to her office.

EDITH TIMMONS, a sixty-year-old realtor who managed the Crown and Palmer office at Madison and 60th Street was at her desk when a young man came into the office. Through her open door she could see him flash some sort of I.D. at the receptionist, and she got up and went to the door. "May I help you?" she said to the young man.

"Mrs. Timmons," the receptionist said, "this gentleman is from the FBI; perhaps you should speak to him."

"Yes, please come into my office," she said. Edith turned back to her desk and began to take deep breaths, composing herself. She sat down at her desk and clasped her hands together to keep them from shaking. "Yes, come in," she said.

The young man showed her his identification. "I'm Special Agent Harding, with the FBI," he said.

"How may I help you?" Edith replied, trying to keep her voice steady. Forty years before, Edith, whose name was not Edith, had participated in a Weather Underground bank robbery in downtown New York, and a bank guard had been killed. She had only driven the getaway car, but she knew that somewhere in the Justice Department bureaucracy there was an arrest warrant with her real name on it and that there is no statute of limitations on murder.

"I understand that your firm handles short-term rentals on the Upper East Side," Harding said. "Is that correct?"

"Yes, it is," she replied, relieved that he did not seem interested in arresting her. "It's a specialty of ours."

Harding handed her a sketch of a middle-aged man. "Have you, during the past few weeks, shown an apartment or rented an apartment to a man who looks like this?"

Edith tried not even to blink. "No, we haven't," she said. "I handle the short-term rentals, myself, so if he had come in here, I would have seen him."

"You're certain you haven't rented to someone who looks even vaguely like this man during the past weeks?"

She shook her head. "I'm sure; I've only rented to couples for the past three or four months. It's been more than a year since I rented to a single man. And none of the men in the couples looked like this. Why are you asking?"

"It's just a routine investigation," Harding said. "We're talking to all the realtors in the neighborhood."

"I see." She stood up. "Well, I'm sorry I couldn't have been more help, Agent Harding. Good day."

"Good day, and thank you." The young man left her offices and turned up Madison Avenue.

Edith closed her office door, sat back down in her chair and rested her face in her hands, trying to tame her wildly beating heart. She took a tissue from the box on her desk and dabbed at the beads of perspiration that had popped out on her forehead, then she got out her compact and repaired her carefully applied makeup.

For a moment, there, she had thought her life would go up in smoke: her partnership in the realty firm, her marriage to a Park Avenue physician, her two sons and her five grandchildren.

What was that man's name? She got out her card file of rentals and began going through them, then stopped at one. Foreman; Albert Foreman. She dialed the number.

TEDDY WAS IN HIS WORKSHOP when the phone rang. He routinely forwarded the calls from his apartment to this phone, but he never got calls, except from telemarketers. He picked up the instrument. "Hello?"

"Mr. Foreman?"

"Who's calling, please?"

"This is Edith Timmons of Crown and Palmer. Is this Mr. Foreman?"

"Yes."

"I'm sure you'll recall that I rented you your apartment at the Mayflower a few weeks ago."

"Of course, Mrs. Timmons. Is anything

wrong? Are the owners returning earlier than planned?"

"Oh, no, nothing like that. I just wanted to tell you about something, purely for your own information."

"Yes?"

"A few minutes ago I had a visit from an FBI agent, who showed me a sketch of someone who looked vaguely like you and asked if I had rented an apartment to such a person."

Teddy's gut clenched. "And what did you tell him?"

"Mr. Foreman, I have to tell you that I have no love for the FBI and I have no wish to help them. I told him that I had not rented to any such person, so you shouldn't be bothered."

"That's very kind of you, Mrs. Timmons. It's just a tax matter. I'll contact them, and I'm sure we can work it out."

"Well, of course, I knew it would be something like that. I just wanted to let you know that you need not be concerned. They won't come looking for you."

"Well, thank you again, Mrs. Timmons. I very much appreciate your concern."

"One thing, Mr. Foreman: if you should have a conversation with these people, I'd appreciate it if you wouldn't mention that you rented the apartment from me. I wouldn't want to be caught in a lie."

"Of course not, Mrs. Timmons, and thank you again." Teddy hung up and breathed a sigh of relief. They were looking for him, but they had missed. He'd be all right for a while longer.

FORTY-SIX

TEDDY NOW TURNED HIS ATTENTION to his next victim. He still had the photographs of the others he had identified as prospects, but he was growing tired of small fry; he wanted a bigger fish, someone who would strike fear into the hearts of America's enemies.

He looked at his watch; time to call Irene. He dialed her cell phone number.

"Hello," she said, knowing who was calling. "It's been a while."

"I've been a busy fellow," he said.

"Believe me, I know all about it. I've completed my investigation of how you're getting the information, and I turned in my report to the director."

"And?"

"And I've blamed it on the FBI."

Teddy smiled. "Good."

"And, I understand, the FBI is blaming it on us."

"Perfect! When are you coming to New York again?"

"Maybe in a couple of days. Can I let you know?"

"Sure, call me anytime on the cell phone."

"Anything I can do for you?"

"Yes. I'm looking for a new kind of target, a bigger fish."

"At the U.N.?"

"That would be good; I'd rather not have to travel to Washington."

"Let me poke around and see who I can come up with. Maybe I can bring you a name when I come to New York."

"Good. I'm looking forward to seeing you. Bye-bye." Teddy hung up. He really was looking forward to seeing her. His increasing interest in Holly Barker was making him horny, and he needed relief.

Teddy went to his workbench and returned his attention to something he had been working on for several days. He didn't have a sniper's rifle, and buying one that would suit his purpose would be too complicated and too dangerous. Instead, he had decided to make one himself that would break down and be easily concealable.

He owned a virtually unused Walther PPK-S, the stainless-steel, updated version of the gun made famous in the James Bond novels. The caliber was .380, which posed a problem, but he could deal with that. He also had a Douglas .380 rifle barrel that he'd ordered more than a year ago.

He cut down the rifle barrel to sixteen inches and built a six-inch silencer to add to that. Then he replaced the pistol's grip panel with an L-shaped piece of flat aluminum plating that came over the top of the gun. He shaped a folding stock of a strip of one-inch alloy that was fixed to the plating by a single screw, so that it could be quickly attached or detached using a dime for a screwdriver.

Finally, he mounted a 6x18 power Leupold zoom scope to the top of the L-shaped plating. He broke down the little pistol, removed the barrel and replaced it with the new, longer barrel, then reassembled it. Then he carved an eight-inch wooden grip and affixed it to the barrel, to protect his hand from the heat buildup when the weapon was fired. What he finished up with was a neat, small, very quiet rifle with a pistol grip that could be broken down and carried in a briefcase or raincoat pocket. This was perfect, but if the rifle were going to be effective at, say, a hundred yards, he was going to have to upgrade the ammunition; the standard .380 round was just not powerful enough.

He hand-loaded a hundred rounds of ammunition with a 115-grain, pointed, lead-tipped bullet and a cartridge packed with five grains of Unique powder. That would give the round the extra velocity, accuracy and destructive power it would need to hit an eight-inch target dead center at a hundred yards. Still, the bullet would drop more than it would from a higher-powered rifle, so he was going to have to fire the rifle to sight it in for the range.

IRENE ARRIVED in New York and followed Teddy's instructions. She went to the fountain in Grand Army Plaza outside the Plaza Hotel at high noon and loitered for ten minutes. Then she set off across 59th Street and into Central Park. Teddy, who had been watching her from half a block away, was occupying a bench along the walkway toward the zoo, reading the *Post*. He dawdled a hundred yards behind her, looking for tails, then watched as she moseyed around the zoo and finally headed north.

He followed her for half an hour, then, when he was sure she was not being tailed, called her cell phone.

"Yes?"

"There's a room booked in the name of Frances Williams at the Lowell Hotel, on East Sixty-third Street, between Park and Madison. Go there and check in, telling them that your luggage was delayed by the airline and will be delivered later. When you've satisfied yourself that you're clean of tails, call my cell from your room and give me the room number."

"Got it," she said.

Teddy followed her all the way to the hotel, then walked past it and around the block again, making sure he was not followed. Halfway around, his cell phone rang.

"Yep?"

"Six one six. All is well."

He continued around the block, then entered the hotel, went straight to the elevator and rode to the eighth floor. He walked down two flights, and, after checking out the hallway, knocked on the door.

There was a pause, and he was inside. Irene was already naked under a terry robe. He was out of his clothes in a flash.

AN HOUR LATER, as they lay, half asleep, in each other's arms, she spoke for the first time. "How about a nice, flashy Saudi prince with financial connections to Al Qaeda?" she asked.

"Oh, yeah," he murmured.

"His name is Ali ben Saud, and he's one of hundreds of Saudi princes," she said. "What sets him apart is that he actually makes money, instead of just lying around and collecting whatever allowance the king allots him. He's invested cleverly, too cleverly, we think. What caught our attention is that he invests more than his allowance, and we think the extra funds come from an Al Qaeda contact in Syria. There is constant activity in his accounts, money being wired here and there, some legit, some questionable."

"How sure are you of his involvement with Al Qaeda?" Teddy asked.

"We're sure, but we couldn't prove it in a court of law."

"Where is he?"

"He lives flashily, right here in New York. He's an assistant secretary general at the U.N., and he has a big duplex apartment in the U.N. Plaza building."

"I love that building," Teddy said. "I remember once a character in a movie saying that if there is a god, he probably lives in that building."

Irene laughed. "He has a penthouse apartment, and the building's security is excellent, so it would probably be very difficult to get to him there."

"What's his work schedule, and how does he get to the office?"

"He leaves his apartment every morning at nine for work and walks to the main entrance of the U.N. building. Then he exits the U.N. building every afternoon at four, regular as clockwork, and walks home."

"That's very cooperative of him," Teddy said. "He must drive his security people crazy."

"He walks with an entourage of six or eight guards, who are heavily armed. Our people have observed this, but we're not allowed to maintain any real surveillance on him, because he's too well connected with Saudi officials in this country who have a lot of influence with the State Department. We haven't even told the New York station of our interest in him, though that's going to happen any day now."

"Good," Teddy said. "That means I'll have to deal with only his personal security people and not worry about surveillance from anybody else. I'll have to go down to U.N. Plaza and take a look at the area."

"Not right now," Irene said, pulling him toward her.

"Oh, no, indeed not," Teddy said, kissing her.

FORTY-SEVEN

HOLLY WAS HOME at lunchtime to walk Daisy, when the phone rang.

"Hello?"

"It's the old man," Ham said.

"How you doin', Ham?"

"Not bad. Ginny and I thought we might come up to New York and do some Christmas shopping."

"Great! It would be wonderful to see you. I can put you up, you know."

"Nah, suggest a good hotel. I told you why."

"There are two good ones in the neighborhood, though, the Lowell, on Sixty-third and the Plaza Athenee, on Sixty-fourth. They'll both have thick walls."

"Okay, I'll book us in."

"When you coming?

"Tomorrow okay?"

"Sure. I'll see if I can get some time off, and if you'll give me your flight information, I'll have a car meet you."

"I'll e-mail it to you. Bye." He hung up. Ham had never been one for long telephone conversations.

Holly got Daisy's leash and left the building, headed for the park. She tried not to be self-conscious, tried not to look over her shoulder, but the thought that maybe Teddy might be following her never left her mind. They entered the park at 64th Street, walked past the zoo and headed north at a fast walk for Holly and a slow one for Daisy, but since she had a lot of sniffing and inspecting to do, the pace was good for both of them.

At the Bethesda Fountain Holly looked around for a cop and, seeing none, un-clipped Daisy and let her range around the open area, while Holly sat on the fountain's edge and kept an eye out for the law. It was a one-hundred-dollar fine to have your dog off the leash in the park after nine A.M.

Immediately, Holly saw two men who could be Teddy Fay: one older looking, in a long topcoat with a short, gray beard, and another in a sheepskin coat and a tweed cap, with a big yellow muffler that partly covered his face. She looked away from both of them, then glanced back when she could. She made sure her cell phone earpiece was firmly in her ear, then she reached into a pocket and pressed the single key that connected her to the team leader.

"I'm here," he said.

"I've got two candidates," she replied without moving her lips. "Old man in topcoat with beard, younger man in sheepskin coat and tweed cap. Can't be sure about either."

"We're on it." He rang off.

Holly gave them another couple of minutes to identify the two men, then she called Daisy and headed back toward 64th Street, still walking quickly. She made the last few blocks in record time, and as soon as she was inside she called Lance.

"Yes?"

"I identified two prospects to the team," she said.

"I know; they're tracking both. The older man with the beard has been eliminated—

he's *really* old—but they're still on the sheep-skin coat. Come on back to work."

Holly left some fresh water for Daisy, told her to guard the apartment with her life, and got a cab back to the office. She went imme-diately to Lance's office.

"What's going on?"

Lance was watching a jerky television im-age on a monitor next to his desk. "There's the sheepskin coat," he said. "He's leading them on an erratic walk, and they're having trouble keeping him in sight without losing him or blowing the tail. I've dispatched an-other team to help. You think it could really be him?"

"Well, it could be Larry David, I suppose."

"I'm never going to be able to watch his show again without thinking about this," Lance said, laughing. He picked up his phone and pressed a button. "I want one team member to get close; Holly's here, and I want her to have a good look. Have some-one approach and pass him from in front."

Holly watched the screen, and a moment later the perspective changed: the camera was a block away, and the man in the sheep-skin coat was walking toward it. The man and his pursuer stopped on opposite sides of the street for a traffic light.

"Zoom in as close as possible," Lance said into the phone.

The camera began a slow zoom, and as it framed the man more tightly, he took off his tweed cap and wiped his forehead with a handkerchief. Holly got a good look at his face; he couldn't have been older than forty-five. "Not him," she said. "Too young."

Lance spoke into the phone again. "He's not our man," he said. "Break it off; everybody back to the Barn." He hung up the phone.

"I'm sorry, Lance, I thought he might be Teddy."

"Don't worry about it; the exercise was good practice for the team."

TEDDY APPROACHED THE U.N. PLAZA BUILDING on foot. The elegant apartment house soared forty stories or more into the New York skyline. Teddy started near the front door and walked slowly toward the U.N. building, perhaps a block away. He wanted to see the area from the target's perspective.

This was not going to be as easy as the

others, since ben Saud would have up to eight armed guards with him. If Teddy tried to do a drive-by from a motorbike or bicycle, they'd cut him to pieces the moment he fired, maybe sooner. No, he was going to have to be stationary and, preferably, elevated. As he walked toward the U.N. he saw, across the street, a building under construction, a small office or apartment building. The steel structure was up, and the floors appeared to be in, but cladding of the exterior had not yet begun.

Attached to one side of the building was an elevator cage to get the workers up and down in a hurry. That would do for access, he thought, but not for escape. He broke off his walk to the U.N. and crossed the street. Two men were conferring on the sidewalk over a set of plans, one of them obviously the construction foreman, in his work clothes and yellow hard hat, the other in a business suit and topcoat but also wearing a hard hat. Building owner? Architect? As he passed them Teddy got a good look at a plastic I.D. badge clipped to his topcoat collar. It identified him as a New York City building inspector.

"You've got a couple of soft spots in the second-story temporary flooring," he was saying, "and I want them beefed up *today*." Teddy couldn't hear the response, but he didn't need to. He was concentrating on remembering as much detail as possible of the I.D. badge the man was wearing. Then he saw something that immediately appealed to him. On the west side of the building, the side opposite the elevator, there was another way out. He liked that a lot.

KERRY SMITH came into Lance's office. "Any luck?" he asked Lance and Holly.

"No," Lance said, "not our man. Good practice for the team, though; keeps them occupied."

"Keeping them occupied is getting harder," Kerry said. "I'm getting tired of writing reports that say, in essence, 'Nothing happened today,' and I suspect that Washington is getting tired of reading them."

"Okay, Holly," Lance said, "just maintain your routine, keep going home every day at noon to walk Daisy, keep putting yourself out there for Teddy to see."

"Okay," Holly said, rising from her chair.

"By the way, Lance, do you mind if I take two or three days off? My dad and his girlfriend are coming into town tomorrow."

"Sure, we'll try to struggle along without you."

"You may as well pull the team off, too."

"Okay. See you Monday."

Holly left Lance's office and went back to her own.

Kerry looked at Lance. "Are you really going to pull the team off?" he asked.

"No," Kerry replied.

FORTY-EIGHT

TEDDY GOT INTO THE CAR, carrying a briefcase, drove over to the West Side and headed north on the West Side Highway, which turned into the Henry Hudson Parkway, which turned into the Saw Mill River Parkway. Near the end he got off at the exit for Katonah and began driving around, looking for a very private spot.

After a few minutes he stopped on a small bridge. A stream passed under him, and on one bank he saw a well-worn footpath. Not likely anyone would be in the woods today, he thought. He pulled past the bridge onto the wide shoulder and got out of the car, carrying his briefcase. He half-walked, half-slid down the embankment to the footpath and began walking quickly upstream, away from the bridge. After a couple of minutes, there was a bend in the stream, and Teddy could no longer see the bridge.

It was cold and silent in the winter-stripped woods, and he walked for another quarter of a mile before he found a fork in the path, away from the stream. He stopped and spotted an oak tree with a knot in its trunk around eight inches in diameter on the other side of the stream. He estimated the distance to the tree to be twenty yards. He walked up the right fork in the path, pacing off another eighty yards, then stopped and looked around. He seemed completely alone in the woods, and the only sound he could hear was the rush of the stream. Looking back, he could see the oak tree with the knot clearly.

Teddy sat down on a large rock and, after checking both ways on the path for company, opened the briefcase and began assembling his new Walther PPK-S rifle. That done, he disassembled it and went through the process another three times, getting faster. After the third time, he was down to thirty-five seconds, and he reckoned that was about as fast as he would get.

Teddy knelt behind the rock and rested the barrel of the silenced rifle on it. He took careful aim at the knot in the oak tree, adjusting the zoom scope, then he squeezed off a round. The rifle was pleasingly silent, emitting only a whispery *pfffttt!* The bullet struck a foot below the knot and barely grazed the trunk on the right side. Part of that must be trigger pull, he thought. He fired one more round, and it stayed a foot low, but was only six inches right.

He adjusted the scope for elevation and turned the knurled knob two clicks to bring it into horizontal alignment. He fired another shot, and the bullet struck the tree at the bottom of the knot and a little left. He adjusted twice more, until he squeezed off a round that struck the knot dead center, then just to be sure, he fired two more rounds, both of which were nearly in the original bullet hole. That's it, he thought. I'm sighted in for a hundred yards.

He got up, walked around a bit, then shoved in another magazine, stood and fired another six rounds from an unbraced standing position. He started wide but gradually brought his fire on target. The center of the knot was now a crater, and he was putting every round into it.

Satisfied, he quickly disassembled the rifle, packed it into the fitted briefcase and began walking back to the car. A few minutes later, he was back on the Saw Mill, heading south for the city, enjoying the drive.

THE PHONE RANG in Holly's apartment.

"Hello?"

"It's your old man."

"You're in already?"

"Five minutes ago."

"How's the Lowell?"

"Very nice; better than I'm used to. Can I buy you lunch?"

"No, but I'll take you. Pick you up in fifteen minutes?"

"We'll meet you in the lobby."

Holly phoned La Goulue, a restaurant at 65th and Madison she passed every day while walking Daisy, and made a reservation. She walked Daisy, played with her for a bit, gave her a cookie and told her to be a good girl, then she went to meet Ham.

* * *

THE RESTAURANT was warm and cozy, and they were given a nice corner table. Ginny, Ham's girlfriend, was a good-looking woman with bright red hair who had taught Holly to fly the year before, and this was her first time in New York.

They ordered, then Ham spoke up. "So, how's the work going?"

"Not so hot," Holly said.

"Can't you find Teddy?"

Holly's eyebrows went up.

"It wasn't so hard to figure out," Ham said. "There've been three or four murders around the U.N. the past few weeks, and I don't believe the Agency is committing them. I always thought he might have gotten out of that airplane."

"He did," Holly said. "Ginny, you can't hear this, and if you do, you have to keep it to yourself."

"Don't worry, Holly, my lips are sealed," Ginny replied.

"She knows how to zip up," Ham said. "Now, why haven't you found this guy?"

"Because he's very, very smart," Holly said. "I figured he might be using the Lexington Avenue subway to get up and downtown, so we staked it out and photographed every likely candidate, but I swear to God, I think he spotted me and got out of there, instead of onto the train."

"You? Why would he know you?"

"Because I met him at the opera, and he invited me to use a spare ticket. He was beautifully disguised, though, and I never tumbled to him until I saw him later, ignoring what he said was a bad hip or knee or something and running like a jackrabbit for a cab."

"Isn't there some way to lure him out from his cover?" Ham asked.

"Maybe me. I think he lives in my neighborhood, so we've had a team following me, in case I see him."

"That would explain the guy across the street who keeps changing places with a woman," Ham said, nodding toward the window.

"Damn," Holly said, looking out the window, "he's one of ours, all right. I asked Lance to pull off the team while you're here, but I guess he didn't."

"Why do you think Teddy would be interested in you?" Ham said.

"I don't know that he would, but he's obviously figured out that I'm Agency or Bureau, and he has the advantage of recognizing me when I can't recognize him."

Ham sat quietly for a moment.

"What are you thinking?"

"I'm trying to think of a way to make you better bait."

"Thanks a lot, Ham. Should I go naked in the street?"

"That might do it, but you'd freeze to death in these temperatures."

ACROSS THE RESTAURANT, Teddy sat with Irene. He was against the wall, while her back was to the room, so he could see Holly clearly. He was wearing his nose and mustache disguise, and Irene was good cover, too. They wouldn't expect him to be with a woman.

"I'm nervous about being in a restaurant with you, Teddy," Irene whispered.

"Just don't use my name; call me Carl," he whispered back.

"Who is it you're looking at across the room?" she asked.

"One of yours," he said. "Holly Barker."

"She's right here in the restaurant?"

"Yep. We followed her here."

Irene sat up straight, so she could see the

reflection of the room in the mirror behind their banquette. "Where?"

"She's sitting next to a redhead, and there's a man with them with his back to us. He looks ex-military to me; could be her father."

"You've got more guts than is good for you," Irene said.

"You're probably right. Have you thought of retiring from the Agency?"

"I would, if I had something to do with myself," she said.

"How much have you got in savings?"

"About three hundred thousand in stock accounts, and I'd have my pension, of course."

"How'd you like to live in the islands?"

"Which islands?"

"Caribbean."

"Now *that* would make an attractive alternative to working."

"It's about time for me to get out of here," Teddy said. "I just want this one more good score, then I want to disappear for good. You want to disappear with me?"

She smiled. "I think I'd like that."

"We'd have to do this carefully," Teddy said.

"Tell me how, and I'll do it."

"I think St. Barts would be nice; I was there for a weekend about fifteen years ago, and I was impressed."

"I've heard good things about it."

"You retire, go down there and look for a house. Use your savings for a down payment; I'll give you a bank name in the Caymans, and you'll apply for a mortgage there. The payments will be made from my funds, and in time, when we're sure they're not interested in you anymore, I'll replenish your savings. It's important that the Agency can see that you're doing this on your own hook, with no help."

"That's true. You're sure this is what you want to do, uh, Carl?"

"I'm sure; how about you?"

"I'm in."

"When you get back, go see Hugh English and tell him you want to retire in, say, a month. Tell him you're thinking about a place in the sun somewhere and ask him for recommendations, then put your place on the market. Is it paid for?"

"Yes, and it's probably worth three-fifty, three-seventy-five."

"Good. With that, an Agency investigator

would see that you can afford the place in the islands."

"This is exciting," she said, putting her hand on his.

"I'm looking forward to it," Teddy replied. "I just want to tie up some loose ends here." He looked across the room at Holly again. He would be sorry to say goodbye to her.

FORTY-NINE

IRENE FOSTER WALKED into the Barn's front desk and asked for Lance Cabot. "Ma'am, may I see some I.D.?" the man at the desk asked.

She noted that, as he spoke, one hand went below the desktop. Security was pretty good here. It was her first visit to the Barn since it had opened, and she was looking forward to seeing the place. She handed him her Agency I.D.

"Thank you, ma'am," the man said, picking up a phone. "Ms. Irene Foster to see you, Mr. Cabot. Yes, sir." He hung up the phone and turned back to Irene. "Please take the elevator to the twelfth floor; you'll be met there."

"Thank you." Irene rode up in the elevator and was met by an attractive, fortyish woman.

"Ms. Foster? I'm Holly Barker," the woman said. "Please come with me to Lance's office."

So this was the girl Teddy was so interested in, Irene thought, following her down the hallway. She was more attractive than she had imagined, and she felt a pang of jealousy.

Lance stood up to greet her as she came into his office. "Irene, it's good to see you somewhere other than on a teleconference," he said, shaking her hand. "You've met my assistant, Holly Barker?"

"Yes, but I didn't even know you had an assistant," Irene replied.

"I wanted to give her a chance at some supervisory work," Lance said. "How's Hugh English?"

"Oh, about the same, I think. He asked me to look in on you and see how things were going in the hunt for Teddy Fay."

Lance sighed. "I'm afraid I don't have much to report," he said. "We keep trying new things, but so far, he's been very slippery."

"That's not going to sound very good to Hugh, Lance, or to the director."

"Irene, you can tell Hugh for me—and the director, too—that if anybody at Langley thinks they can do a better job up here, I'll step aside in a flash. Quite frankly, I'm getting tired of being Langley's cop, and as nice a guy as Kerry Smith is, I'm tired of having to deal with the FBI on everything I do."

"Now, Lance," Irene said placatingly, "everybody at Langley, including the director, knows how good you are, and we all know we don't have anybody better. You just keep plugging away at this, and, eventually, you'll get a break and capitalize on it."

"I hope to God you're right," Lance said.

"I read your report on the extra surveillance you're putting on likely targets; I think that's a very good idea."

"Well, we were a little late coming up with it," Lance said. "You'll recall we lost the first name on the list before we could act."

"It happens," she said. "Don't be discouraged. By the way, you got my e-mail about Ali ben Saud, I hope."

"Yes, but I don't understand why we've had to pull surveillance on him. I should think he'd be a prime target for Teddy."

"Things are pretty tense with the Saudis right now," Irene said, "and Hugh felt it could hurt the political situation with them if ben Saud or his people made your people."

"I understand," Lance said. "Is this something the president has asked for?"

"No, it was Hugh's decision, on his own authority."

"How are Hugh and the director getting along these days?"

"As well as can be expected."

"Is he ever going to retire?"

"Not until he has to." She paused. "I'm thinking of putting in for it, myself, though."

"Really? I thought you'd outlast Hugh."

"Even if I did, I'd never get his job, and I'm a little weary, Lance. I think I'd like to live in a sunnier climate, bake my bones a bit."

"Have you said anything to Hugh about this?"

"Not yet, but I've pretty much decided to go and see him on Monday morning."

"You don't want to see the Teddy Fay thing through?"

"Look, it's just another operation; there've been hundreds before it, and there'll be hundreds after it. Anyway, I feel helpless on this one. You're at the pointed end of this effort; all I'm doing is shuffling papers."

"Well, I'll be sorry to see you go, Irene. Where'd you have in mind?"

"I don't know, someplace in the islands, I guess. Have you spent any time down there?"

"Ten years ago I was acting station chief, working out of St. Thomas."

"Did you like it there?"

"It was all right; I liked the islands farther south—St. Kitts, St. Barts—better. Those were really nice."

"I've read good things about St. Barts," she said. "Maybe I'll get on the Internet and have a closer look at it, check out the property prices." This was working out well, getting a recommendation from Lance.

"What else can I do for you while you're here?" Lance asked.

"I'd love to take a look at your facility," Irene replied. "Could Holly show me around?"

"Sure." He buzzed Holly and instructed her.

THEIR TOUR FINISHED, Holly escorted Irene back to the front lobby.

"Thank you so much, Holly," Irene said, taking her hand. "It was very kind of you to take the time to show me the building."

Holly shook her hand. "I was very pleased to do so."

"By the way," Irene said, "we hear good things about you from time to time. Keep up the good work."

"I'll do my best," Holly said.

Irene went out into the cold streets, the jealousy burning in her breast. She needed to get Teddy out of New York fast. She knew him well enough to know that he wasn't going to leave Holly Barker alone.

FIFTY

TEDDY WALKED SLOWLY DOWN Fifth Avenue,
wearing what appeared to be a broken nose,
a brown Vandyke beard and a reversible topcoat with the tweed side out. He wore a soft
felt hat and carried a shopping bag with a
few wrapped empty boxes peeking out, and
he could still see Holly, who had obligingly
worn a bright red woolen tam. The tall, thin
man, whom Teddy had now identified as her
father, Hamilton Barker, from his military records, was with her. He didn't know, yet, who
the redhead on his arm was, and he suspected that she was an Agency or Bureau
colleague of Holly's.

The three of them passed St. Patrick's Cathedral, paused in front of Saks Fifth Avenue and gazed at the giant Christmas tree in Rockefeller Center. Then they crossed the street and walked into the arcade that led to the skating rink.

Teddy dallied in front of Saks for a minute or two, since he didn't have to worry about losing the three while they looked at the skaters and the tree. He used the pause to try and identify Holly's tailing team.

There would be four of them, he knew, and they would dress against type, as he had. He had his doubts about a woman pushing a baby carriage, who was ignoring the Saks windows and looking at the crowd instead. Chances were, a doll occupied the carriage. He liked a man, too, wearing a fat down jacket and a lumberjack's cap with earflaps. The man should have been smart enough not to wear suit trousers and wingtips with that outfit. The other two team members, he reckoned, would be working closer to Holly.

He crossed the street when the pedestrian stoplight changed, and he had just reached the other side and was entering the arcade when he heard three gunshots. A

.45, he thought immediately, and the sound came from near the skating rink.

Suddenly, the thick crowd in the arcade became a tidal wave of people, all running away from the gunfire. Teddy flattened himself against a shopfront and his hand closed on the little Keltec .380 in his coat pocket. He looked back toward Saks and saw that the mother with the baby carriage had abandoned her young and was crossing Fifth Avenue as best she could through the traffic and against the running crowd. So much for the safety of her "child."

As the crowd quickly drained from the arcade, Teddy looked toward the skating rink and saw a man carrying a semiautomatic pistol in each hand, spinning like a dervish and firing random shots at people and through shop windows. Two shoppers were down, and there was broken glass everywhere. Then Teddy saw the man with Holly, one hand behind his back, walking quickly toward the shooter. Teddy began edging up the arcade toward Fifth Avenue, keeping his back to the buildings and his hand on the gun.

Then, for no apparent reason, the shooter stopped spinning and started walking backward, directly toward Teddy. His attention seemed occupied with something further down the arcade, and Teddy saw that it must be Ham Barker, who was walking calmly toward the man. He knew that Barker held a gun behind him, and that, as soon as he was a little closer to the shooter, he was going to start firing himself. Teddy was behind the shooter, in a direct line. If a slug from Barker missed or overpenetrated the shooter, Teddy was in line to catch it, and he didn't want that.

He backed into a doorway, took the Keltec from his pocket and held it at waist level, keeping it close to his body. The shooter was maybe eight feet away now, and that was close enough. Teddy fired two rounds at the man's spine; almost simultaneously, he heard two other shots, probably from a 9mm. He left the doorway and walked quickly toward Fifth.

Teddy didn't look back to see what was happening. He put his gun hand back into his pocket, turned left and headed for the corner of 50th Street. A sea of people were rushing across Fifth Avenue through the stalled traffic, and he joined them and headed down 50th toward Madison. As he reached the other side of Fifth he checked the reflection in Saks window and saw in the crowd the man in the down coat and lumberjack's cap coming toward him. He seemed to be speaking into his left fist.

Teddy continued down 50th Street, then, as he approached the side entrance to Saks, he ducked down in the crowd and pushed his way toward the revolving door. He was inside the store in a second, and he didn't wait to see if his pursuer was behind him. He turned left and walked as quickly as he could toward the long bank of elevators. The white dial over one turned red, and Teddy ran for it, pushing his way inside just as the doors began closing. Looking back the way he had come, he saw the man in the lumberjack cap come in through the revolving doors. The elevator doors closed, and the crowded car started up. Teddy thought the man saw him at the last possible moment.

BACK IN THE ROCKEFELLER CENTER arcade Holly was running toward Ham, her 9mm in one hand and her I.D. wallet in the other. She held the I.D. in the air, with the wallet open, and the gun out in front of her, the safety off and her finger alongside the trigger guard. She heard four shots, spaced very close together and saw the shooter go down. It was unlike Ham to fire more than twice, since he always hit what he was shooting at.

The shooter was on the ground, but he was moving, and there was still a gun in each hand. Ham was approaching him, his gun in both hands, and Holly ran up beside him. "I'll get one hand," she said.

"Right," Ham said, but his eyes never left the shooter.

Holly saw a woman from the Barn approaching from Fifth Avenue, holding a gun. There seemed to be guns everywhere. Holly walked up to the shooter and put her foot on his right wrist, while Ham did the same to his left. She put her weight on his wrist, and his hand opened. She bent and picked up his gun, while Ham took the other one, but she did not let her attention stray from the shooter.

"Ham," she said, "do you still have that Orchid Beach P.D. badge I gave you?"

"Yep," Ham said.

"Get it out and wave it when the cops come. We don't want them shooting at us."

"Right." Ham was digging in his pocket.

Then cops came from everywhere.

* * *

TEDDY GOT OFF the elevator on the sixth-floor men's department, turned right and walked into the men's room. He went into a stall, reversed his coat so that the raincoat side was now out, folded his felt hat and put it into the coat pocket, took a tweed cap from the other pocket and put that on, then pulled off the Vandyke and nose and put those in his pockets.

He left his shopping bag on the toilet seat, went to a sink and turned on the water, then checked his reflection. There were bits of spirit gum clinging to his face and he wiped it clean with a damp towel. He left a dollar for the attendant, then walked out of the men's room, past the elevators to the escalator, donning a pair of heavy, black-rimmed glasses as he walked. As he started down he saw two men walking very quickly away from him through the men's department, gun hands in their pockets, talking into their fists. He began walking down the escalator to make his descent faster.

HOLLY FRISKED THE DOWNED SHOOTER for more weapons and found none, just the two .45s, but he had half a dozen full magazines in his overcoat pockets. He had stopped moving, now, and she thought he must be dead. "Ham, how many rounds did you fire?"

"Two," Ham replied.

Two holes in the man's chest were oozing blood.

"I heard two more," Holly said.

"So did I, but it wasn't me. The gun noise was a little light, maybe a .380."

Holly looked at the woman from the team. "Did you fire your weapon?"

"No," the woman said.

"Who did?" Holly asked.

"I think it was Teddy Fay," she replied.

Then the police were in charge. Holly identified herself and Ham, and they talked to a detective for half an hour as he covered the scene.

"He's got two holes in his chest and two in his back," the detective said. "Who was the other shooter?"

"I've no idea," Holly replied.

FIFTY-ONE

LANCE WAS SITTING AT HIS DESK, disconsolately working his way through some administrative paperwork, when his cell phone vibrated on his belt.

"Yes?"

A man's excited voice riveted his attention. "He's in Saks!" he panted.

"Who?"

"Teddy Fay. There was some sort of commotion and gunfire over at Rockefeller Plaza, and I spotted a man who fits the description crossing the street and ducking into the store. Request maximum backup!"

"Easy now," Lance said. "Did anybody else make him?"

"Martin did; she radioed me, and I was on my way when I saw the guy. He matched the description."

"Give me the description?"

"Six feet, slim, wearing a tweed overcoat and a regular felt men's hat, broken nose, mustache and chin whiskers, brown. He was carrying a shopping bag, a red one, filled with wrapped presents."

"I'll have people there shortly," Lance said. "In the meantime, have your team cover the main floor exits; don't let him leave the store."

"Got it."

Lance closed his cell phone, picked up his desk phone and entered a twelve-digit number that would ring the cell phones of every man and woman in his unit. "Listen up, everybody; Teddy Fay has been spotted at Saks Fifth Avenue, that's between Forty-ninth and Fiftieth. Everybody converge on Saks *right now*, no delay. When last seen Fay was wearing a tweed topcoat, a felt hat, a broken nose and a brown Vandyke beard. He's carrying a red shopping bag with wrapped gifts inside." He repeated the instructions, then dialed the front desk. "This is Cabot; I want a car out front *now.*" He ran for the elevator.

HOLLY WAS TALKING to a police detective when her cell phone rang and she got Lance's message. "I have to go," she said. "I'll talk to you, Lieutenant, later."

"You can't go," the detective said. "This is a police investigation."

"No," she said, "it's a national security matter. Mr. Barker will continue to talk to you." She sprinted toward Fifth Avenue, grateful that she had not worn high heels. Traffic was at a standstill, and she threaded her way through it and ran into Saks through the center revolving doors. She immediately spotted a team member guarding the entrance and ran up to him. "What's the word?"

"He's upstairs somewhere," the man replied. "Lance is scrambling everybody. In the meantime, we're to watch the exits; we can use your help."

"How did he get upstairs?"

"Elevator. An agent saw him."

Holly ran for the rear of the store. She was about to go for the elevators when she saw the escalator. That would give her at least a quick look at each floor. She got on and headed up. On the second floor she got off, looked slowly around for as far as she could see. No tweed topcoat, not that he would still be wearing that. She got back on the escalator and began ascending, looking for a man with no coat at all.

As TEDDY REACHED the fifth floor he caught sight of someone coming up the escalator whose clothes he coveted. The man got off on five, and so did Teddy. He followed the man, who turned immediately through a door marked "Employees Only."

Teddy followed him to a men's room, and as the man stood at a urinal, Teddy fetched him a hard chop across the back of his neck. The man collapsed as if he had no legs.

Teddy stripped off the man's outer clothing and got into his outfit. He put his tweed cap in a pocket, then pulled off the man's beard and put it on. A quick check of the mirror, and he was out of there, headed for the escalator.

He had no sooner stepped onto it than he saw, coming up, a red tam. Holly looked up and directly at him, then looked away. Had she spotted him? Maybe, but she wouldn't recognize him. He kept his eyes fixed straight ahead as she passed him going up.

Teddy continued to the ground floor and got off the escalator. He walked, but not too quickly, toward the 49th Street exit, and as he did, people passing him waved and said, "Merry Christmas!" to him. "Merry Christmas!" he said back, and occasionally, "Ho, ho, ho."

He saw the woman with the baby carriage standing between him and the door. She no longer had the carriage, and she was looking desperately around the ground floor. "Merry Christmas," he said as he passed her.

"Yeah, same to you," she said, not looking at him.

Out on the sidewalk Teddy started walking toward Madison Avenue, looking for a cab. The air was filled with sirens, and people were still running away from Rockefeller Center. He made it to Madison and got lucky with the bus. A moment later, he was riding up Madison, and at 50th Street, he got a glimpse of the continuing chaos. He sat down next to a little boy.

"Hi, Santa," the boy said.

"Hi, there. Merry Christmas," Teddy said.

"Can I have a micro-motorcycle for Christmas this year?"

Teddy had no idea what a micro-motorcycle was, but the boy's mother was shaking her head violently and mouthing "No!"

"You bet!" Teddy said, and the woman looked shocked. "If you're really good, I'll bring you two."

He couldn't very well take off the Santa suit on the bus; the kid would go nuts. He waited until he got off at 63rd Street before he stepped into a doorway, stripped off the costume and dumped it into the nearest trash basket, then he continued east, toward Lexington and his shop.

LANCE STOOD ON THE STAGE of the little theater on the twelfth floor of the Barn and stared at his agents. Kerry Smith sat beside him, looking depressed.

"Holly, what's the story on Rockefeller Center?"

"Some cab driver went nuts," she said. "He abandoned his taxi in the middle of Forty-eighth Street and walked into the Plaza with a gun in each hand. He shot a skater and two people in the arcade before Ham shot him. Oh, Teddy Fay shot him, too. Twice."

"What happened with Teddy?" Lance asked. "I thought we had him trapped in Saks."

A man stood up. "We sealed the place immediately, like you said, and when backup arrived, we scoured every floor. We found nothing."

"Then he couldn't have been in the store. Maybe he went up one flight, then came back down and left the building."

"We had it sealed very quickly," he said. "I can't explain what happened."

"Any theories?" Lance asked the group.

Holly tentatively raised her hand.

"Yes, Holly?"

"Maybe a Santa Claus suit," she said.

"You think he was wearing a *Santa Claus suit*?" Lance asked incredulously.

"Maybe. There was a Santa Claus going down as I was going up. On the fifth floor there was a commotion; apparently, somebody had found an unconscious man in the men's room. I'm just connecting the dots."

Another woman stood up. "A Santa Claus walked right past me at the Forty-ninth Street exit and wished me a Merry Christmas," she said.

Holly raised her hand again. "We found a

red shopping bag in the sixth floor men's room," she said. "It was full of gift-wrapped, empty boxes. It's being checked for prints right now, but I'm not holding my breath."

Another agent stood up. "Listen," he said, "how are we ever going to take this guy without a description? I mean, we had a good description this time, but nobody was looking for a guy in a Santa Claus suit."

Lance wished to God he had an answer to that one.

FIFTY-TWO

IRENE FOSTER WAS BACK from New York in time for work on Monday morning, but she was a little late getting to her office at Langley. As she passed Hugh English's office, she saw him looking through a stack of papers on his desk. "Morning, Hugh," she said, sticking her head through the doorway. "Sorry I'm late; I just got back from New York." She didn't like it when Hugh got in before she did. Every time that happened, something invariably went wrong.

"Irene," English said, "do you know somebody in Operations called Charles Lockwood?"

She did not, and she immediately had an awful thought. "Sounds familiar," she said, trying to breathe normally. "Why?"

"I got a memo from payroll this morning, saying Lockwood is three weeks behind on his time sheets, and they won't pay him, until he's up-to-date. That's what troubles me."

"What's that, Hugh?"

"If he's turning in time sheets, that means he's executive level, not just a clerical worker, and I swear, I know every mother's son at the executive level who works for me."

Irene walked forward and held out her hand. "Give me the memo," she said. "I'll sort it out."

"Thank you," he said, handing it over. English hated dealing with any administrative matter.

Irene took a deep breath; she might as well get it over with, she thought. "Hugh, have you got a second?"

"Sure. Take a pew." He waved her to a chair.

She took off her coat and dumped it on the other chair, then sat down. "I've been thinking about this for a while," she said, "and I've decided to put in for retirement."

English blinked in surprise. "How long have you got in?" he asked.

"Twenty-seven years."

"Then you're fully vested in your pension, I guess."

"I guess I am."

English sat back in his chair. "Irene, I just can't imagine the place without you. I mean, you've been in this office with me for as long as I've occupied this chair, and we knew each other a long time before that, didn't we?"

"Yes, we did, Hugh. Better than twenty years, anyway."

"I'll probably have to assign two people to do your job."

"Thank you, Hugh, but my shoes won't be all that hard to fill."

"I'm not going to count on that. What are you going to do with yourself?"

"Funny you should mention that; I was on the Internet last night, looking at houses in the Caribbean."

"Where in the Caribbean?"

"I've heard good things about St. Thomas and St. Barts."

"St. Thomas was looking overgrown, last

time I was there," English said, "but St. Barts is very nice."

"It seems a bit more expensive than the other islands, but I'll take a harder look at it."

"Twenty-seven years," English said, shaking his head. "I'm coming up on thirty, myself. It's probably time I got out of here, too."

"I can't see you in retirement, Hugh."

"Well, it's become clear that I'm never going to get the top job, unless Kate Rule Lee drops dead, and I'm not going to count on that. When do you want to go?"

"I guess as soon as I can break somebody in," she said.

"You got some ideas on who that might be?"

"I think either Bergin or Masters," Irene replied. "They're both good men; I suppose you should pick whomever you like best."

"You can't think of any women for the job?"

"There are a couple a level down who are comers," she said, "but you need somebody with more field experience, I think. As much as I'd like to see a woman in the job, I think you're going to have to make do with Bergin or Masters for the time being."

"Or both of them," English said. "Okay, I'll

try and make a decision today, and you can start working with him."

"Thanks, Hugh. It's been fun, and I appreciate all you've done for me." He had done fuck-all for her, she recalled. She was only in this job now because Kate Rule had wanted a woman high in Operations.

"I was glad to do it," English said benevolently. "You deserve a happy retirement."

Irene got up and walked to the door. "I'll take care of this," she said, holding up the memo. "Don't worry about it."

"Hey," English said, "maybe Mary and I will join you in St. Barts."

"Happy thought," she said, quivering with disgust. She headed for her office, the memo clutched tightly in one hand, her coat in the other.

She hung up her coat and got behind her desk. She inserted her computer card into the machine, and it came on automatically, having read her codes. "Dear God," she said, looking at the memo while the computer booted. "Don't let this be Teddy."

IT WAS TEDDY. Fifteen minutes later she had read the complete file of Charles Lockwood, and while it was credible, Teddy hadn't bothered to do his usual thorough job on background. Lockwood was Princeton '88 and before that, Groton, but the Groton transcript was missing, and there wasn't much on his parents. She'd have to call Teddy as soon as she got out of the office. She picked up a phone and called payroll.

"Payroll, Miriam Walker speaking."

"Miriam, it's Irene Foster in Operations."

"Hi, Irene."

"I'm calling for Hugh English about Charles Lockwood's time sheets for the past three weeks."

"Can you get them to me today, Irene? I'd really like to pay the guy."

"I'm afraid not."

"Why?"

"Lockwood is on special assignment, and he's unreachable for administrative matters."

"For how long?"

"Another month, six weeks. It's impossible to put a date on it."

"All right, I'll mark his record as such, but I'm going to rely on you to get him up-to-date when he returns." She'd be gone by then.

"I'll ride herd on him. Where are you sending his paychecks?"

"Let me check," she said, shuffling some

papers. "An account in the Caymans," she replied, finally.

"That sounds like our Charlie," Irene said. "Thanks, Miriam. Bye-bye." She hung up. It was unlike Teddy to be greedy, but she supposed that if he had created Lockwood—and after all, it had been her suggestion—the man would have to be paid in order to be credible.

She was relieved that she had announced her retirement to Hugh English, because she had just painted herself into a very tight corner. She had used her authority to authenticate Lockwood and thus, to protect Teddy, and Miriam Walker was certainly going to remember every detail of their conversation. She would remember that Irene had sounded as if she had known Charles Lockwood well. Maybe that "Our Charlie" had been a mistake.

She fed the memo from payroll into her shredder, which immediately reduced it to ash, then she logged on to the Agency mainframe and began looking at any assets they might have in St. Barts. To her relief, there weren't any: no station, no resident, no stringers. How many places were there left in the world where the Agency didn't have, at the very least, a stringer? She wouldn't have to worry about bumping into somebody she knew while she and Teddy were walking on the beach. Except in the unlikely event that Hugh English followed through on his retirement threat. She shuddered again.

As IRENE WAS LEAVING the office that evening, Hugh English shouted at her as she passed his office.

"Yes, Hugh?"

"It's going to be Bergin; you can start on him tomorrow morning."

"Right."

"Did you get that payroll thing sorted out?"

"Yes. Turns out he's an analyst in Intelligence. Somebody in payroll had entered the wrong division code on his pay record. You won't hear from them again."

"Thanks, Irene. Good luck on the house hunt."

"Good night, Hugh."

FIFTY-THREE

TEDDY WAS BACK in his shop with a spray bottle of Windex and a cloth, wiping everything down. He was going to have to move, soon; he was seeing way too many people on the streets who were looking for him. He had been very lucky to get out of the Rockefeller Center imbroglio without getting collared.

He went carefully over every doorjamb, every work surface, every piece of equipment, erasing any trace of himself. It took him more than two hours, and when he had finished he got into latex gloves. He would wear them whenever he was in the shop from now on. His apartment was next. He left the shop and walked back toward his building on Park, looking forward to a good dinner from Restaurant Daniel, served in his suite, and maybe a movie on TV.

As he approached the building he was stopped in his tracks by the sight of a woman in the lobby, talking to the doorman and the super. He turned and walked back toward Lexington. The woman was the one with the baby carriage outside Saks earlier in the day. Had they traced him to the building, or were they just canvassing?

He went back to his workshop, donned his latex gloves, looked up the number for the doorman and dialed it. "Hello, William? It's Mr. Foreman."

"Good evening, Mr. Foreman."

"Have I had a package delivered in the last hour or so, or anybody looking for me?"

"No, sir, but we had a lady from some government agency in here looking for somebody, she wasn't sure who."

"What was it about?"

"She wouldn't say. She showed me a sketch of some guy that didn't look like anybody I know. The super, neither. Is there anything I can do for you?"

Teddy thought quickly. Was there anything

in the apartment he needed? Fingerprints— he needed to wipe the place down. "No, William. See you later." He hung up and walked back to the building, holding his breath as he walked in, waiting for somebody to shout "That's him!" He made it to the elevator and went upstairs.

He ordered dinner from downstairs, then put on his gloves and began wiping down the suite. He stopped for dinner, then went back to work. When he was satisfied, he began packing his clothes; he certainly wasn't going to give them DNA from the sweat on a hatband or from his dirty underwear.

When he was nearly done, he called the doorman. "William, the building has a car service, doesn't it?"

"Yessir. Can I get you a car?"

"Yes, going to Kennedy Airport." He looked at his watch. "I have a flight for London at ten o'clock."

"I'll have a car for you in twenty minutes, sir," William said. "I'll buzz you when it's here."

Teddy changed into a business suit and packed the remainder of his clothes. He set his two suitcases and briefcase by the front door and sat down to wait for the car to arrive, increasingly nervous. They must be canvassing every building in the neighborhood, he thought. It's what he would have done, if he were Lance Cabot. From what the doorman had said, though, he and the super had given the agent nothing. The phone buzzed.

"Yes?"

"Your car is here, Mr. Foreman. Do you need any help with your luggage?"

"No, just meet me at the elevator." Teddy collected his two bags and briefcase and went down in the elevator, where William met him. A black Lincoln was idling at the curb.

"How long will you be away, sir?" William asked as he put Teddy's bags into the trunk.

"A week or so. Please hold my mail."

"You never get any mail, Mr. Foreman. You're the only one in the building that doesn't."

"Oh, that's right," Teddy said, chuckling. "It goes to my office. Would you let the people at Daniel know that they can pick up my room service dishes?"

The doorman held the car door open, and Teddy got in. "Have a good trip, Mr. Foreman."

"Thank you, William," Teddy said, slipping him a fifty.

"Thank *you*, sir!"

The car drove away. "Which airline?" the driver asked.

"British Airways," Teddy replied and settled in for the ride.

As THE DOORMAN WALKED back into the building, the super emerged from his ground-floor apartment. "Willie," he said, "I just thought of something."

"What's that, Rich?"

"That agent who was here earlier this evening. The sketch didn't look familiar, but you know, the description she gave sounded kind of like Mr. Foreman."

William shrugged. "I hadn't thought of that, but I guess it could describe a lot of guys."

"Only one in this building, though," the super said. "Have you still got her card?"

William rummaged in a drawer and came up with it. "Here it is," he said, handing it over.

The super went back into his apartment, looking at the card.

Twenty minutes later the woman agent, accompanied by a dozen other men and women, flooded into the lobby of the building.

"Can I help you, ma'am?" William asked.

"What's the apartment number for Albert Foreman?" she asked.

"Fourteen B," William replied, "but Mr. Foreman left about twenty, twenty-five minutes ago."

"Do you know where he was going?"

"Yes, ma'am, I got him a car from our service; he was going to Kennedy Airport to catch a ten o'clock flight for London." He looked at his watch. "That means he'll be taking off in about an hour and a half."

The super emerged from his apartment. "Please take these people up to Mr. Foreman's apartment," she said to him.

The super handed her the key, and she handed it to another agent. "You take the group up there and go over the place with a fine-toothed comb. I'm calling this in." She turned to William. "How was Mr. Foreman dressed?"

"He was wearing a dark business suit, a topcoat and a gray hat, a fedora," William replied.

The agents headed for the elevator, and Martin called Lance.

"Cabot."

"Lance. It's Martin. We're at the building, and Foreman left twenty-five minutes ago for Kennedy Airport. Said he was taking a ten o'clock flight to London."

"Then he'll be arriving there in ten or fifteen minutes, with decent traffic," Lance said. "I'm on it. You and your people do the apartment."

"We've already started." She gave Lance Foreman's description.

LANCE TURNED to Kerry Smith. "This guy, Foreman, who sounds like Teddy, is going to be at Kennedy airport shortly. How many people do you have there?"

"Half a dozen agents," Kerry replied, "but we can mobilize the NYPD unit out there, plus airport security."

"Good. Have them go directly to the departing-passenger set-down and the departure lounge for every airline with a London flight tonight. He's traveling as Albert Foreman, and he's wearing a dark suit, a topcoat and a fedora. Go!"

*　　*　　*

AT KENNEDY, Teddy got out of the car, paid the driver and carried his own luggage into the terminal. He took the escalator down one floor and emerged at the curb where passengers from arriving flights waited for taxis. Upstairs, unknown to him, FBI, the police and airport security were flooding the departure areas, looking for him.

Teddy waited in line patiently for a cab, and ten minutes later, he was headed back to the city. He gave the driver the address of his Lexington Avenue shop. He didn't feel like carrying his luggage anymore.

"Where you in from?" the driver asked.

"London," Teddy said without thinking.

"London flights don't arrive this time of night," the man said. "They get in during the afternoon."

"We had the mother of all flight delays," Teddy said.

FIFTY-FOUR

LANCE AND HOLLY WALKED into the Foreman apartment on Park Avenue and looked around. "Looks like nobody lives here," Holly said. An agent came up to them.

"Clean as a whistle," he said. "Not so much as a partial on any surface."

"Then Foreman is Teddy," Lance said. "Get a sketch artist up here and put him with the doorman and the super. Maybe we'll at least get a better sketch."

"You know," the agent said. "When we were canvassing realtors last week I interviewed the woman whose office is the rental agent for this building, and she denied having rented anything in any building to a single man during the past couple of months." He handed Lance a rental agreement. "We found this in the desk drawer, wiped clean, of course. Her signature is on it. The woman lied to me."

"Find out why," Lance said. "Maybe she's an old acquaintance of Teddy; maybe she knows something else that could help. Pick her up, scare the shit out of her and milk her dry. Print her and do a background check, too. See if her path has crossed Teddy's at some time in the past."

The man left.

"He's not going to be at Kennedy," Holly said.

"Maybe not," Lance replied.

"*Certainly* not," Holly said. "Teddy's not going to tell a doorman where he's going, then go there."

"We checked the car service; it dropped Teddy at Kennedy fifteen minutes ago."

"Then he's not there anymore. My guess is, he's on the way to LaGuardia—if he's running—and he's on the way back into the city, if he's not."

Lance called Kerry. "He may be headed to LaGuardia or back into the city," he said.

"Turn out as many people as you can at the other airport; I'll deal with the rest." He closed his phone and shouted, "Everybody listen up!"

Everybody stopped talking and moving around the apartment.

"Teddy may be headed back into the city," Lance said. "I want you to divide into three groups and cover the Triborough Bridge, the Fifty-ninth Street Bridge and the Midtown Tunnel. Call the bridge and tunnel authority and have them squeeze traffic down to as many lanes as you can manage. Check the occupants of every cab that goes through."

"Lance," Holly said. "I know it's a stretch, but shouldn't we check the Brooklyn and Manhattan bridges, too?"

"Oh, all right," Lance said, and gave the instructions.

TEDDY'S CAB WAS on the Van Wyck Expressway now. "Tell you what," he said to the driver. "Let's go to Brooklyn on the way. I've never been over the Brooklyn Bridge."

"Whatever you say, Mister," the driver said. "It's your meter. I'll take you over the Verrazano Bridge, if you feel the urge to visit Staten Island."

"Why not?" Teddy said. "We'll take the ferry back. It'll be fun."

"Tourists," the driver chuckled to himself, shaking his head.

BACK AT THE BARN, Lance, Holly and Kerry took the phone reports from the teams on the bridges and tunnel.

"Zip," Kerry said. "We didn't move fast enough."

"Yes, we did," Lance said.

"Maybe he did a costume change, and he's still at Kennedy or LaGuardia, waiting for a plane."

"Every gate agent was alerted," Lance said. "Anyway, we have a confirmation from the cab starter at Kennedy; Teddy definitely got into a cab. He must have left his car and gone directly to the arrivals area."

"Then where the hell is he?" Holly asked plaintively.

"I think you were right, Holly," Lance said. "I think he's back in the city. He's not done yet; he's going to kill somebody else."

"But where is he?"

"He's got another place, a workshop; has to have. There was no sign that he'd done any work in the Park Avenue apartment. He didn't move any equipment out when he left."

"Then that workshop has got to be near the apartment," Holly said. "You can't have a workshop on Park, Madison or Fifth Avenues; that kind of industrial space just isn't available."

"Lexington Avenue would be the nearest place," Kerry said. "There's all sorts of shops there, and semi-industrial places like dry cleaners and shoe repair shops. He could rent a room on Lex."

"All right," Lance said, "we'll canvas every building on Lexington from, say, Seventy-second to Fifty-seventh Streets, and if we don't come up with anything there, we'll start on Third Avenue, but we're going to need manpower." He picked up the phone. "Get me Lieutenant Dino Bacchetti at the One-Nine," he said. "That part of town is on Dino's patch; let's let him earn his consulting fee. He's going to have to work without warrants, so tell him to tell his men to tread lightly and get permission from supers."

TEDDY ARRIVED back at his Lexington Avenue workshop at midnight. He had bought the cab driver dinner on Staten Island, paid a two-hundred-dollar cab fare and tipped the driver a hundred, making his day.

He had just gotten his luggage up the stairs when his cell phone rang.

"Yes?"

"It's Irene."

"Hi, there. You okay?"

"Well, you scared the shit out of me this morning."

"What did I do this morning?"

"When I got to work, Hugh English was poring over a memo from Payroll about the absence of time sheets for one Charles Lockwood. Sound familiar?"

"Uh-oh."

"Don't worry, I squared it. I told Payroll that Lockwood was out of town on assignment for another month or six weeks and couldn't be reached."

"What did you tell English?"

"That Lockwood works in Intelligence, and Payroll had sent the memo in error. You need to do some more work on Lockwood's background; there was no transcript from Groton. I also told Hugh I'm retiring, and he recommended St. Barts. So did Lance Cabot, for that matter."

"So nobody will think it odd when you start looking there."

"Nope, I've put them on notice. Hugh says maybe he'll retire there, too, and be my neighbor."

Teddy laughed. "Fat chance."

"Right. He won't go until they shoot him."

"I see you're having Lockwood's pay sent to a Cayman bank. Is that going to give them a trail to follow?"

"Nah, it's being sent from there to a bank in Singapore. They can look for me in Singapore, if they like."

"How long before you can meet me in St. Barts?"

"I'll probably get there first," Teddy said.

"You're winding it up?"

"Just one more little job to do."

"Ben Saud?"

"It's better if I don't tell you who or when. Or how I'm going to get to St. Barts."

"Fine by me. Will you let me know when you're there?"

"I'll call you on this phone and say that I'm somewhere in the Middle East."

"Okay."

"If I'm blown and shouldn't go to St. Barts, say, 'I hear Iraq is nice this time of year.'"

"Got it. Teddy, is this really going to work? Are we really going to make it?"

"Yes, it is, and yes, we are. All I need is a few more days, and I'll be lying on that beach. Shortly after that, I'll be lying on it with you."

"I'm looking forward to that. I figure I'll be able to get out of Langley in a couple of weeks. Tom Bergin is replacing me, and he already knows eighty percent of what he'll need to know before I go. I'll put in my papers in the morning, and I'll put my town-house on the market, too. There's always a line of people waiting to buy in my development, so I'll be out of there pretty quick. I'm going to try to sell it furnished, so all I'll want to send south is a few books and pictures. I'm going to give my clothes to Goodwill and start over."

"They were looking for me in my building today," he said. "I'm out of the apartment for good, now."

"How did they find the building?"

"I think they canvassed every building in the neighborhood. The doorman and super didn't tell them anything, but I'm operating on the premise that the apartment is burnt."

"Where are you now? Oh, sorry, I don't want to know, do I?"

"No, but I'm safe enough. I'll call you in a few days, if I can."

"I miss you."

"I miss you, too. Bye-bye." He hung up, and it surprised him to realize that he really did miss her.

FIFTY-FIVE

DINO BACCHETTI WAS ON THE PHONE when his captain came into his office.

"What the hell is this search on Lex?" he demanded.

"The Feds called and needed our help. They're trying to nail this Teddy Fay guy."

"*What?* I thought the guy blew himself up in an airplane."

"Just between you and me and the Feds, he didn't. He's the guy who's been knocking off people around the U.N. the past few weeks."

The captain shook his head. "Nobody ever tells me anything." He left Dino's office.

Dino continued calling his men. They were down to 65th Street on Lex, now.

TEDDY HAD BEEN UP most of the night putting the final touches on his plan. He had made two bombs with the remainder of his plastic explosives, both wired to be ignited by a garage-door opener, which he tucked into the pocket of his overcoat.

His last item was the finishing of his building inspector's I.D. The New York Brotherhood of Construction Inspectors website had thoughtfully supplied a facsimile of a real I.D. All he had to do was scan it, put on his makeup, photograph himself, then print and laminate it. It wasn't perfect, but it would do for what he had in mind.

Finally, he whipped a loop into a length of elastic shock cord, took off his belt and hooked on the shock cord before running the belt through the loops again. He whipped a larger loop in the other end and let it dangle down his back. It would be hidden by his topcoat. He dismantled his little sniper's rifle and placed the parts in inside pockets of the topcoat, put on a battered felt hat, picked up his luggage and left the building for the last time, locking the door and tossing the key into the nearest street corner wastebasket.

HOLLY SAT AT HER DESK, bored. They were waiting to hear that Dino Bacchetti's people had completed their canvas of Lexington Avenue, and all she had to occupy her was the *New York Times.*

IT WAS 7:30 A.M. as Teddy moved down Lexington, carrying his luggage, a canvas satchel containing the two bombs and wearing a wig, a new nose, muttonchop whiskers and his heavy, black-rimmed glasses. He lugged everything the three blocks to the garage where his RV was stored, stowed his luggage in the rear and began driving downtown. The vehicle now had a valid Florida registration and plates.

HOLLY WALKED INTO Lance's office just as the phone rang. He picked it up.

"Lance Cabot."

"It's Dino; my guys found the workshop. It's a third-floor studio apartment over a dry cleaners on the west side of Lex between Sixty-third and Sixty-fourth."

"I'll get my people over there right away," Lance said.

"Don't bother; the man is gone, and my guys got the impression he wasn't coming back. What made them think that is that they found a very nice drawing of a homemade sniper's rifle made out of a Walther PPK and some custom-made parts. But they didn't find the rifle, so he must have taken it with him. They also found some debris left over from making a bomb, and plastic explosive residue was detected on a workbench."

"Oh, shit," Lance said.

"If you've got any idea who the target is, you'd better get your people on the spot fast," Dino said.

"Thanks, Dino," Lance said and hung up. He told Holly and Kerry Smith what the cop had said.

"So who's the target?" Holly asked.

"We've still got the two names we identified earlier."

"So why don't I think he's going after who we think he's going after?" Holly asked.

Kerry spoke up. "Maybe because he's always been a step ahead of us?"

"Ben Saud," Lance said.

"Why do you think so?" Kerry asked.

"Because he's not on our list, and because Washington wouldn't let us surveil him."

"That's perfect for Teddy," Holly said. "And I'll bet you anything he *knows* we're not on the guy. I still think he's got an insider at Langley."

Lance looked at his watch. "Ben Saud is going to be walking to work from U.N. Plaza in a few minutes, as he does every day. We don't have time to make a plan, so I'm just going to flood the area with everybody I can lay my hands on, and it'll be every man for himself." He picked up the phone and pressed the code that rang everybody's cell phone, then gave the orders.

TEDDY DROVE DOWN Second Avenue to the Forties and parked the RV in a garage around the corner from his destination. He went into the rear of the vehicle and removed a pair of aluminum crutches, the kind hinged at the elbow, and his satchel containing the bombs. "I'll only be about an hour," he told the attendant, "so please don't bury the vehicle." He gave the man a twenty to help him remember.

He walked down the street toward the

building under construction at the corner of First Avenue. Outside the structure, he stopped, looked around, and placed the crutches in a corner of a large Dumpster, which contained scrap drywall and lumber, then he went looking for the construction superintendent. He found the man alone in a little shed, checking over some blueprints.

"Morning," he said, showing his I.D. card, which was hanging around his neck on a beaded chain. "I'm Morrison; I'm your regular guy's supervisor, and I want to take a look around, see what kind of job he's doing."

"Oh, he's a good man," the superintendent said. "He's really put us through the ringer around here."

"I'm sure he has, but I still have to do my job."

"I'll come with you," the man said.

"Not necessary," Teddy said, holding up a hand. "I'd rather do it alone."

"Whatever you say; the elevator is right over there." He nodded toward the construction lift. "Oh, by the way, we've got a homeless guy who's made himself a little hutch in the basement of the building. I know it's against code, but I haven't had the heart to throw him out so close to Christmas."

"I'll leave it out of my report." Teddy left the shack and walked over to the elevator. He rode up three stories, looking through the grillwork toward the U.N. Plaza apartment building. He stopped on the third floor. The angle was perfect.

The floor was empty of workers, since they were hanging steel on the higher floors, so Teddy didn't have to shoo anybody away. He walked around the third floor looking for options. It wasn't a very big building—ten or twelve stories—and fairly narrow. Immediately next door, on the side of the building opposite from First Avenue, was an empty lot where steel, lumber and other building materials had been stored. Teddy placed his two bombs at the corners of that side of the floor, then armed them. All he had to do now was to press the button on the garage-door opener. He checked his escape route again and found it satisfactory, then took a look at the box that housed the structure alarm.

He glanced at his watch: twenty minutes to go, if ben Saud and his security team were on time. He took the parts of his sniper rifle from his inside coat pockets and assembled it carefully, checking everything as he went. He inserted a full magazine, then leaned against a steel beam and sighted down to the street. The distance was right, about a hundred yards; his only correction would be for his height above the target. Since his position was elevated, the tendency would be to shoot high, and he would have to correct for that on the fly. Fortunately, he had six rounds, plus two more magazines in his pocket.

Ten minutes to go. Teddy set down the rifle and began doing stretching exercises. He hadn't tried this for a while, and he was going to have to be limber to make it work. He repeatedly stretched the thigh muscles of his left leg, pulling his foot higher and higher to the rear. Finally, satisfied, he picked up the little rifle and began sighting through the scope again.

At one minute before the stroke of nine, the first of the security detail left the U.N. Plaza building and did a quick survey of the sidewalk to the U.N. Headquarters building. They signaled the rest of the party, and the group left the apartment building, with ben Saud at their center, dressed in a business suit but wearing an Arab headdress.

As they walked quickly toward U.N. Headquarters, Teddy checked through the scope and suddenly realized that the man in the Arab headdress was not ben Saud but a decoy. Ben Saud was three paces behind him, between two security guards. Good camouflage, Teddy thought as he sighted on the man's Adam's apple.

FIFTY-SIX

HOLLY WAS RIDING DOWN Second Avenue in a car with Lance at the wheel, and traffic was very bad.

"There must be an accident or some construction a few blocks ahead," she said.

"Well, we're stuck with Second Avenue, so we're just going to have to ride it out," Lance replied. He held up his cell phone and used it in the walkie-talkie mode. "This is Cabot. Has anybody made it to U.N. Plaza yet?"

"It's Martin," a woman's voice said. "Three of us have got it staked. I hope more are on the way."

"*Everybody* is on the way," Lance said. "Be as unobtrusive as possible; we don't want him to know we're there, if we can help it."

"Roger."

Lance closed the cell phone. They were inching past 48th Street, now.

"Maybe I should walk," Holly said.

"No, I checked out the pedestrians; we're doing better than they are."

"God, I hate just sitting here."

"So do I."

Traffic suddenly sped up, for no apparent reason, and they were moving at thirty miles an hour, keeping up with the changing lights.

"Drop me here," Holly said.

"Right. I'm going to cross to First Avenue at the next street. I'll see you there."

Holly hopped out of the car.

TEDDY SQUEEZED OFF a round, and ben Saud's head erupted, spraying everyone around him with blood and gore. Security men were throwing themselves across his body, too late. There would not be an opportunity for a second shot, but one was not needed. He dropped his beautiful little rifle onto the floor; he wanted them to find it.

Teddy walked quickly to a red metal box

fixed to a beam and broke the glass with his elbow. An alarm began to sound and a mechanical voice began to repeat. "Structural failure; abandon the structure, abandon the structure." He could hear people shouting on the higher floors.

Teddy quickly headed for his escape route. He had spotted this on his earlier visit to the building: it was an aluminum tube about three feet in diameter that was fixed to the side of the building, so that construction debris could be tossed into it. Teddy looked up the tube to be sure nothing was coming, then he jumped into it and began to slide down.

The tube made two 360-degree turns, then spat Teddy out into the Dumpster at curbside, creating a cloud of dust. He beat at his clothes for a moment, then collected the crutches he had placed in the corner of the Dumpster, and looked up and down the street. On First Avenue, all hell had broken loose, but the block he was in was oddly quiet.

Teddy jumped out of the Dumpster, and, keeping it between himself and First Avenue, he reached down, grabbed his left foot and pulled it up behind him, sticking his toe through the loop of shock cord hanging there. He dusted himself off again, squared away his hat, picked up the crutches and began swinging slowly toward Second Avenue, picking up a rhythm and making good progress. Then, at the end of the block, on Second Avenue, a woman got out of a car and began walking quickly toward him. She looked oddly familiar.

HOLLY WAS ALREADY OUT of the car when she saw the commotion at the other end of the block, on Second Avenue. This was not good, she thought; she began walking quickly up the block. The only person between her and First Avenue was an elderly, one-legged man on crutches, making his way toward her.

TEDDY RECOGNIZED HOLLY BARKER, and he was relieved to see that she was looking not at him but past him, toward the action on First Avenue. She had begun to run, and he continued toward her. It occurred to him that she would run past the building, so he had no more time. He stopped, reached into his left coat pocket and pressed the button on the garage-door opener. The two explosions went off simultaneously.

HOLLY STOPPED IN HER TRACKS and gaped at the sight of the steel skeleton ahead of her collapsing slowly and noisily into the vacant lot next door. The old man on crutches stopped, looked over his shoulder at the noise, then continued more quickly. Good idea, she thought; get the hell out of here. She stood and watched the building, waiting for the danger to be over so she could proceed. The old man continued past her, and she looked into his face for a moment. Sweat was streaming down it; he must have been frightened by the collapse of the building. "Are you all right, sir?" she asked.

"YES, TANK YOU," Teddy replied, using a vague mittel European accent. "Vot hoppen?"

"I don't know," she said, truthfully.

"I get out of here," he said, starting to move again.

"Good idea."

AS HOLLY WATCHED the dust settle, men in hard hats were running out of the cloud of dust ahead of her. There was much shouting. Then she froze as a horrible idea came to her. She turned and saw the old man on crutches nearing Second Avenue. "Teddy," she said aloud. Then she shouted, "TEDDY!!!" He seemed to pause for a moment, then continued on his way, not looking back.

"Look out!" someone shouted from behind her. She turned and just managed to avoid a group of men who were running past her, apparently escapees from the building. One of them stopped and stood beside her.

"What happened?" she asked him.

"I don't know," the man said. "The structure alarm went off, and everybody abandoned ship. Then there was a loud noise, and the building started to go. I think everybody got out."

Holly turned and looked back toward Second Avenue. The man on crutches was gone. She made her decision; she started to run toward Second Avenue.

TEDDY REACHED THE GARAGE, unhooked his left toe from the shock cord and tossed the crutches ahead of him into the RV. He didn't bother with his coat, just jumped in and closed the door. He was about to start the engine when Holly Barker ran past the garage entrance, headed downtown, never looking into the garage. He turned the key and pulled across the sidewalk and into traffic.

Holly was running down the east side of the street, looking around her for something, looking for him, he was sure. He rolled up his side window, which was tinted dark and, slowly, overtook her. She was, perhaps, ten yards away, jogging down the sidewalk, looking up and down the street, and there was a gun in her hand. Traffic stopped for a light.

HOLLY SEARCHED DESPERATELY through the crowd on the street for the old man on crutches, but he had vanished, as if into thin air. She grabbed for her cell phone and pressed the walkie-talkie button. "Lance. Holly. Do you read?"

"I read you, Holly."

"What happened over there?"

"Ben Saud is down, single shot to the head."

"I think I made Teddy."

"Where? Where are you?"

"An old man on crutches passed me going toward Second, just as the building under construction collapsed."

"Teddy probably fired from that building," Lance said.

"I can't see the old man," Holly said. "I saw him headed toward Second, and I yelled his name, and he paused, but he kept going. Then I got distracted for a second, and when I turned around he had apparently turned the corner. I'm searching on Second, now, but I can't see him anywhere. It's like he just went *poof* and vanished into thin air. I mean, how far could he get on crutches?"

"Well, if it's Teddy, he's not on crutches anymore. Maybe he had a car waiting. I'll send help. Start looking in vehicles."

"Roger."

THE LIGHT CHANGED, and Teddy drove on, watching Holly running along the curb, looking into parked cars. He made his way across traffic and managed to turn right onto 42nd Street. His last glimpse of Holly was in his offside rearview mirror. She was standing stock still, looking in his direction, the gun still in her hand.

Teddy continued on, toward the Lincoln Tunnel, New Jersey and I-95 South to Florida.

FIFTY-SEVEN

IT WAS NEARLY MIDNIGHT before Holly, Lance and the whole team got back to the Barn, every one of them streaked with dirt and dust from their search through the debris of the collapsed steel structure. Lance called everybody into the big conference room. There wasn't room for everybody to sit down, so they stood along the walls, every one of them looking exhausted.

Lance, appearing exhausted himself, looked around at the group. "I want to thank you all for sticking with this and bringing this hunt to a close at last. What I'm about to tell you is above your pay grade, but you deserve to know." Lance set a shopping bag on the table, reached into it and pulled out a small, odd-looking rifle.

"Teddy Fay made this in his workshop; the NYPD found the drawings for it. It's simply a Walther PPK-S .380 pistol, to which Teddy added a scope, a longer barrel, a silencer and a folding metal stock. He shot Ali ben Saud with it this morning.

"The weapon was found a few feet from the unidentified body that the firemen located in the search. Because the structure alarm went off when the building started to collapse, everybody working there survived, a few with minor injuries. Only this one corpse was unidentified. I've just spoken to the medical examiner, who has done a preliminary autopsy, and it seems certain that the corpse is that of Teddy Fay."

There was a stir of approval in the room, and applause broke out.

"Since, for public purposes, the corpse of Teddy Fay was supposed to have been eaten by fish off the coast of Maine many weeks ago, no inquest will be held, and no public announcement will be made. And no one in this room will ever discuss this subject again with anyone outside it.

"Our job is done, and that's it. Our task force is officially disbanded or rather, unofficially, since it never existed. Tomorrow morning, all Bureau personnel will report to the New York City field office downtown at nine A.M. the day after tomorrow for reassignment. All Agency personnel will report to Langley at nine A.M. next Monday in the director's conference room. She would like to thank you personally before you are given new assignments.

"Everybody is *ordered* to get a good night's sleep. Kerry Smith and I would like to thank each and every one of you for your hard work on what must have seemed like a fruitless assignment. You will all have commendations placed in your personnel files, and you will all get new assignments that are better than you would normally expect at this stage of your careers. Good night and good luck."

Lance and Kerry walked out of the room, and Lance tapped Holly on the shoulder as he went. "Follow me," he said.

Holly followed Lance down the hall to his office. He stopped, said goodbye to Kerry Smith and motioned for Holly to come in and sit down.

"You look upset," he said. "Do you have any questions? If so, ask them now and never again."

"Who was the corpse found in the wreckage?"

"It was Teddy Fay, and don't you ever let me hear you doubt it."

"Was the homeless man who lived in the basement ever found?"

"These people move freely about the city; now that his home no longer exists, I'm sure he has taken up residence elsewhere."

"I *saw* Teddy Fay on the street; he *spoke* to me."

"Oh? Do you *know* that?"

"I know it."

"How?"

"Instinct."

"Instinct isn't good enough when you have to sign your name to the kind of report that Kerry and I are submitting to our superiors. You were mistaken; you simply saw an old man. Is that clear?"

"Can we talk, off the record, for a moment?"

"Just this once, then we're done with it."

"Do you really think this is over?"

"I do. Teddy pulled up stakes: he abandoned his base and a workshop that he went to a great deal of trouble to assemble."

"Did we find anything of use among his papers or on his computer?"

"All the paper in the place had been shredded and burned; the computer hard drive had been reformatted, so every byte was scrubbed from it."

"So we still don't know exactly how he got into the Langley mainframe or who his contact was?"

"We have no hard evidence that he ever got into the mainframe, and a very thorough internal investigation has determined that no one at Langley aided him in any way."

"Suppose he starts killing again?"

"I've no reason to suppose he will, but should that happen, I'll screw that elephant when it sits on me. If he pops up someplace else and starts killing, he won't be Teddy Fay, he'll be someone else. Are we done?"

"Won't we all have to answer to our superiors, if that happens?"

"Let me give you an important lesson in politics, Holly: Kerry's superiors and mine— at every level, right up to and including the president of the United States—are going to be vastly relieved when they read our report. All of them participated in covering up the fact that Teddy was still alive; the president told the congressional leadership of both parties the truth, and they helped cover it up, in the hope that we would stop Teddy before his continued presence became known to the press. They're all going to feel very good about this."

"But it will come out, eventually, won't it?"

"Certainly not. Teddy Fay's body will be cremated before the day is out, and his ashes will occupy a landfill on Staten Island. If rumors start, they'll have nowhere to go."

"But the *president* will be part of a big cover-up."

"No, he will not. He will receive our report and accept it, because it is in his interest to do so. He will have no knowledge of anything outside that report, and thus he will have nothing to cover up. *Now* are we done?"

Holly took a deep breath and nodded. "We're done."

"If you think about it, you'll know that you have nothing to be anything less than proud of. Don't let your mistaken identification of an old man trouble you; there is nothing what-ever to support that identification."

Holly nodded. "I understand. Do you know what my next assignment will be?"

"You're not going back to the Farm or to Langley. You're going to be staying here, with me. It's been intimated to me that the Agency's New York station will be reorganized in this building, under me. You're going to like your assignment."

Holly smiled. "Good. What's next?"

"Something interesting."

"Tell me."

"After you've had twelve hours sleep and a couple of days off. Go home, see your father and his girl and Daisy. I'll see you Monday morning. Merry Christmas."

Holly got up and went home.

FIFTY-EIGHT

BOB KINNEY CAME HOME from the Bureau at midnight. Nancy was waiting up for him.

"Want some eggs?" she asked, kissing him.

"Love some," he said. "I didn't get any dinner."

"Can you tell me what was going on?"

"You know I never tell you Bureau secrets."

"Of course not."

"Teddy Fay is dead."

"Well, *that's* a relief."

"You know it. I expect that opinion is being voiced at a number of residences around the city, including the big white one on Pennsylvania Avenue."

"Is there going to be an investigation of all this?"

"You can't investigate something that never happened."

"That's your story, and you're sticking to it?"

"You got it."

"I hope you're right."

"I hope so, too, baby."

"You want bacon or ham with your eggs?"

"I want you with my eggs."

"Done."

FIFTY-NINE

WILL LEE WAS IN BED, watching a DVD of *Casablanca*, when Kate came home from work.

"You're pretty late," he said. "I didn't know people at your level of government service worked after midnight."

Kate dropped her clothes on the floor and crawled into bed with him, snuggling her warm body against his. "Why, Mr. President, you're not wearing any clothes."

He groped around. "Why, Madame Director, neither are you."

"Hang on," she said. "I've got some news that will put you in the mood."

"I don't need any news to get in the mood," he said, turning toward her, "but I have a feeling you're going to tell me anyway."

"You're right. It was Teddy Fay who shot Ali ben Saud this morning, then blew up an office building under construction across the street from the U.N."

"Tell me something I don't know."

"I just thought you'd like it confirmed. What you don't know is that they found Teddy Fay's body in the wreckage of the building, along with the homemade gun he used."

"So, it's over?"

"It's over."

"Are we going to announce anything?"

"*I'm* certainly not, and you're crazy, if you do. Tell your congressional leaders and tell them to sit on it."

"What happens if they don't?"

"Then they're guilty of hiding the whole business from the American people."

"I don't know if I'm comfortable with this."

"You made that decision weeks ago, pal; learn to live with it."

"I suppose you're right."

"You *know* I'm right."

"Now can I molest you?"

"You'd better."

They reached for each other.

SIXTY

THREE WEEKS LATER, Irene Foster got home, tired and not a little drunk. Her living room was piled with boxes; her walls and bookcases were bare; there were still sheets on her bed, but that was the only comfort of home left in her little townhouse.

From somewhere, she heard the muffled ring of a cell phone, and she tore at her handbag looking for it, finally dumping the contents on the floor.

"Hello?"

"Hello, yourself."

"Thank God, I was beginning to think . . ."

"Don't ever think that."

"Where are you?"

"Somewhere in the Middle East."

She laughed. "Oh, that is *very* good news."

"I thought so, myself. What have you been up to?"

"Today was my last day. There was a party; I'm roaring drunk."

"I wish I were there to take advantage of you."

"If I can join you in the Middle East, we'll arrange that."

"Come ahead."

"Really?"

"There's a little inn; I can't pronounce it properly, but it translates, literally, as the Hostelry of the Three Forces. I've no idea what that means."

"You're there now?"

"When you check in, a Mr. Charles Lockwood will be waiting for you, and he'll have half a dozen houses for you to look at. When will you check in?"

"You can't use that name!"

"I'm not using it; it's the name of the real estate agent who's going to show you the house."

"Are you serious?"

"Perfectly."

"And what name are you using?"

"We'll invent one when you arrive. When will that be?"

"The sale of the house closes at ten tomorrow morning. If the airlines cooperate I can be in the Middle East by tomorrow night."

"Perfect. Tell me, how did that little matter that so concerned your people work out?"

"It's dead and gone, and so is the subject of the matter."

"Really? Do they really believe that?"

"Probably not, but they would prefer to."

"That's almost as good as if they believed it."

"Better. They'll be covering their asses for the rest of their careers."

"Is anyone going to come looking for that employee who didn't turn in his time sheets?"

"That gentleman resigned from the service, effective last week. I turned in his resignation for him."

"So that's a dead issue?"

"It's not even an issue."

"Call me before you take off tomorrow."

"Will do.

*   *   *

TEDDY BROKE THE CONNECTION and lay back on the chaise longue, looking up at the stars. A warm, tropical breeze wafted across his bald spot. He sighed and drifted off into a doze, dreaming of doing nothing forever.

AUTHOR'S NOTE

I am happy to hear from readers, but you should know that if you write to me in care of my publisher, three to six months will pass before I receive your letter, and when it finally arrives it will be one among many, and I will not be able to reply.

However, if you have access to the Internet, you may visit my website at www.stuartwoods.com, where there is a button for sending me e-mail. So far, I have been able to reply to all of my e-mail, and I will continue to try to do so.

If you send me an e-mail and do not receive a reply, it is because you are among an alarming number of people who have entered their e-mail address incorrectly in their mail software. I have many of my replies returned as undeliverable.

Remember: e-mail, reply; snail mail, no reply.

When you e-mail, please do not send attachments, as I *never* open these. They can take twenty minutes to download, and they often contain viruses.

Please do not place me on your mailing lists for funny stories, prayers, political causes, charitable fund-raising, petitions, or sentimental claptrap. I get enough of that from people I already know. Generally speaking, when I get e-mail addressed to a large number of people, I immediately delete it without reading it.

Please do not send me your ideas for a book, as I have a policy of writing only what I myself invent. If you send me story ideas, I will immediately delete them without reading them. If you have a good idea for a book, write it yourself, but I will not be able to advise you on how to get it published. Buy a copy of *Writer's Market* at any bookstore; that will tell you how.

Anyone with a request concerning events

or appearances may e-mail it to me or send it to: Publicity Department, Penguin Group (USA) Inc., 375 Hudson Street, New York, NY 10014.

Those ambitious folk who wish to buy film, dramatic, or television rights to my books should contact Matthew Snyder, Creative Artists Agency, 9830 Wilshire Boulevard, Beverly Hills, CA 90212-1825.

Those who wish to conduct business of a more literary nature should contact Anne Sibbald, Janklow & Nesbit, 445 Park Avenue, New York, NY 10022.

If you want to know if I will be signing books in your city, please visit my website, www.stuartwoods.com, where the tour schedule will be published a month or so in advance. If you wish me to do a book signing in your locality, ask your favorite bookseller to contact his Penguin representative or the Penguin publicity department with the request.

If you find typographical or editorial errors in my book and feel an irresistible urge to tell someone, please write to David Highfill at Penguin's address above. Do not e-mail your discoveries to me, as I will already have learned about them from others.

A list of my published works appears in the front of this book. All the novels are still in print in paperback and can be found at or ordered from any bookstore. If you wish to obtain hardcover copies of earlier novels or of the two nonfiction books, a good used-book store or one of the online bookstores can help you find them. Otherwise, you will have to go to a great many garage sales.

ACKNOWLEDGMENTS

I want to thank, once again, my agents of twenty-five years, Morton Janklow and Anne Sibbald, for their hard work on my behalf. They have been instrumental in the formation and longevity of my career, and I will always be grateful to them.

I also want to thank my editor, David Highfill, who is responsible for getting the book through the publishing process intact, for his always insightful view of my manuscript. All the people at Putnam have done fine work on my behalf, especially Michael Barson and Elizabeth Hazelton, who schedule all my publicity and book tours twice a year, and I thank each one of them.